BLIND
DATE

BOOKS BY WENDY CLARKE

BLIND DATE

WENDY CLARKE

bookouture

Published by Bookouture in 2021

An imprint of Storyfire Ltd.
Carmelite House
50 Victoria Embankment
London EC4Y 0DZ

www.bookouture.com

ISBN: 978-1-80019-553-0
eBook ISBN: 978-1-80019-552-3

For Tracy

PROLOGUE

I know your secret, but you don't know mine.

That's my confession.

You've gone silent, Melanie... Why's that? Is it because you're afraid of what I'll say? That this call will no longer be about me but about you? What would be the fun in that? It's enough that you know I know.

But that's not my only confession. What I want to tell you tonight is that I hurt. Right deep inside my chest, the way it would feel if a knife was thrust into my heart to the hilt. Then further still. And all this because I've experienced the most perfect love.

The purest love.

Can you understand that?

When you feel love like that, passion like that, madness like that, you will do anything to keep it. Anything to make sure that no one will ever stand between you and that perfect state.

But what if that love is taken from you? Maybe you'll seek that person out or perhaps you'll seek out another. Always chasing. Always searching. And when you have them, you will make them understand they are yours, that you won't let them leave you as the other one did. You will cling to that love with fingers capable of tenderness but also capable of much worse.

And yet, even though you have someone new, you will never

forget that first perfect love. How they left you empty. How can you forget when the space they left in your heart has become filled with something harder? Darker. When that darkness threatens to turn you into a monster you don't recognise, it's hard not to wonder if it really was your fault.

What do you think, Melanie? Now you've heard my confession, my secret, does it surprise you that I might not be who people think I am? That I'm worse... so much worse. Maybe it does or maybe you knew all the time because, perhaps, we're not so different.

And yet, something still bothers me. Something I wanted to ask. It's a question that comes to me when I walk the dark streets at night or see the cold moonlight reflected in the canal.

I've made my confession, Melanie.

When will you make yours?

ONE

It's funny how sometimes you know change is coming. You have an inkling. A small nudge. Maybe just the ghost of a feeling. That hadn't happened today. When I'd woken at 4.15 a.m., my back-up alarm shrill in my ear, there had been nothing. Just bleary-eyed, crushing tiredness and the need for strong coffee.

It's five now, still dark, the sky not yet showing even a hint of pink or peach, but there's something in the air that tells me it's no longer night. A softer tone that's more like a bruise than solid blackness. A certain expectation to the silence, as if it's waiting to be broken by something: the first note of birdsong, the soft rumble as a bin is wheeled out for collection, the bark of a dog as it's let out into a garden. In my case, it's the slam of my car door before I lock it and hurry across the car park to the rather uninteresting-looking red-brick building in front of me.

Reaching up a hand, I punch at the buttons on the keypad, my fingers numb with cold, glad that I'm not the first one here even if it means that I'm late. I let myself in and the door clicks shut behind me, shutting out the security light that illuminates the puddles that have formed in the potholes of the car park overnight.

Once, when I was new and enthusiastic, I would have taken the time to pause before pushing open the door. With the flat of my hand pressed to its cold face, I'd have taken in the blue lettering on the panel attached to the wall beside it... the one spelling out the name of my place of work. Lock Radio. For most of my first year of working here, although I've never admitted this to anybody – not even my husband, Niall – I'd whisper the name to myself. Wondering as I did how I'd managed to bag my dream job against such stiff competition. Asking myself what good-luck fairy had been looking down on me when I'd arrived on the doorstep that first day. Giving thanks for the lucky series of events that had led me from an internship all those years ago to the prestigious post I now have on breakfast radio.

But now I'm older and wiser, I know it wasn't luck at all. I've watched other young hopefuls come through the doors. Seen who's made it and who hasn't. It's their hunger and enthusiasm that keeps the successful ones here... along with hard graft. Nowadays a lot don't get in the same way I did – three years of media studies at university, followed by a stint on hospital radio, broadcasting from a tiny room with no windows – but by other efforts. Vlogs and podcasts done in their spare time, making them current. On the pulse. Accessible to the younger members of our audience.

I smile to myself as I shrug off my jacket, thinking about my first few months here. Remembering how happy I'd been when after months of making tea and running around after everyone, I'd been taken on as part of the promotion team at events. Even though it had only been handing out flyers, it had been a foot in the door. The highlight, though, had been when Simon had suggested I sit in on the Breakfast Show. From my stool at the back, I'd scribbled frantic notes, taking in everything he and his co-hosts, Chris and Nadine, did and said, longing to be one of them.

Now, of course, I am.

The reception is brightly lit even though Dawn, the reception-ist, won't be in for a few hours yet. I lay my jacket on the desk, next to the sheaf of fliers and other promotional material and dig in my bag for a mirror. Holding it up to each ear to make sure I've not put in mismatching studs – a distinct possibility after managing to sleep through my alarm. If it hadn't been for my back-up alarm waking me, I'd still be tucked under my duvet.

Tipping my head to the light, I wipe a smudge of black from under my bottom lashes then put the mirror back in my bag. Applying mascara when your eyes are glazed with tiredness is no mean feat. Still, at least with Niall sleeping in the spare bedroom, I no longer have to worry about waking him.

On the wall, a large flat-screen TV is showing a demonstration that happened in Manchester yesterday. Although the sound is muted, subtitles chase each other across the bottom of the screen. As I watch, the picture changes. A newsreader sits behind a desk, and on the screen behind, I recognise the wide-open mouth of the tunnel that burrows through the hillside a little way down the canal from where the radio station is situated. The subtitles tell me what I already know. It's the place where two years ago, a young woman, a prostitute, disappeared... presumed dead. Today the police are going to do an anniversary appeal.

That poor woman.

I turn away not wanting to see, even though it will be something to add to today's schedule, along with anything else of interest my co-presenters and I find in the papers. Speaking of which, where are they?

As if in answer to my unspoken thoughts, a burst of laughter comes from the kitchen area on the other side of reception. It's Chris, probably responding to one of Dan, the producer's, filthy jokes. They're going to love the fact that I'm late as it's well known at the radio station that I take pride in my punctuality. I sigh.

Picking up my coat, I'm about to join them when the board with our photos on catches my eye. Under the heading *Breakfast Team*, Simon, Chris and I smile out from behind the glass. I pause and press a finger to my face; the picture was taken a few years ago

ounger and more fresh-faced.

godawful hours had started to take their toll.

home life had fallen apart and divorce had become

ething that happened to other people.

Before I knew the misery of betrayal.

I look at the happy young girl in the photo, her shiny, dark hair falling to her shoulders, the one who believed her marriage would last forever, and wonder what happened to her. The photos are long overdue an update, and a few weeks ago, someone came in to take some new ones. When he'd turned his camera round to show me what he'd taken, I couldn't help thinking that although my smile was the same, it had lost some of its sparkle, the hair some of its shine.

I lift my hand to it, surprised, as I always am when my fingertips touch nothing but the soft skin at the back of my neck. My straighteners still sit on my chest of drawers next to the mirror in my bedroom, but they're no longer needed. After years of getting up at the crack of dawn, I decided a pixie cut would be simpler to manage. I just hadn't realised how long it would take for me to get used to it.

The boys' photos are either side of mine, flanking me like bodyguards. Theirs need changing too, though neither will admit it. Chris's hair was shorter than it is now when the photographs were taken, and Simon was clean-shaven and boyish, without the stubble he's recently started sporting. He looks out at me now, his expression calm and reassuring. At least *he* won't join in with the ribbing I'll get when I open that kitchen door. He's not like that.

Suddenly I feel weary. I used to laugh at all Chris's jokes, but now the thought of responding to whatever he's going to say feels like too much of an effort. I push the door open with my shoulder and sling my coat and bag onto an empty chair before heading to the coffee machine.

'Morning, gang.'

Normally, there'd be chat and joshing or a companionable silence as each member of the team gets ready for the show. This morning though, I can already tell that the hush has a different quality to it.

I get myself a black coffee, tearing a corner from a sugar packet and adding it to the dark liquid. Needing the energy. I wait for either Dan or Chris to get their first joke in at my expense. When it doesn't happen, I turn my head and look from one to the other.

'What's up?'

Chris has been looking at his phone, his large fingers tapping at the screen. He raises his head, a frown on his face. 'Eh?'

I point at the digital clock on the wall. 'It's five-fifteen. I'm late. You should be taking the piss out of me. That's what you do, Chris.'

Chris breathes in sharply but just as quickly he rallies. 'Were you catching up on your beauty sleep, Mel? You certainly need it.'

I laugh but there's something about his quip that feels forced. Maybe I'm imagining it. 'I slept through my first alarm. Anyway, are you all right? When you're this quiet, you make me nervous.'

'Of course I'm all right. More than all right.' There's a lag in his response that worries me, but when his face creases into a smile I relax again. I'm probably just imagining things. Chris cups his round face in his hands and strikes a pose. 'Just look at this face. With good looks like this I'm every girl's dream.'

'Nightmare more like,' Simon says, throwing Chris a disapproving look. But I catch the warmth in his voice. The boys have, after all, been friends for years. He looks back at me. 'Anyway, don't fret about the time, Mel. You won't be the first to miss an alarm and you won't be the last. It happens.'

'Not to me it doesn't.' I take my coffee over and sit down on the settee next to him. 'I never oversleep.'

'It could be your body telling you something – that you need to take things a bit easier. You *have* been quite anxious lately. Not surprising with everything that's been going on at home. No wonder you're tired.'

I frown. 'I thought it was the other way round... that anxiety keeps you awake.'

'Yes, usually but sometimes your body just gives in to it. I remember last year after Anne lost the baby...'

He stops and looks away. I want to say something to make it

better, but I can't. I've never been good at that sort of thing. Instead, I say something mundane. Less emotive.

'Yes, you're probably right. I think I might have read something similar or maybe it was one of our callers who mentioned it. Anyway, I'll be fine with a shot of caffeine inside me.' I glance up, wondering if the others are listening in to our conversation but they don't seem to be. 'Niall and I are doing okay, as it happens. We've been grown up about the divorce thing.'

I pick up my mug, hoping it will be the end of the conversation, but he hasn't taken the hint.

'I'm glad.' He turns in his seat to look at me with concerned eyes. 'It must be hard still living under the same roof, now you're not married.'

The mouthful of coffee I take is too hot, burning my throat as I swallow it. I put the mug down again, annoyed with myself.

'It's fine,' I say. Recently, *fine* seems to have become my default word. I don't know what's got into me today. It's not as if Simon means anything by it. 'Ignore me.'

Simon leans across and gives my hand a squeeze. 'Sorry, I should never have brought it up.'

'Stop being so bloody nice. Mr Bloody Nice Guy.'

Chris picks up a pen from the coffee table and throws it at him. It misses and rolls to the edge of the desk. So, he *had* been listening. 'Say it like it is. That's what I do. I'm sure Mel doesn't mind sharing a bathroom with a guy she can't stand the sight of.'

'That's not true. I—'

He cuts me off. 'Any more than she minds being late. Or looking like a tired sparrow that's been plucked.'

'Fuck off, Chris,' I say, my hand rising to my head, smoothing the wisps at the nape. 'At least I don't look like an ageing hippie.'

Chris has his feet on the coffee table, one crossed over the other, and I lean forward, whacking at the one nearest to me. I immediately regret it as the side of his trainer is covered in mud.

I look at my hand. 'Jesus, Chris. You didn't walk here, did you?'

Now I think about it, I hadn't seen his car in the car park.

He shrugs. 'I like it. It helps me to wake up.'

'Sober up, more like.' Producer Dan closes the lid of his laptop and scratches at his ginger beard. He gets up and takes his mug over to the sink, rinsing it under the tap before hanging it on the cup stand.

'None of you bloody lot touch this mug or you're dead,' he says, pointing a finger at us all.

'As if we'd want to catch what you've got,' Chris fires back, bullet fast.

Dan looks at the clock. 'Come on, slackers. Let's get this show on the road. We've only thirty minutes until we go live and we've a lot to talk about. It's the anniversary appeal for the woman who disappeared in the canal tunnel. The police are hoping to refresh the public's memory and maybe pull up more witnesses. They want us to mention it on the show.'

My eyes move to the window although there's nothing to see but darkness. 'Crazy that it was so close to here. Her poor family.'

Dan nods. 'Crazier still that they never got anyone for it. Hopefully, the appeal will jog someone's memory. I'll see you all in the meeting room. Get your arses into gear, you lot, or we'll have Di on our backs.' He looks meaningfully at me. 'You know how she hates tardiness.'

Di, our programme controller, is a dour woman with little sense of humour, and she and I have little in common other than our commitment to Lock Radio, but she knows what she's doing. I've also learnt that it's wise to keep on the right side of her, as she's the one who puts the programme schedule together and keeps the station running smoothly.

'And no one wants Di on their back.' Chris points to his soft stomach. 'Or on their front. Jesus the thought.'

I laugh but he's right. If we had the choice, we'd all avoid her. But we don't have that option as, every day after the show has finished, the four of us meet with her to go through a snagging list of what's just gone on air. We don't enjoy the feedback much, but we know it's a necessary evil if we want to make the show as good as it can be. Her feedback usually consists of a slapped wrist for Chris when one of his jokes has been too near the mark, or a suggestion to Simon that he keep things tight and move into a story quicker. I've been lucky. In all the years I've been doing the show, I've come off lightly in comparison.

'Don't worry. She won't even know I was late and, even if she did, I'll get Si to sweet-talk her.'

Chris looks up and winks at Simon. 'Good luck with that, lover boy.'

He's right, despite his ridiculously boyish good looks and old-fashioned charm that make women want to mother him, even Simon finds Di difficult to deal with at times.

'Five minutes,' Dan bellows, and as he leaves, Chris gives his disappearing back the finger. I have to laugh. Despite the snipes and the banter, we really are one big happy family and I'm relieved that the odd tension I'd felt in the room when I'd first walked in has gone.

Sometimes it's easy not to see the clues. Or maybe it's just easier to ignore them.

TWO

We're almost finished with the preparation meeting, and are about to go into the studio, when there's a knock on the door.

I look up, surprised. There's not normally anyone else here this early in the morning.

'Who's that do you think?'

Simon shrugs, but I see how his eyes slide over to Chris, who doesn't look up but shifts in his seat uncomfortably.

It's Dan who breaks the silence. 'That'll be Charl.' He pushes back his chair and goes to open the door, but I catch his arm as he walks by me.

'Who the hell is Charl?'

'Come on, you must have seen her around. She's the new intern who's been sitting in on Lee Carden's afternoon slot. Di got her in after seeing her YouTube channel. Bright little thing. She's certainly got the patter, I have to say.'

I frown, trying to remember if I've seen this girl, Charl, or not and decide that I haven't. After our morning meetings with Di, I'm usually straight out of the door. Desperate for a hearty breakfast at the Canal Café on the corner, followed by a run in the park to stretch legs that have been sitting too long.

'I don't think I've seen her, no.'

Dan smiles as he opens the door. 'Now's your chance then.'

The girl who walks in looks to only be in her early twenties, but she exudes a confidence that I never had at that age. Her hair is dark blonde. Her smile wide.

'Hi.' She throws her denim jacket on the back of the nearest chair and looks at each one of us in turn, her eyes not faltering. 'Thanks for having me.'

It's a strange expression to use – like she's a child who's just arrived at a birthday party, rather than someone who's burst in on a breakfast show meeting. Still unsure as to what she's doing here, I make myself smile back.

'It's nice to meet you, Charl. I'm Melanie, or Mel... whichever.'

She doesn't answer but nods, her large blue eyes taking in my rather run-of-the-mill appearance. Suddenly, I'm seeing myself through her eyes. Knowing that she's looking for something that sets me apart from other dull women my age... finding nothing. In her young eyes, the pixie hairstyle I chose because I thought it looked youthful will have done nothing but push me closer to middle age, the jeans and long-sleeved T-shirt I'm wearing testament to my ordinariness.

'You don't mind if I sit in then?' The question is directed to me, not to Si or Chris... or even Dan.

I look to them for help but it's like they've suddenly found very important things to do. Chris's head is bent to his phone and Simon is shuffling through the papers on the table in front of him, like a newsreader at the end of the ten o'clock news.

'No, of course not. I'll find a stool for you to sit on.'

'Great. Thanks.'

The dress Charl has on is made of some sort of chiffon material, pale pink and blue with an asymmetric hem. She's teamed it with opaque indigo tights and Doc Martens and the bow of the tangerine-coloured scarf she's twisted around her head flops onto her smooth brow.

An outfit like that on me would look odd, as if I'd dressed in the dark, but on her it's creative and arty. Feeling a prick of envy, I tear my eyes away from the tiny stud in her nose and the full blood-red lips and pick up my bag and notes.

'Come on then. Or the listeners will tune into Radio One instead.' I laugh but the sound is hollow. Nothing feels right this morning.

As we leave the meeting room, I feel the touch of Simon's fingers on my arm. Thinking he's going to say something, I turn and look at him with a question in my eyes, but he's already gone, striding down the corridor after Chris, leaving me alone with Charl.

'I really do love your show,' she says. 'Really, really love it.'

It's said with such surprising passion that I find myself smiling back at her. A genuine smile this time. 'Thank you. I'm glad.'

She tilts her head at the boys who are going into the studio at the end of the corridor. 'What are they like to work with... I mean really?'

I think of how I should answer her then decide to give her the truth. 'Annoying. Frustrating. Fun. Silly. That sums it up pretty well.'

'I envy you,' she says, her hand on my forearm. 'I really do. How long have you been doing this?'

I lead the way down the corridor. Her question has made me feel suddenly old. 'Nearly eight years.'

'And you've never thought about giving up? Doing something else?'

'No, never. What makes you think I would?'

'Oh, no reason. I just wondered if you ever got itchy feet. I certainly do.'

I let her into the studio, where Simon is already at his control desk, studying the monitor in front of him, and show her where to sit. Then I take the seat next to Chris and put on my headphones, swinging the mic round on its arm until it's in the right position.

Simon gives me the thumbs up, and I smile back, leaning back in my chair as the words I've listened to for the last eight years sing out.

Lock... ray... dee... oh!

Then I wait and listen as he gives his usual introduction.

'Morning folks. This is Lock Breakfast Radio with Simon, Mel and Chris. The Three Musketeers. All for one and one for all. It's six o'clock and time for the news and weather in your area.'

I look at the monitor in front of me and draw a breath in before letting it out slowly through my mouth. Preparing myself.

The next few hours go by in a blur as they always do. The three of us have been working together for so long that sometimes we forget there are people listening to us.

Simon leans forward, the microphone grazing his lips. 'In a minute we'll be talking about the five things women over forty should never wear but first I'll leave you with Taylor Swift.'

I watch as Simon pushes the fader button to bring in the next song then takes off his headphones. I do the same. Each song is a precious breathing space, and we like to make the most of it. The screen in front of us will tell us when it's coming to an end.

'So,' he says, looking thoughtfully at me. 'Any plans for tomorrow evening?'

I shrug. 'I haven't really thought. I'll probably just watch something on Netflix then have an early night.' My happy mood fades a little. It seems to be what I do most evenings. Niall in one room, me in another. Trying our best to be civil to one another if our paths cross in the kitchen or hallway, as they inevitably do from time to time. Making careful small talk that won't threaten to crack the delicate shell of our carefully built equilibrium.

Next to me, Chris slides his own headphones down so they're resting on his shoulders. He pushes his seat back and puts his feet up on the desk in front of him, eliciting a frown from Simon.

'Come to The Junction with us. You haven't had a good night out in ages.' He rubs at his cheek. 'I remember when we used to go out all the time.'

The Junction with its fake dark wood panelling and even

faker leather-look seating is situated a little way down from the lock that gives the radio station its name, in a strangely attractive spot where road, canal and railway meet via bridges. The pub's red-brick frontage looks out onto the water and in summer, when the weather is good, the punters sit out on the grass slope in front or stand in groups on the towpath, getting in people's way. On Friday and Saturday nights it can get quite busy, and later, when everyone's had a few, the space between the long bar and the tables that line the wall fills up with people wanting to dance to the landlord's choice of cheesy music. Of course, it's not everyone's cup of tea but the three of us love it. Or rather, we used to. Now Chris goes on his own. Or sometimes with Simon when Anne lets him.

'We were younger then,' I say, surprised at his suggestion. He's right, it *has* been a while. I narrow my eyes. Why has Chris decided to invite me? 'I wasn't married then. Simon wasn't either.'

'Since when has that stopped him?' Chris flicks a paper clip in Simon's direction. It hits the edge of the monitor then drops onto the floor.

Simon bends to pick it up, holding it up to Chris's face before placing it with an exaggerated flourish into the plastic desk organiser beside his keyboard. His smile has slipped a little. 'Very adult, Chris. Very mature.'

Chris ignores him and turns his grin to me. 'So you'll come out tomorrow night then? Have some fun?' He leans over and nudges my arm. 'Come on. It'll be like old times. You, me and Mr Grumpy over there.'

'I don't know.' To be honest, I haven't felt like doing much recently. It feels as if those carefree days are long gone.

'Leave it, Chris.' Simon flashes a warning at him. 'If Mel doesn't want to go, she doesn't want to go.'

'It's not that I don't want to go, it's just that things are a bit difficult at home at the moment.'

Chris pulls a face. 'Come on, spoilsport. You know what they say. All work and no play makes Mel a dull girl. Or maybe we should open up the invitation to newcomers.' He turns his head to look behind him. 'You up for a night out, Charl?'

I twist in my seat. For a moment, I'd forgotten all about her. Our eyes meet and she holds my gaze before looking away.

'No, you're all right. I'm out with friends Saturday. Another time.'

'Bring them too,' Chris says, his grin widening. 'The more the merrier.'

'No, I don't think so. But thanks anyway.'

Chris turns back to me. 'Actually, I didn't mention it before but there's someone I thought you might like to meet. A mate of mine. He's a good bloke.'

I widen my eyes in surprise and horror. 'Are you trying to tell me you're setting me up with someone?'

I look over at Simon but from his expression, I can see he's as surprised as I am.

'Setting you up? Me?' Chris gives a loud laugh. 'What a terrible expression. Think of it more like a blind date... a lorra laughs. What's your name and where do you come from? Here's Our Graham with a quick reminder. If you don't like him, you can leave.'

I cringe at his bad Cilla impression. 'You have to be kidding me. I'm not ready for anything like that.'

Simon gives him a pointed look. 'Yes, give it a rest, you idiot.'

The monitor is telling us the song will be over any second. I pull my headphones onto my ears and glare at Chris. 'Anyway, it isn't going to happen.'

It's true. I'm not ready. I know Chris is thinking it's because I'm not over Niall, but the truth weighs heavier. It's because my secret is there with me wherever I go... and I can't trust myself.

THREE

It was dark when we arrived this morning, so the blinds in the meeting room where we've gathered for our feedback are still closed. Before sitting down, Di crosses to the window and twists the plastic rod, letting in the daylight. It feels strange to be confronted by the day like this, reminding me of the sensation when you walk out of a cinema after an afternoon show.

Except for when it's the middle of summer, it's always like this. We enter the building in the dark, the following hours fly by, and when we finally emerge from our windowless studio, we're tricked into believing that it's still night. Now the evidence that the world has awakened is in front of us. The sky blue, the sun glinting off the water of the canal.

Like I say, time is an odd thing.

Chris and Simon have taken seats either side of the large table in the middle of the room. I pull out the chair next to Chris and Di sits opposite me. I smile to myself; wind back ten years and this could almost be my interview.

'Charl not joining us then? I thought it would do her good to hear the feedback. That we don't always get things right. That there's always something to improve on.'

As an intern to the station, we must seem like the unattainable.

Celebrities almost. It makes me feel strangely maternal towards her.

Simon looks uncomfortable. 'Di didn't think it would be a good idea.'

'So, how do you think it went?' I turn to our programme controller and smile, confident in the knowledge that it went well. In fact, we were all pretty much on top form today.

Di laces her fingers together. She looks down at her notebook then back up at me. 'I'm satisfied with this morning's programme, Mel. It was up to its usual high standard.'

I nod. Di's pleased which means we can all leave early. I picture the white froth on the latte I'm going to have at the Canal Café and wonder how guilty I'd feel if I paired it with a Danish pastry. In the months since the divorce, I've put on half a stone through comfort eating and should really make more effort to get rid of it. As I think this, I run my thumb around the waist-band of my jeans, feeling the small roll of flesh that emerges over the top. I'm not there yet, but in two years' time, I'll be the age of the women we were talking about in our feature on mutton dressed as lamb after forty. After I've passed that milestone, will people be looking at *me* and thinking I should be dressing my age?

'Your thoughts, Mel?'

'Sorry?' I'd been staring out of the window at the morning walkers and joggers on the towpath, thinking I must do more exer-cise, but now my eyes focus back on Di. I'm embarrassed that I haven't been listening.

Di leans forward, her arms resting on the shiny pale wood of the table, her fingers still linked. 'I was saying that ratings are down. Have been progressively for the last few months.'

It's not the first time she's said this, and we haven't been unduly worried. Fluctuations in listener figures isn't unusual. 'I'm sure things will turn around. They always do. It's simply a blip.'

'We usually have upwards of three hundred thousand listeners for the Breakfast Show. Last month it was down to about two hundred thousand. That's not just a blip, Mel. That's a huge great speed bump.'

I look at the boys. Their faces mirror each other's misery.

'Come on.' I throw Simon a smile. 'We can get ourselves out of this.'

Di clears her throat. 'I'm sorry, Mel. It's too late. Any changes would be minor and have no impact on audience figures. We need to take more decisive action. Have a complete overhaul.'

My stomach starts to twist. 'What do you mean?'

'I mean that things have to change, and we can only do that by juggling our presenters.' I get a sudden ridiculous picture of the three of us spinning above my head. I'd laugh if wasn't so serious.

The atmosphere in the room has changed. It's weighted with expectation.

Di is looking at me steadily. I try to hold her gaze but find it slipping away. For suddenly my heart clenches and I know what she's going to say. The last thing I want is to see her face when she lets the words fall into the silence.

'You're dropping us, aren't you?' The little bit of control I've gained by saying it first is tiny compared to its significance. How it will impact our lives.

Di brings her fingers to her lips, steepling them as if in prayer. 'No, Mel. That's not what's happening. Not entirely.'

I look first at Chris then at Simon for help. It's then I realise that Dan isn't here with us. Why isn't he? A glance through the glass panel shows me he's in reception talking to Charl. I spin my chair back to face the others, feeling riled. As our producer, Dan should be in here supporting us, not outside with her.

'Simon, did you know about this?' His hesitation tells me everything. 'You did, didn't you?' I turn to Chris. 'Jesus, not you too.'

'I'm sorry, Mel.' Chris's voice is laced with embarrassment. 'Di told us yesterday.'

'And you went through the whole of the show this morning as though nothing had happened.' It beggars belief. 'Even though you knew that soon it wouldn't be you sitting in that chair but someone else.'

Di clears her throat. 'It won't be someone else. The boys will still be doing the show.'

I stare at her, trying to follow her thread. Wondering if I've heard her right. 'It's just me? I'm going but the boys are staying? You can't do that, Di. We're a team. We've been a team for the last eight years.' My body feels light as if, at any moment, it might float away. 'Simon, Mel and Chris. The Three Musketeers. It's what the listeners know. It's what they want.'

Di shuffles her papers. 'Not according to the latest listening figures it's not.'

'You can't get rid of me. It's not fair. Why me and not one of the others? They're both older than me. You realise it's sexism, don't you?'

Outside the window, a narrowboat slides by. Normally, I'd enjoy watching its painted side. Smile at the holidaymakers' attempt at steering her, ducking under overhanging branches and squabbling over who's going to steer it into the lock and who will open the heavy gates.

Not today though. Today, my gaze goes right through it.

'It's nothing personal, Mel. We just have to get the balance right,' Di continues. 'Simon is the anchor and has always been the lynchpin of the show. Chris is his foil. If we got rid of either, there'd be an outcry. The audience like you too, of course, but the triangle hasn't been working for a while now and getting someone in who will attract a fresh new audience is something we have to try. We need someone—'

'Younger? Say it, Di. That's what you mean, isn't it?'

'It's nothing to do with age. We need to add someone to the mix who can connect with a different demographic. The format hasn't changed in years. It's imperative we're aware of what's on trend and the way we can do that is to have someone on the Breakfast Show who already has a fan base and knows what people want.'

Suddenly, it all becomes clear.

I stare at her wide-eyed. 'Jesus. It's that girl, Charl, isn't it? That's why she was sitting in with us today. You're putting her in my place? Simon, Charl and Chris. What a lovely ring it has.' I point an accusatory finger at Simon, livid at his treachery. 'And you knew, didn't you? You both knew.'

Simon runs a hand down his face. 'We wanted to tell you, but—'

'I told them not to, Mel.' Di takes off her reading glasses and places them beside her notes. 'We have to follow procedures.'

I stand, my chair scraping on the floor as I push it back. 'So that's it then. I'm out. Thrown on the scrapheap because some young upstart thinks she's better than me simply because she looks good on YouTube.' I think of the money I've been trying to save so that I can move out of the house I share with Niall and feel near to tears. 'The audience won't even see her face, for Christ's sake.'

Di doesn't rise to my anger. 'You're overreacting. And we're not throwing you on the scrapheap. It's not like that at all. We're moving you, that's all.'

My despair ebbs a little as I sit down again, trying to think of who might be leaving. It can't be Luke on Drive Time... he's too popular. Maybe it's one of the afternoon crew.

I look at Simon and Chris, knowing I shouldn't be angry with them. These decisions come from the top. They would have fought to keep me, but there would have been nothing they could have done.

'Where are you moving me to?' I ask, holding my breath. Waiting for her reply.

Di taps her pen on the table and fixes me with her stare once more. 'We're moving you to the late-night slot from Monday. Alan's leaving.'

Simon's head shoots up. 'So soon? Doesn't he have to work out a notice or something?'

'No. The details are confidential but it's better this way.'

I close my eyes in disbelief. Suddenly, the room feels too hot. I want to throw open the window and take gulps of the fresh morning air.

Di is waiting for me to say something. Simon and Chris are too, and through the glass panel of the door, I sense that Dan and Charl are watching me, waiting for my reaction. I feel humiliated. Know I need to compose myself. But no matter what I say, I know my voice will betray what I'm thinking, for no one wants to do the late-night radio slot. Not if they're in their right minds anyway.

Without realising it, my arms have crossed over my body as if protecting it, rubbing at the flesh above my elbows.

'The graveyard shift, you mean.'

'Yes.'

I look around the room at the people I've worked so closely with for the last few years, the people I'd thought had my back, feeling an intense anger at their disloyalty.

It makes me want to lash out, take myself away from all this and do something stupid to forget. Like I did once before when resentment made me want to be anyone except the person who had been made to feel insignificant. I close my eyes and take a breath. Remembering.

Look where that got me.

FOUR

I let myself out of the radio station and, leaving my car in the car park, take the path that leads down to the canal. It's eleven o'clock, and if this was a normal day, I would make my way to the café, already imagining the first sip of my latte – so much nicer than the coffee from the machine in the kitchen that we drink during the show to keep ourselves awake. But this isn't an ordinary day. Far from it.

So instead of turning right, I turn left. Away from the town. Not wanting to do what I'd usually do. Needing time to think.

The sun is unusually warm for an autumn morning. Normally, I'd walk slowly, taking pleasure in the way the sky reflects in the water's dark surface. The clear image of the clouds and buildings only broken by an angler casting his invisible line or the slow nose of a narrowboat heading for the lock gates. Today, though, there's a smell of diesel in the air and I'm blind to the beauty. Seeing only the rusting metal hulls of the barges, windows thick with grime. Nudging the boats in front like an inquisitive dog.

I walk with purpose beside the canal. Head bowed. Jaw set. Following the artery of slow-moving water that moves from town to countryside. With every step, the bank becomes more tangled, more overgrown. The buildings fewer.

When I hear my name being called, I don't look up. I'm too

angry. I know it's Simon whose feet are slapping on the mix of tarmac and compacted mud and gravel that makes up the towpath.

'Mel, wait.'

I don't stop but carry on walking, only turning when I feel the tug of his hand on my sleeve. I pull my arm away. 'Just leave me, Simon.'

'Please, Mel.' The breeze lifts his hair. It looks better that way, mussed and uncontrolled rather than gelled. Anne should tell him that.

'Leave me alone. I really don't want to talk about it.'

Simon pushes his hands into the pockets of his leather jacket. 'It's not so bad... the late-night programme.'

'That's easy for you to say. You're not the one who's been assigned to it. You're not the one who's been pushed out by a girl young enough to be your daughter.'

He frowns, considering this. 'Not quite.'

'Well, close enough.' I don't feel angry now, just sad and disillusioned. 'I loved it on the breakfast team, Si. You know I did. The three of us... we always had each other's backs.'

'We still will. You moving won't change that.'

On the other side of the canal, trees lean in towards the water like respectful mourners. Even though it hasn't happened yet, I'm mourning too. I watch their reflections move in the sluggish water.

'It feels like a break-up. It feels like my divorce all over again.' I know I'm being melodramatic, but I can't help it.

My throat is closing. I don't want to cry, not in front of him. But it's too late – a tear slides silently down my cheek. Angrily, I brush it with the heel of my hand and turn away, but Simon has seen.

'Please don't cry, Mel. Me and Chris are here for you. Always have been. Always will. The Three Musketeers have nothing on us. All for one and one for all and all that. You might be changing programmes, but you can't get rid of us that easily.'

I have to laugh. Taking a tissue from my pocket, I swallow back my emotion and blow my nose. 'No, I probably can't. The way

Chris follows me around, you'd think he was my guard dog.' I smile and stuff the tissue back into my pocket. 'It's kind of sweet though.'

Simon pulls a face. 'If you say so. What he needs is to get a girlfriend. A proper one... not someone he picks up to screw. He's forty next year for Christ's sake; he's too old for all that. Maybe I should have a brotherly word with him.'

'Some people are never too old.'

We stand side by side at the water's edge, contemplating what he's just said. As we watch, a moorhen darts into the reeds at the side of the canal. A flash of black and red.

'Do you think I should take it then? The late slot?'

'I think you should talk to Alan. Ask him about it – how he finds the hours, what makes his show special to him. Di wouldn't have suggested you take it over if she didn't think you'd make a success of it. It might not be what you're used to, but you could find you like it better. No more stupidly early mornings. No producer to interfere. Being your own boss and making your own decisions. Look at me, Mel. You won't know unless you try it.'

I do look at him then, considering what he's said. I'd been thinking about going back, telling Di where to stick her stupid job. But if I do, I'd only be cutting off my nose to spite my face. What if I can't find another job? Or, worse still, what if I do? The thought of nine-to-five in an office makes my heart sink. It's unlikely I'll ever find anything half as rewarding as what I do now. Radio is all I know.

I drag my eyes away from the water. 'What should I do, Simon?'

'I already told you. Speak to Alan.'

I know I should, but something is holding me back. Alan's not the most approachable of people. 'I suppose it wouldn't hurt. Do you know why he's leaving?'

'Haven't a clue, but whatever it is, it must have happened suddenly for there to have been such a quick changeover.'

I look at him. 'Do you think he's been sacked?'

He shrugs. 'Who knows?'

There's a splash of an unknown, unseen animal near the opposite side of the bank. A rat maybe? I wait to see if it will emerge, but it doesn't, the only evidence of it the ripples that move slowly outwards.

'I feel like shit. I really do.' It's true. I haven't felt this way since my marriage fell apart.

'Then come out with us tomorrow, Mel. You need cheering up. We'll have fun like we used to, and we can help you drown your sorrows.' He nudges my arm. 'It's been ages and I miss it. I know Chris does too.'

'Really?'

'Yes, really. It's about time you had some fun.'

I fold my arms. 'Tell Chris I'm not interested in his crazy blind date ideas.'

Simon smiles. 'That's not what I was talking about, but you can tell him yourself when we're there.'

'Except that I won't be going.'

I'm not going to admit to Simon that for a moment I was tempted. That I liked the idea of being that person again – the one who drank and flirted and laughed. It's a long time since I've been on a date, and I have to admit a small part of me is intrigued to know who it is Chris has chosen for me.

Quickly, I put the old Mel back in her box and press firmly on the lid. The Mel I've been remembering was still new to the radio station and life hadn't yet thrown her a curveball. I'm no longer that person. I might have been tempted but the temptation is only fleeting. There's no point in trying to recapture the past. None of us are those people anymore.

Simon picks up a small round pebble from the path and throws it into the water. Ripples radiate from it long after it's sunk. 'There's nothing I can do to change your mind?'

'I don't think so,' I say.

Simon hesitates. He's looking at me. Assessing me. 'And you're sure you're all right?'

'Yes. You know me, Si. I always bounce back.'

He nods and smiles. 'Yes, you do.' His smile wavers a little. 'I've always envied you that.'

I wonder if he's thinking back to when he and Anne lost the baby... the pregnancy that came to nothing. When he'd mentioned it this morning, I'd been surprised as he doesn't usually talk about it. I smile back at him, wondering if he's okay. For months after it happened, he wasn't himself. I suppose, as his friend, the kindest thing would be to ask him, but I can't bring myself to. It's too sad. Too personal. Instead, I shift my bag on my shoulder and move away from him. Making it clear I want to be left alone.

'I'll leave you then,' he says, nudging another stone with the toe of his shoe. 'But promise me you'll talk to Alan.'

'I will. I'll give him a call.'

'Good. Do you have his number?'

'I don't think so.' Why would I have it? There are three hours between when Alan lets himself out of the radio building and we let ourselves in. It's not as if he's the most sociable of presenters either, never bothering to go to the get-togethers we sometimes have or the Christmas meal. His sociability is saved for his radio show... knowing his listeners are there for him and him alone.

Simon scrolls through his phone. 'Here, I'll text it to you.' When he's done it, he puts his phone back in his pocket. 'I'll see you soon.'

He turns and starts to walk away but I call after him, having a sudden need for him to know I appreciate that he came after me.

'Thanks, Simon.'

He doesn't turn, just lifts his hand in acknowledgement, and I watch as he walks back the way he came. Trying not to think how, in a few days' time, the breakfast jingle will have changed. *Start the day the Lock Radio way with Simon, Charl and Chris.*

Taking my phone out of my bag, I ring the number Simon gave me, surprised when Alan answers immediately.

'Yes?' It's only one word but his voice is instantly recognisable. Low. Drawn out, with an upward tilt at the end. To my shame, I've only listened to the Late-Night Show a couple of times since I joined. But in the short hour I listened, lying prone on my bed, the ceiling spinning, after a night at the pub with the boys, I'd heard the intonation of that one syllable time after time as Alan answered the phone to his late-night callers.

A narrowboat passes by, an upturned wheelbarrow on its roof, and I press my hand to my ear to block out the *chug, chug* of its engine.

'Alan.'

'Melanie Abbott. I wondered when I'd hear from you.'

'How did you know it was—' I stop, realising how stupid the question is. He'll know my voice just as much as I know his. I clear my throat. 'I'd like to talk to you about the show.'

'I'm listening.' Again, that low, slow voice. The drawing out of vowels. So different to the pistol-crack patter of the Breakfast Show where our words duck and weave around each other.

'There's a lot I need to ask you, Alan, and I'd rather do it face to face.'

'I see.' He sounds amused. 'Let me look in my very full diary and I'll see if I can fit you in.'

It feels as if he's playing with me, but I ignore it. 'I can do any day after eleven. We could meet in the pub if you like. I'll buy you a pint as a thank you.'

'I don't drink.' He gives a mirthless laugh. 'Clearly no one's mentioned I used to have a little problem.'

I try and think but have no memory of it. Either the people I work with don't know, or they've been very professional. I can imagine that of Simon but certainly not of Chris.

'No, I hadn't heard anything.'

'Hmm. I have a habit of misjudging people. It's a fault of mine. One of many. Well now you know... my secret's out.'

I watch the play of light on the water, pondering what he's said. 'Is that why you're leaving?'

He gives another sharp bark of laughter. 'No, that's not the reason.'

I wait for him to say more but he doesn't.

'A coffee then?'

'I haven't time for that. If you can be at the studio at nine tonight, I might be able to spare you a moment before I get ready for my show.' He pauses. 'My last show.'

'Yes, I can do that. Thank you.'

'Save your thanks until we've spoken. You may want to keep them.' He gives a phlegmy cough. 'Just one thing before you go, Melanie Abbott.'

I feel wrong-footed by his use of my surname. Is he making fun of me? Can he tell by my voice that I'm worried I'm already setting myself up to fail? I decide not to comment on it. If I'm to succeed in my new role, I'll need his help.

'What is it?' I ask.

I think he's going to ask me how I feel about the change or let me in on something Di's said to him. He doesn't. What he says next couldn't have been further from my thoughts.

'The graveyard slot. Heed my advice. Don't take the job.'

FIVE

When Niall comes home later, I expect to hear him go upstairs to the spare room to change as he usually does, but instead he comes into the living room. The bang of the front door had already woken me, and now I sit up, realising I'd drifted off and rub the sleep from my eyes.

He leans his back against the door frame and folds his arms. 'Hi. Sorry, I didn't mean to wake you.'

Beside me, on the settee, is the notebook I'd been writing in before I'd given in to my tiredness. In it are the questions I want to ask Alan when I meet him this evening. I look at my watch. 'It's fine. I've had nearly an hour. That will keep me going until bedtime. Did you want something?'

By some unspoken agreement, I've started using the sitting room at the front of the house and Niall has created a man cave in the dining room. Consigning the dining table to the garage and replacing it with a settee from which he can watch football on the flat-screen TV he's fixed to the wall. I don't mind about the table as, even if I'd felt like it, there's no one I want to entertain.

'I did want to ask you something, yes.' Niall takes out his phone, checks it then puts it back in his pocket. 'If you're not busy.'

'No, it's fine.' I still can't get used to this new politeness. I miss the people we once were. Miss the laughter and the bickering. The mess we made when we cooked and the arguments we had about what to watch on the TV. Recently, I've had to remind myself about the parts I don't miss: those last months of our marriage. The silences. The recriminations. The lingering suspicion of betrayal.

No, I don't miss that.

Niall chews at his lip. 'I've tried to be mindful of your feelings. I know it's difficult to live in the house together and it's certainly not what we imagined we'd be doing after the decree absolute came through.'

I nod, remembering the twin brown envelopes that had landed on the doorstep the morning it became official. How sad they'd looked lying side by side. How official.

'We weren't to know the house wouldn't sell.'

'I offered to move out.'

'I know you did but this house was yours before you knew me, and you've always loved it more than I have. I said I was happy to rent if something suitable came up and I haven't changed my mind.'

Niall forces his hands into the front pocket of his jeans. He looks down at the floor then back up at me. 'Thank you... but I need to tell you something. I'm not asking your permission or anything; it's just I thought you should know.'

I note the seriousness in his voice. 'What are you talking about?'

Niall comes over and sits on the arm of the settee. 'I've invited Fiona round tomorrow night. I hope that's okay.'

For a moment, I want to laugh. He's like a son telling his mother he wants to bring his girlfriend home.

'Of course,' I lie. 'Why wouldn't it be?' I think of the casual rota system we've set up to organise our separate lives and try to be grown up about it. 'It's your day to have friends round. I'll go out for dinner like I always do.'

Niall rubs at the side of his neck. 'She's not just a friend, Mel. You know that.'

'Don't I just.'

He ignores me. 'And I'm not just talking about dinner. I want her to stay the night.'

'Stay the night?' I repeat, wondering if I've heard him correctly. Though I suspect she already has. In those heady earlier days of their relationship when they couldn't keep their hands off each other. There would have been plenty of opportunities when my mum had been ill and I'd spend the weekend at her house on the other side of town.

'Yes,' he continues. 'I can't go to hers as her parents don't approve of me. They think—'

'That you're too old for her,' I finish for him. 'And they'd be right, Niall. She's only twenty-three.'

I put the flat of my hands to my face. This is the second time today I've been replaced by someone who could almost be my daughter. If it was possible to feel any worse then this is that moment. But, of course, you can only replace something that's already there. In Niall's head at least, I've been gone a long time. That's what marital affairs do to you. They cancel you out.

'Christ, Niall. You're going to sleep with your girlfriend while I'm under the same roof?' I shake my head in disbelief. 'Please tell me you're joking.'

'I'm not joking, Mel. You were the one who said you wanted to move out and you must admit it's been a long time. I know you've wanted to find the right place, and I want that for you too, but I feel like you've been stalling. I'm truly sorry about everything, but life goes on and it's time ours did too. Whether you like it or not, Fiona and I are a couple now, and we need space.'

'You've only known her five minutes.'

'You know that's not true.'

He stands and walks to the window. It looks out across the road to a row of identical houses. Starter homes they call them, and most of the young couples who were living here when I first moved in with Niall have moved on. Maybe it was because, unlike us, they had children and the houses grew too small. Or maybe it was because, also unlike us, they aspired to something grander.

'Have you thought about maybe staying with your mum?' he carries on. 'This can't be easy for you either. There must be times when you want to...' He stops and has the decency to look embarrassed.

'You know that wouldn't work.'

The thought of staying with my mum, trapped in her suburban semi while she tells me how I've wasted my life, is too much to contemplate at the moment. It's not as if she was exactly supportive when I told her Niall and I were splitting up. Her reaction had been typical of her. *What do you expect if you marry a plumber?* I hadn't spoken to her for several months after that. If I go there now, I'll have to tell her about my job and bite my lip while she tells me, as she always does, that I should have chosen a different career path. Accountancy or something in the medical line like my perfect anaesthetist brother.

'I'll look again tomorrow,' I say.

'Or I could move. I told you that before.'

I shake my head. 'No. You don't have to do that.'

But there's no way I'm going to be staying here tomorrow night while my ex-husband shags his girlfriend. I need to do something.

It's then I remember Simon and Chris's invitation to go out. I hadn't given it any serious thought because I knew I wouldn't be going, but now I wonder if this might be the solution. If it's anything like it used to be, I won't be back until well after midnight and hopefully, by then, Niall and Fiona will have done what they need to do and be tucked up asleep in the room next to mine. I think of the friend Chris said he'd bring along. The blind date. I'd rejected it out of hand, but would it be such a bad idea to let my hair down and have some fun? I only need to talk to him. It doesn't have to lead to anything.

I fold my arms across my stomach and contemplate Niall's back, wondering if I feel jealous of how he's moved on. 'I'll be out until late so you can do what you want. It's none of my business anymore.' Something occurs to me then. Something I hadn't thought of before. 'What does Fiona think about staying the night while I'm still living under the same roof?'

Niall doesn't look at me but continues to stare out of the window. 'She's cool with it.'

'Meaning you haven't told her yet.'

He frowns, annoyed that I've always been able to read him. 'I'm going to tell her later. She'll be fine with it... I know her, Mel.' He turns now, a smile on his face. 'I'm getting fish and chips later – I could get you some too, if you like.'

It's his way of thanking me.

I look at my watch. 'No, I'm all right. But thanks anyway.'

'Okay. I'll see you later then.'

Niall leaves the room, closing the door behind him. I'd considered telling him about what happened this morning, but now I think I won't. Not until I've spoken to Alan, or at least, not until I've made a firm decision.

I pick up my notebook and put it in my bag, then check I have my car keys. As I drive to the station, my mind's not on what I'm going to say to Alan but on tomorrow night and my decision to go.

There's a strange excitement inside me but also a kernel of dread. For months I've been avoiding anything that could make me vulnerable, and a little voice is telling me this might have been a very bad decision.

SIX

It's odd going into the Lock Radio building now that it's dark once more. Even though I know it's evening, not early morning, my brain has been tricked into thinking that I'm about to start work again and my head is filled with the images I'd seen in the anniversary appeal. In the reconstruction, a young woman, chosen for her likeness to the girl who had disappeared, had walked towards the gaping mouth of the canal tunnel, late afternoon sunlight catching her long dark hair. She'd been wearing clothes similar to those the missing girl had worn when she'd last been seen – a short denim skirt, white T-shirt exposing an inch of flesh above the waistband and platform sandals. I'm wondering how I might incorporate some of this into the next Breakfast Show.

I stop with my finger on the first digit of the keypad, realising how stupid I'm being. Thinking about this now is a pointless exercise. Not just because it's evening or because I won't be working tomorrow as it's a Saturday, but because, by Monday, there will be no Breakfast Show... not for me anyway.

The brightly lit reception is a stark contrast to the darkness I've left outside in the car park. It's eerily quiet too. I'm not often here this late and the place has a different feel to it. Lifeless, somehow, as though the soul of the building has left it.

A glance at the kitchen door shows no light through its round glass window. I think about making myself a coffee before going to find Alan, then decide against it. The sooner I do this, the sooner I can get home to bed.

I find Alan in Studio Two, headphones on, eyes closed. He's leaning back in his chair, his fingers laced behind his head, blue veins visible beneath the pale skin on the underside of his forearms. In repose, the thin face slack, he could be any age between fifty and sixty but I'm sure he must be younger; the station would have axed him long ago if he wasn't. How old he really is is anyone's guess and I'm certainly not about to ask him.

'Hi, Alan.'

He doesn't acknowledge my greeting and it's only when I walk across the studio and stand in front of him that I realise his lack of response is because he's listening to some music on his headphones. His head nods, his mouth soundlessly forming the words of a song.

I sit in the chair opposite him and wait for him to notice me, feeling like a schoolgirl who's been sent to the headmaster to explain herself. The seconds turn to minutes and I'm just wondering whether he even knows I'm here when he speaks.

'Melanie Abbot.' There are those long, drawn-out vowels again. The low, soporific voice. Alan doesn't open his eyes and his head continues to nod in time to a tune I can't hear.

'Is it still convenient to talk to you?' I'm unsure now. From the way he's acting, speaking to me appears to be the last thing on his mind.

'Maybe.'

Very slowly, he unlaces his fingers and lowers his arms. He lifts the headphones from his head, then, finally, he opens his eyes.

'I wonder if you've got what it takes,' he says, a smile hovering on his thin lips. 'Whether you're up for the challenge.'

I feel myself bristling. 'I'm not afraid of a challenge. I never have been. Ask anyone here.'

The smile stretches. 'Oh, believe me, I have.'

His eyes are dark, slightly protruding. Hawk eyes. They sweep my face as though searching for something, though what that might be I have no idea. No wonder he's on the margins of our tight-knit radio family. I've often felt sorry for him when Chris jokingly calls him the Grim Reaper, but now I don't blame him. Alan's social skills are severely lacking.

Suddenly, I can't be bothered with any of it. 'If you've changed your mind, just say, Alan. It's been a long day and, to be honest, my bed will be a lot warmer than your welcome.'

Not answering my question, Alan pushes his chair back and crosses his feet at the ankles. 'Warmer still if I was in it. Tell me, what are you wearing under that pretty top of yours? I'd say you favour black lace.'

His voice is lazy. Uninterested. He could have just asked me what the weather was like outside. But what he says still makes me freeze, wondering whether I've heard him correctly.

Seeing my expression, Alan shakes his head, wearily. 'Oh, for goodness' sake, Melanie. Get over yourself. Is that how you'd react if a caller said the same thing to you?' He leans his sharp elbows on the shiny surface and looks at me. 'There are people out there, driving their lorries, finishing their shift at the hospital, maybe simply unable to sleep, who are lonely. You don't want to be caught off guard.'

'Couldn't you have just told me that?'

Alan places his hands on the desk and spreads his fingers. They're long and thin, the hard bones of his knuckles pressing against the white skin.

'Would it have been as effective? You're going to have to learn how to deal with all types of people if you're to do this job properly. If you're not sure you can manage that, then may I suggest you don't waste my time or yours.'

I'd thought the Late-Night Show would be a doddle compared to what I've been used to, but now I'm beginning to wonder whether I was wrong. But I've never been a quitter.

And I've never been so intrigued.

'If I'm going to take over, Alan, I'm going to need to know everything.'

He glances at the clock on the wall. 'Near impossible in forty-five minutes but I'll do what I can to fill you in. Could I make a suggestion though?'

'Of course.'

'Sit in on my show, or at least the beginning of it. That way, you'll get more of a feel for it. I think you'll find that the late-night programme is at the other end of the scale to what you're used to. It doesn't have the structure for a start – the news, the travel. There's no fast, upbeat music, no inane chat with your co-host chums. Just you and your listeners. Intimate. Slow-moving like that big old canal out there. And unlike the Breakfast Show, you don't talk at your audience, you talk *to* them. *With* them.'

I nod and stifle a yawn. Despite my afternoon nap, the early morning is catching up on me, but at least tomorrow is Saturday, and I won't have to get up early. 'Yes, I'll sit in, but can I ask you some questions first?'

Alan looks at me steadily. 'Ask away. If I can answer, I will.'

I get my notebook out from my bag and look at the questions I want to ask. They seem stupid now, naïve. Closing the book, I ask instead something from the heart.

'What's it like, Alan, really like, to be here alone doing your show? No co-host. No producer?' The image has a certain romance to it. A darkened studio. A single light picking out the one person who can brighten up someone's life in the darkest hours.

He steeples his fingers to his lips. 'The best way I can describe it is having a date with someone who has an advantage over you – where you don't know them, but they know all about you. Or a stalker. Once you get established on the show, there will be people out there who will have been listening and following you for weeks, months even. They'll know your voice, will have noticed the small things you give away about yourself. What you do. What you like. Of course, you'll have experienced a little of this already, but the late-night audience is different.'

I put my head on one side, fascinated. 'How so?'

'There are thousands of people listening, but halfway through the show, you'll lose your daytime audience and be left with the people on the fringes. Delivery drivers, factory workers, cabbies, care workers... anyone on a night shift. Then there are the breast-feeding mothers, the worriers, the insomniacs. Faceless, nameless, real people. All with a reason to be listening to you... and you alone.'

I look around at the empty studio wondering how I'd feel if it was just me here. Alan's slightly protruding eyes watch me, then he answers my unspoken question.

'Being here alone is my favourite part of what I do... or should I say *was*. With viewing figures for the late show low compared to daytime radio, the budget doesn't extend to a producer, but I like it that way. To all intents and purposes, you are your own boss. It's *you* who decides what song to play and when to play it. Not Simon. Not Dan. *You* who decides who to let speak and who to cut off.'

I raise my eyebrows. 'Cut off?'

'Yes. Unlike the daytime shows where a call is recorded during a song, these calls are live. You are the only censor. Late at night, you grow a loyal fan base. While they're listening, you become the object of their affection, or at least their attention.' He points to the monitor beside him, where the callers' numbers will appear, and gives a tight smile. 'Be careful. That feeling can be powerful.'

I think about this. On the Breakfast Show, there are four of us involved, if you count the producer. Being in sole charge of my own programme has a certain appeal.

'The people who call in... What are they like?'

Alan draws in a long breath and thinks about it. 'Some are lonely, some are sad, some are hyped up after a good night out, some are drunk, some are desperate to tell you some news. Mostly, though, for whatever reason, the people who call in are wanting someone to talk to. You are that person. In their eyes you become their friend. Their confidant. Their confessional.'

The mention of the word confessional reminds me of something I wanted to ask him.

'A main part of your show is the True Confessions slot. I'd like to know more about the type of things they confess to.' I've never listened to this part of the show myself but have heard Simon mention it. It's at midnight, and despite the late hour, listener figures always go up when it starts.

Alan pushes his chair away from the desk and swings one long leg over the other. 'Sometimes it will be someone remembering a prank they pulled on someone when they were a child. Or it could be as bad as someone admitting to sleeping with their married boss. Some things will make you laugh, but some will be shocking. Remember that because they know you can't see their face, a radio caller will be duped into thinking they have a certain anonymity.' He chuckles. 'If only they knew. A voice can sometimes be as recognisable as a face.'

I think of the number of people who call me on my mobile. People whose voices I know instantly without reading their names on the screen.

'Yes, you're right. But what if they say something... controversial?'

Alan locks his fingers around his knee and studies me. 'It's not what they say that's important. It's how you respond to it... hence my own little prank earlier. You always have the option to end the call, cut them off with some music, but I've found it's not always the best way. Not if you want to avoid them calling back the next night or the next. You may think being a radio presenter is all about talking but it's about listening too. Thinking how you can turn something around. How to keep the listeners interested.'

My breath quickens. 'Has something like that ever happened to you? Has someone ever phoned in with a confession that has made you feel uncomfortable?'

'A couple of times.' He massages the back of his neck. 'Not for a while though.'

'Do you mind telling me what happened?'

'It was a few years back. A guy phoned in and told me his

confession was that he wanted to kill himself. He'd apparently been having these thoughts for a while and decided that doing it on air might be a cool thing to do. I won't lie to you – it shook me up a bit.'

My hand shoots to my mouth. 'He didn't, did he?'

Surely I would have heard if that had happened.

'Thank God, no. I managed to talk him round and got him to promise he'd seek help once he came off the phone.'

'Do you think he did?'

He lifts his shoulders in a half shrug. 'Who knows? The phone numbers come up on the monitor, but this guy had withheld his. He never called back, and I just have to hope that it was because he didn't need to, that his cry for help had been heard. The alternative is too gruesome to think about. What I do know is that listener figures rocketed the next evening. Some people are just damn morbid.'

I give a small shiver. Would I be able to cope in a situation such as that? I want to ask him something else but he's already sliding his chair sideways so he can look at his computer screen, and a glance at the clock shows me there isn't long until the show starts.

While Alan prepares, I open my notebook and write some headings. I want to make sure I understand how everything works before Monday. Before Monday... the graveyard slot hasn't even started, and it sounds as if I've already made up my mind.

Have I?

After all Alan's said, a part of me is excited to be sitting in on the show. But another part is uneasy. I don't have time to consider my feelings though as he's already got up and dimmed the lights. From my dark corner, I watch him go back to his seat, pick up his headphones and put them on. He leans forward. A lone figure picked out in the single bright light.

He slides one of the fader knobs and music fills the studio. It's something I recognise but can't place. Haunting. Emotional. From a musical perhaps?

Alan lets it play for a moment and then fades it out, replacing it with his low, slow voice. A voice that reminds me of dark chocolate. Of night-time. A cold chill runs down my spine. If the Grim Reaper was real, it's what his voice would sound like.

'This is Lock Radio. It's ten o'clock and time for the Late-Night Show.' Alan's eyes flick over to me then back to his monitor. 'My *last* Late-Night Show if truth be told. I'll miss you, really miss you, and I want this to be a night we can truly remember. Talk to me. You know the number, but in case you've forgotten...'

His voice is hypnotic, each word drawing me in. Like the other thousands of listeners, he's making it feel like we're in a private conversation. That it's just the two of us.

I study his closed eyes, with their hooded lids, the relaxed way he sits, long legs stretched in front of him, fingers linked behind his head, arms wide, just as he was sitting when I first came in. He could be a grandfather telling his children a bedtime story in front of the fire. I'm mesmerised. Too fascinated to make notes.

'Welcome, children of the night,' he says, a smile on his thin lips. 'Welcome to the Late Show.'

As Alan's words linger, I think about how it will feel being alone in the studio with just these nameless, faceless callers for company. Is it true that it's easier to confess a secret to someone you don't know?

Would *I* find it easier?

With difficulty, I push the thought away, not wanting to go there.

SEVEN

I get out of the cab and pay the driver, buttoning up my coat as he drives away even though I'll be taking it off in a few minutes. It's nearly eight thirty, the time I said I'd meet Chris and Simon. But despite the late hour I got to bed last night, on top of yesterday's ridiculously early morning, I'm feeling okay. Usually, on a Saturday morning, even with no alarm set, my body clock kicks in and I'm infuriatingly wide awake soon after four. Not this morning though. No, this morning, I'd slept in until eleven, only waking when Niall knocked on the door to say there was a cup of tea waiting for me in the kitchen if I wanted it. No longer comfortable entering the bedroom we once shared.

It's a lovely star-filled evening and rather than go straight into The Junction, I stand a moment by the lock, looking at the moon reflected in the water of the canal. It feels odd to be here again, as though I've been transported back in time. When I first started drinking in this pub, I was a young, new presenter. Wanting to be seen, hoping I might be recognised even though people only knew me from my voice. How silly that young girl was. How needy.

Now I'm older and wiser... so old, in fact that, I've been bumped off my prime-time spot. I give myself a mental slap. I'd told myself I wouldn't spoil everyone's evening by getting bitter, and I won't. To be honest, I couldn't wait to leave the house this evening. Couldn't stand watching Niall in the kitchen, chopping peppers and putting wine in the fridge to cool.

I turn away from the canal and lean my back against the black paddle of the lock gate so I can watch the Saturday night punters who are milling outside the pub smoking. Thinking about Niall and his preparations has left a hollow feeling inside me. It's hard not to remember the first time he invited me over for a meal... perfectly cooked steak and chips. Harder still to forget how, later, he'd led me upstairs to his room. Not that we'd made it there; our lust had got the better of us and the landing floor had become our bed. My hand reaches round to the small of my back remembering the sting of the carpet burn I'd received.

Although Fiona is a lot younger than I was then, from the look of her – the carefully straightened hair and the even more carefully applied make-up – I can't see the same thing happening. And at forty-two, I know that Niall will prefer a soft bed for his seduction.

Christ, what was I thinking of when I said I was okay with her staying over? No one in their right mind would agree to it! I take a deep lungful of cool night air... but neither would anyone in their right mind still be living with a man they'd divorced.

Pushing myself away from the paddle arm, I cross the towpath and head up the steps beside the grassy bank to the pub. Hoping that the boys will already be here. Wondering if I can face standing on my own at the bar if they're not. It never used to bother me but I'm a different person now.

Lock Radio is situated on the outskirts of town on a stretch of canal where the office and residential buildings have started to give way to patches of open field and the odd dilapidated brick structure that must have had a use in bygone industrial times. The Junction, in contrast, is closer to the heart of town, the red-brick warehouse buildings that flank the pub now converted into upmarket flats for young professionals. It's a place to see and be seen and I wonder if I'm still up to it. Now I'm happy to stay in the background and leave my breakfast programme persona in the studio.

I push open the door and peer inside. The place is full already, most of the tables taken. Several groups of people stand in the space between them and the bar, but it doesn't take me long to see Simon. He's sitting at the end of the bar on a high stool, contemplating his phone. I can't see Chris though. As I make my way towards him, he looks up and raises his hand to register he's seen me. Putting one foot on the ground, he puts his phone in his jeans pocket then holds out his arms, kissing me on the cheek when I reach him.

'You made it.' He settles himself on the stool again. 'Chris and I were worried you'd change your mind... again.'

After checking no one's using it, I move a stool from further along the bar and sit. 'There was no way on God's earth I'd be staying in tonight. Niall's got his little girl coming round for a *look at me aren't I a great cook and therefore a great shag* meal.'

'Fiona?'

'That's the one. Can you believe he actually had the bare-faced cheek to ask me if she can stay the night... like I'm his mother?'

Simon takes a sip of his drink, eyeing me over the top of it. 'Or like the ex-wife who's sharing the marital home.'

I narrow my eyes at him. 'That's not fair, Si. You know I'd move out if I could. I know better than anyone that it's not ideal. Anyway, I didn't know what to say so I agreed to it.'

'That's very nice of you.' He puts down his glass and looks at me thoughtfully. 'I thought you said she was just a flash in the pan.'

'That's because I thought she was. She's so *young*, Simon. What's he playing at?'

'Maybe he just likes her. Maybe they're right for each other, did you think of that? It happens, and you can't dictate where or when.'

Not wanting to have this conversation and annoyed that Simon's not taking my side, I turn to the bar and try and catch the attention of one of the bar staff.

Simon's voice is placatory. 'Don't be mad at me, Mel. All I meant is that Niall's not your responsibility. You're divorced and what he does or doesn't do is no longer your concern. I don't want you getting hurt, that's all. Here, let me get this. What are you having?'

I let him buy me a gin and tonic and allow my irritation to dissipate. 'Where's Chris?'

'He's here somewhere. I lost him soon after we got here.'

'Have you been here long then?'

Simon has a mouthful of his drink. 'Half an hour or so. You know Chris: he doesn't like to waste good drinking time.'

I frown. 'Look after him tonight, Si. Don't let him get wasted.'

'I'm not his bodyguard or his conscience. If he wants to drown his liver then that's his problem.'

'You don't mean that. You worry about him as much as I do. God knows how he gets up in the morning for the show.'

'All I can say is thank God we're on air and no one can smell his beer breath or see his bloodshot eyes.' He picks up a beer mat and rolls it along the bar top. 'We're never going to change him. He is who he is... a giant, longhaired, overweight, shit-funny guy who the housewives love.'

We both laugh but I'll be happier if I know where he is. Looking out for him tonight will give me a purpose for being here. It used to be to drink too much, dance and flirt but that's not me anymore.

The pub is busier now, but as the person on the other side of me moves away with their drink, leaving a gap, I see Chris. He's standing at the other end of the bar, a pint in his hand, a chaser in front of him. My heart sinks. It's only just gone nine. This could be a long night.

I wave to him, and he gives me a thumbs up back. Soon he's pushing between the groups of drinkers and when he reaches us, he looks down at me and grins.

'Glad you decided to grace us with your presence.' He thumps Simon on the back. 'Got our third musketeer back. Oops, miss your mouth, did you?'

'Fucking hilarious.' Simon wipes at the drink that's gone down the front of his shirt. It looks new, well fitting and with a subtle stripe. The unusual indigo shade brings out the colour of his eyes.

'New shirt?' I ask.

'Yes, Anne bought it for me. She has more of an eye for these things than I do.'

Chris pulls a face. 'Makes you look like a fucking ponce.'

I tap him on the leg with the toe of my boot. 'Shut up, Chris. Are you drunk already?'

He's made no mention of his friend. Maybe he didn't turn up.

'You must be kidding. The night is young. I haven't even got close to starting.' He bends and leans a heavy hand on my shoulder. 'Tonight's going to be great... just like old times.' He raises his pint. 'To The Three Musketeers.'

Simon raises his glass. 'All for one and one for all!'

Their words make me sad. 'Except we're not, are we. Have you forgotten I won't be with you on Monday?'

Chris rubs the side of his face with the flat of his hand. 'Damn it, yes I had.'

'So, what happened?' Simon rests his elbow on the bar and looks at me. 'Did you get to speak to Alan?'

'Uh-huh. I went back to the studio last night and sat in on the programme.' I think of the laid-back music Alan had played, the topics he'd discussed and the conversations he'd had with the callers. How he'd spoken to each one as though they were family. 'It was odd. He knew so much about the people who phoned in. Details like whether they were married or divorced, whether they had a pet and what they did for a living. He chatted to them as if they were old friends.'

Simon raises his eyebrows. 'That sounds the other end of the spectrum to what we do.'

I nod in agreement. 'It really is. But you know what? I had this weird sensation of being sucked in. On our show, we don't really know anything about our callers, but last night it was different. Intimate. I found myself wanting to know more about their lives. Why they'd want to listen to a show at an hour when most other people are asleep. And why chatting to Alan is so important to them. Especially the regular callers.' I lean forward, hands on knees. 'Because some of them have been ringing in for months... years even.'

Chris rests his elbow on my shoulder and, with his other hand, raises his pint to his lips. He takes a gulp then smiles glassily at me.

'So, what are these regulars going to think when they find out it's you and not Alien Alan on the other end of the line.'

I frown. 'I don't know. I hadn't thought about that. A lot of people phoned in to ask why he was leaving and to say he'd be missed but no one asked about who was taking over.' I take a mouthful of my gin, thinking I should pace myself so I don't suffer tomorrow. But then I remember what I'll be going home to and drain my glass. 'Speaking of which, do you know why Alan's leaving?'

It's Chris who answers. 'No idea. He's an oddball... everyone thinks so. It's all very sudden and hush-hush, so I wouldn't be surprised if he's done something he shouldn't have and is leaving under a cloud.'

Simon scratches at his chin, considering this. 'Wouldn't Di have said?'

'No,' Chris replies. 'She can be very discreet when she wants to be.'

I think back to last night. 'Whatever the case, I'm going to have to do something to win the audience over.'

The truth is, I'd been fascinated by how Alan had responded to his callers. So much so that I hadn't considered how his close relationship with them might affect me. I'm going to have to start from scratch to win their confidence. Build fresh relationships and trust with those who are already part of the late-night family. If I don't do that, the ratings will plummet, and I really will be out of a job.

'You'll be great. Everyone will love you.' Simon smiles reassuringly.

'Really?' I don't want to sound needy, but I really need the boys' encouragement if I'm to do this.

'Of course – why wouldn't they?'

Moving away from me, Chris reaches behind him and thumps his pint of beer on the bar. Brown liquid runs down the outside and pools on the wooden counter. He leans his arm on it, not noticing.

'Stop being so fucking nice about it, Simon. Christ almighty, you'd be the one covering your eyes and pretending it wasn't happening when the Christians were being thrown to the lions. I'll tell it to you straight, Mel. You won't find it an easy change. There are some loons out there at that time of night. My advice is to get the hell out of it before you make a decision you might regret.'

He turns away from me and waves a hand to get the barman's attention. I know he's only looking out for me, but I'm shocked at his negativity. I'd started to feel more confident about the change. Viewing it as a challenge. Determined to make it work. But after what Chris has just said, the doubts start creeping in again.

EIGHT

It's late. It's noisy. Although I'd decided I wouldn't have too much to drink tonight, the boys keep ordering. We haven't moved from the bar but I'm okay with that. I like watching people, even though it's just occurred to me that most of the people in here are quite a bit younger.

'Do you ever feel like you've moved on from this?'

I'm addressing no one in particular, but it's Simon who answers. 'Not really. We might be a bit older but we're still the same people.'

I look at him, then away again. 'No, we're not. Not really. We've had things happen. Good and bad. We've celebrated our successes, mourned our tragedies and, hopefully, learnt from our mistakes.'

'Get you, the great philosopher.' The word is thick in Chris's mouth. He's clearly quite far down the road to inebriation. 'The biggest mistake you made was to marry that idiot, Niall.'

I wonder if Simon is going to have a go at him for being so blunt, but he doesn't. When I first got here, he had seemed on good form, but in the last half hour or so he's been quieter. More pensive, as if something's on his mind.

Chris's voice brings my attention back to him. 'I'm going to love and leave you guys. There's someone I want to talk to.'

Giving me a pantomime wink, he pushes himself from the bar and walks unsteadily over to the other side of the room where a dark-haired man is standing on his own, his back to us. Could this be the guy Chris mentioned? The blind date?

'Who's that?' I gesture towards him with my head.

Simon looks over and shrugs. 'No idea. You forget, Chris knows everybody. He's a ridiculously ugly bugger but there's something about him that makes everyone want to be his friend—'

'If I didn't know you better, Simon, I'd say you were jealous.'

The thought is ridiculous. Of the two of them, Simon has the edge when it comes to looks. Chris might have the humour gene, but there's a sensitivity to Simon that I think makes him more appealing.

'Do you think it could be my blind date?'

Simon looks but turns back straight away. 'Who knows?'

He sounds distracted. Usually, he enjoys his nights out, but this evening there's clearly something up with him. With each drink he's becoming more maudlin. It's starting to irritate me. It was, after all, his idea we came out. The two of them were supposed to be cheering me up, but Chris has buggered off and Simon looks as though he'd rather be anywhere than here with me.

I crane my neck around a girl who's stopped in front of us to look at her phone to get a better view of the guy Chris is with, but they've moved out of sight. If it had been him, wouldn't Chris have brought him over by now?

I look at my watch. It's nearly eleven. 'Maybe we should call it a night.'

The music that had been on in the background has been turned up louder and a group of girls, in unseasonably skimpy clothing, have taken to the small dance floor. They've formed a circle, their arms raised, index fingers pointing to the ceiling as they laugh and sing the words of the cheesy song that's playing through the speakers. I'd been looking forward to a dance but now the desire has left me.

'Anne's pregnant.'

My head snaps around. His words have come so out of the blue that for a moment I wonder if I heard Simon correctly. I look at him, unsure what I should say in reply. From his tone of voice, it's impossible to tell how he feels about it. Losing their last baby at twelve weeks was a tragedy none of us had expected.

I would probably never have known about the miscarriage if I hadn't made Simon tell me. He'd been strangely off with me, and I knew him well enough to know that something was wrong. I'd been shocked when he told me, but how I felt was nothing compared to the hell Anne must have been going through. He'd made me promise not to say anything to Chris and I hadn't. Di's not the only one who can keep a secret.

'That's great news, Simon. You're happy, aren't you?'

I'm pleased for them both but worried too. I know how much the loss of their baby affected them. Affected us all in some ways... even Chris, who had suddenly lost a drinking buddy.

'Yes, of course I'm happy.' Simon downs the final inch of his pint and waggles it at the bartender. 'Why wouldn't I be?'

'I don't know, it was just the way you said it.' I hesitate before asking. 'How many weeks is she?'

'Eight weeks. She's only just told me, but I couldn't keep it to myself. You won't tell Anne I told you, will you?'

I cradle my goblet in my hands and look over at Chris, wishing it was him he'd told. Now the pressure is on me to support Simon, and it was so hard to talk to him about everything that happened last time.

'No, of course I won't say anything. You shouldn't worry though. Most women who miscarry go on to have a perfectly healthy baby afterwards.'

I cringe at my thoughtless words, wondering how I'd have felt if someone had said to me, *I'm sorry about your divorce. You shouldn't worry though. If you meet someone else, there's no reason to think it will happen again.*

Not that I'd had any plans to meet anyone else. Once bitten twice shy is a cliché but the truth. I'd been realistic enough to know that the people I'd be likely to meet would be boys too young to want to settle down, divorcees looking for someone to help with their children on the weekends, or much older men with a good reason for still being single. I've spoken out on the merits of online dating agencies and Tinder on the Breakfast Show, but the thought of doing it myself leaves me cold. Meeting a stranger could be dangerous.

And yet, there's this guy Chris has been talking about – the one I've yet to meet. He wouldn't be a stranger but someone chosen by one of my best friends. It's hard to admit, but a tiny part of me is disappointed that Chris hasn't brought him over yet.

'How *is* Anne?' I say, not wanting to dwell on my change of heart.

'Sick as a dog, if you must know. Morning, evening... you name it. Once she's asleep she's okay. I've moved to the spare room so the alarm doesn't wake her at stupid o'clock.' He sighs. 'The trials of breakfast radio, eh. To be honest, I nearly didn't come out tonight, but she says there's nothing I can really do for her whilst she's puking her guts up in the toilet or sleeping it off.'

'And she said she was happy for you to come out?' I find it hard to believe.

'Not in so many words. But, also, I didn't want to let you down. I know how difficult things are for you at the moment.'

'I'm not the priority here, Simon – Anne is.' I shift on my stool. 'I think it might have been nice of you to have given her the choice.' I shake my head at Simon's thoughtlessness. If it was me who was pregnant, I'd want my husband home with me. 'Maybe I'll give her a ring tomorrow and see if she fancies meeting up,' I continue. 'I haven't seen her in ages, and I feel bad about it.'

Anne and I used to see each other every now and again, usually on an evening when Simon was out with Chris and Niall was at his snooker club. Now I realise we haven't met since the miscarriage. Nearly a year ago now. 'We could go to the café one day next week after she's finished work. Have a coffee or something. That's if she's drinking coffee. Isn't that one of the things you're not allowed when you're pregnant?'

Simon really has put me in a difficult position. How can I meet with her without giving away what I know? Chatting normally with the spectre of her pregnancy between us would feel wrong.

'I really wish you hadn't told me, Si. It would have been so much better if you'd waited until she'd had the scan.'

He bows his head. 'I told you because I'm worried and there was no one else I wanted to tell... who would understand. Chris certainly wouldn't.'

I feel myself soften. 'I'm sorry. Of course you're worried, but tonight is the ideal opportunity to take your mind off it.' Taking his drink from his hand, I put it on the bar top and slip down from my stool. 'Come on. You're here now – let's dance.'

Simon reluctantly allows me to pull him into the crowd of people dancing in the space between the tables and the bar. The song that's playing is one from our morning playlist. Normally, the song irritates me, and when it comes on, I make Simon mute it in the studio, relying on the screen in front of him to let me know when it's coming to an end. Tonight, though, the gin has made me warm and fuzzy. The beat of the music pulses in my head, making my feet move in time to it. Maybe it's not such a bad song after all.

Christ, I'd forgotten how much I love to dance.

A group of girls to my right, a couple of them barely out of their teens, are staring in our direction, but it's not me they're interested in, it's Simon. They've recognised him, giggling to each other as they edge closer. He's like the sun, and the women are the planets orbiting around him. Nothing's changed. It's how it used to be when we were younger, when Simon's hair was longer, and he looked more like the photograph on the board in reception. He needs to be careful. I hope he's not going to be weak. But it's just the gin that's making me think like this. He's devoted to Anne now.

The music has gone up a notch, the base reverberating through my body, right to my very core. I dance as I haven't danced in years, arms above my head, eyes closed.

It's been too long.

Way too long.

One song blends into another. Then another. The music is like a drug and I'm getting high on it. It blocks out everything that's happened in the last couple of days. Niall and Fiona. The Breakfast Show that's been taken away from me. Simon and Anne's baby. It's just me and the music.

Simon reaches out. He catches my hand and turns me under his arm. It takes me by surprise and sends me off balance. I laugh and catch hold of his shirt to steady myself, realising how drunk I am. It's like the old days. A time when we had nothing to think about except the following week's playlist. Nothing to worry about except keeping the listener ratings up.

Listener ratings. The words pull me up short. Sobering me momentarily. Maybe if I'd worried about them more I wouldn't now be leaving the show. Leaving my best friends. I look at Simon who's in a world of his own. Dancing as if no one is watching. He's a good dancer. I've always thought so.

I look for Chris. Through gin-glazed eyes, I see him. He hasn't moved from where he was earlier, but others have joined him. A young guy who's laughing at something he's just said and one of the girls who was ogling Simon a while ago. She's reaching up to him, pulling his big head down to meet hers so she can whisper something in his ear.

All around me people are moving, bodies knocking against me. Voices singing out the words to the song that's playing. The room is starting to spin, and I stop dancing, trying to focus on something that isn't moving in the hope that it will help. And that something, the person my eyes choose to fix on, is a man with dark hair. Chris's friend. He's leaning against one of the tables, his face turned towards me. Watching me.

I look away but it's as if my eyes have a will of their own and it isn't long before they're back, taking in his light brown skin. The dark eyes and hair.

What is it that's keeping my eyes locked with his? What spell?

He's not good-looking – not in the traditional sense anyway. His brow is too heavy, the eyebrows almost meeting in the middle. But his nose is straight and strong, his top lip sensitively bowed, the bottom plumper. All this I take in while I'm standing there, trying to still the roundabout motion of the room.

There's something about this man that I can't fathom. He looks out of place here in The Junction bar. His hair too long, pushed back behind his ears. His expression sharp. Eyes watching.

He unnerves me but fascinates me too.

'I'm going back to the bar.' I tug at Simon's arm to get his attention. 'Are you coming?'

'What did you say?' Simon cups his hand to his ear to hear me better.

'I said I'm going back to the bar.'

He catches hold of my arm. 'Stay. I'm having fun. Don't be a spoilsport.'

I shake him off. 'No, Simon. I need to sit down. I shouldn't have drunk so much tonight.'

Simon's nearly as drunk as I am. He looks blearily at my face, tying to focus, and despite the large amount of alcohol inside me, I feel a twinge of concern. Unlike Chris, Simon isn't a happy drunk. In the blink of an eye, the polite, sensitive man we know can morph into a taciturn teenager. But at least if he's dancing, he won't be drinking. That's one consolation.

I push through the crowd and go back to the bar, leaning heavily on it to steady myself. When I feel up to it, I turn and survey the room. It's still busy but, despite the approach of autumn, some of the drinkers have gone outside. The people who stand on the terrace or sit at the wooden tables are illuminated by the lights that run beside the steps leading down to the towpath. Every so often a train passes by on the other side of the cut, but they're largely ignored.

Most of the drinkers are younger than me, laughing and chatting in mixed groups. There are a few people of around my age too, but they all seem to be in couples, facing each other across the wooden tables, some holding hands.

Although I came here with Simon and Chris, seeing them just brings it home to me that I'm on my own. I liked being part of a couple, and although I don't *want* Niall anymore, I miss him. Miss the physical closeness you can't get from a friend: the touch of fingertips on skin; the warmth of a back and the lace of fingers as you lie in bed, whispering things you wouldn't say to anyone else. *The intimacy...* that's the word my intoxicated brain is looking for. The coming together of both body and mind.

With a shock, I realise my eyes have filled with tears. It takes me by surprise as I've always prided myself on my emotional strength. Tears are a weakness, that's what Mum used to tell me. *Wipe those eyes now. Brave girls don't cry.*

I rummage in my bag, searching for my phone... for anything that will distract me from the way I'm feeling. But as I draw it out, my mobile falls through my fumbling fingers and drops onto the dark, beer-drizzled boards.

Fuck.

People are too close, the soles of their shoes and sharp heels threatening to crush the delicate screen. I bend down to recover it, but someone's hand is there before mine, holding it out to me. Hands that are larger and stronger than mine, the fingers long and tapered.

As we both stand, and he hands the phone to me, I recognise him as the man Chris had brought along for me to meet, even though I'd told him not to. The blind date. He says something, but the bar is noisy, his voice accented, and I don't know what he's said. I shrug to show I haven't heard, and he says it louder.

Just one word.

Malik.

Not *My name is Malik* or *I'm Malik.* Just those two short syllables.

I look at his face. At the long straight nose, the black hair pushed behind his ears and the skin that's lightly pockmarked.

His demeanour is intoxicating, strangely dangerous, but I don't know why.

But even as I'm thinking this, I feel the first stirrings of attraction. A heightening of my senses. An awareness of how close he is and the musky scent of his skin. How easy it would be to take that hand and press it to my lips.

Malik.

I don't know it now but it's a word that will change my life. And not for the better.

NINE

For a few seconds, I don't say anything. There's something about this man that's magnetic, every hair on my body reacting to him as though they're made of iron filings rather than something softer.

Eventually, I find my tongue, fighting to keep my voice from slurring, desperate to appear sober. 'I'm Melanie.'

'I know.' His own voice is low.

I sense rather than see Malik beside me. It's as if the air in the space between our arms is warmer than the rest of the room. The pint of beer on the bar beside him is hardly touched and I'm surprised, seeing as it's a Saturday night. I find myself struggling to get words out – scared that if I speak too much, I might spirit him away.

But it's Malik who speaks, and as he does, I watch his lips part and move as though it's the most fascinating thing I've seen.

'Tell me why you're here,' he says.

Even in my gin-dazed state, I recognise the strangeness of what he's said. It's not a question at all but a command – direct to the point of being rude. Normally, I'd counter it with something equally blunt but, instead, I find myself answering.

'Why does anyone come to a place like this? To drink. To dance.' There's a bar stool behind me and I grip the edge of it to stop myself from swaying.

'No, that is not an answer. Why are you here? What are you looking for?'

The situation is odd. He's not making polite conversation or asking the usual things you'd expect when you first meet someone, such as where I live or what I do for a living. It's as if he knows these things already and has moved on to something more intimate, like in the closing hours of a first date. Maybe Chris already told him...

Chris is talking to someone further along the bar, the girl hanging on to his arm, but every so often I see him looking at us. Usually, I'm careful when I speak to men I don't know, but tonight my inhibitions have been swallowed down with my gin. I want to tell him: *You. I was looking for you.* But thankfully I've enough sanity left to know that I can't. That anything I say while I'm drunk could have repercussions that I might regret.

'I suppose I came here to look for the person I used to be.' I laugh. 'Jesus, I sound like a self-help manual.'

Malik gives a warm smile that puts me at my ease. He leans against the bar and studies my face. 'You didn't need to find your-self. *I* found you.'

His words fall into the space between us and hang heavy. There's no irony in what he's just said. It's as though he's simply stating a fact. Malik is no longer looking directly at me but has turned towards the bar. His elbows are on the wooden surface, his drink in between them. The skin on his forearms below his rolled-up sleeves is the colour of dark caramel. Smooth. He's looking at my reflection in the mirror. Excitement has changed my face. Brought a rose flush to my cheeks. I want to ask him so many things but, for the first time in my life, I'm tongue-tied.

Luckily, it's Malik who breaks the silence. 'It's too hot in here. Why don't we go outside?'

He holds out his hand and I take it, as though I've known him for months rather than for a few short, perfect minutes. He guides me between the groups of people standing around the bar and as we pass the dance floor, I look out for Simon but he's no longer dancing. I hope he's okay and that he hasn't gone home to Anne in the maudlin state in which I left him. But equally, I don't want him to come and find me, to break this odd spell Malik has cast upon me.

Clutching my drink to my chest with my free hand, I follow Malik through the wide-open doors leading onto the outside terrace above the grassy bank. There are no tables free but that's not where he's taking me. Instead, he leads me around the side of the building to an alleyway that separates The Junction from the building next door. A window with small dark panes and a heavy stone sill that contrasts with the red-brick wall makes a perfect rest for our drinks. Malik takes mine from my hand and puts it next to his. He leans against the pub wall and smiles.

'This is better. Now I can hear you. What do you do?'

At last, he's asking me an ordinary question. One I don't have to think about.

'Hasn't Chris told you?'

He takes a mouthful of his drink, then puts it back on the ledge. 'Maybe he has, but I want to hear it from you.'

I rest my shoulder against the cold brick. 'Okay. I work at Lock Radio. Chris and I co-present the early morning show. Simon too.'

I expect Malik to make some comment, but he doesn't, and I find myself prompting him. As I speak, my words echo off the brick walls. 'Have you heard the show?'

'No.'

The word is sharp. A pin popping my ego. Without realising it, I'd wanted him to know who I was. To be impressed by what I did. I feel foolish now. 'I don't blame you. It's not everyone's cup of tea.'

From the terrace, I can hear voices, bursts of laughter, music. But here, in our own private space, with the stars twinkling in the small rectangle of sky above our heads, it feels like another world.

'I don't listen to the radio.' His dark-brown eyes are unblinking, and I wonder if he's telling the truth.

'Come on... never?' For some odd reason, I'd thought that everyone listened at some time or another. Before getting up, while eating breakfast, on the drive into work. Clearly not. I desperately want to convert him. 'If you tune in on Monday, I can dedicate a song to you.'

As soon as the words are out of my mouth, I realise how stupid they sound – how crass and patronising. As though by dedicating a song to him, I'll win his affection. Then another thought occurs to me. I'd wanted tonight to push what had happened on Friday from my thoughts and it clearly has.

'Ignore everything I've just said. How could I have forgotten? I won't be doing that show anymore as I've been moved to the late shift. My evenings will no longer be my own. They'll be shared with the insomniacs and night workers of Greater Manchester.'

Hearing the catch in my voice, I feel myself colour. Malik says nothing but his fingertips graze the outside of my arm. With not enough light in which to see his face properly I can't read his expression, but his touch is enough. I've never felt an attraction like this before and I'm not sure what to do.

Malik remains silent and I wonder if I've blown it. Whether he'll make his excuses and leave. It's been so long since I've been interested in someone, I'm nervous. My heart thumps and nerves are making my hairline prickle. I can't keep my eyes from his.

Before I can work out my feelings, Malik pushes himself from the wall. Reaching out a hand, he cups the back of my head and draws me to him. It's sudden. Breathtaking. I know I should resist, pull away before I lose myself, but I can't. Any willpower I might have had when I was sober has long gone.

And in that dark alleyway, he kisses me with such passion that for a moment I forget where I am. I put my hand against his chest feeling his heartbeat beneath his shirt. Tasting him. Losing myself in him.

Then the spell is broken. I can hear my name being called. It's Simon.

I pull away from Malik and curse under my breath. 'I'd better see what he wants.'

I find him on the terrace. He's looking around him, his jacket over his arm. He doesn't look happy.

'I was just getting some air,' I say. 'What do you want?'

'I've been looking for you for ages. I think it's time we went home.'

I look at my watch, but the numbers are blurry. I think it might be after midnight. 'I'm not ready.'

He holds out his hand. 'Come on. Chris is calling a cab. We'll drop you home first.' He goes to take my arm, but Malik is behind me.

'Look, mate. I don't think she wants to go.'

I lean against Malik, feeling the solid weight of him. Glad that he's intervened. 'Malik will make sure I get home okay.' I look up at him. 'Won't you?'

'Yes, of course I will.'

Simon's forehead puckers. 'Are you sure, Mel?'

I feel Malik's arm slip around my waist, the pad of his thumb grazing the soft skin above the waistband of my jeans, and make a decision. I'm drunk but not so drunk that I don't know that I want this man. He's a friend of Chris's and Simon shouldn't be so concerned. I force my eyes to focus on him. I'm a thirty-eight-year-old independent woman, not a teenager. I don't need chaperoning. And I certainly don't want to go home to Niall and Fiona.

'Of course I'm sure. You go, Si.' I give him a reassuring smile. 'I'll be fine.'

Simon has known me long enough to realise there's no point in trying to persuade me to change my mind once I've made a decision. He shrugs and zips up his jacket.

'Good luck for Monday then.' He gives a sad smile. 'The Breakfast Show won't be the same without you.' He jerks a thumb towards the door of The Junction. 'I'd better kick Chris's fat arse into gear. I'm late enough as it is.'

I watch him leave and then it's just the two of us. Malik and me. The part of me that's still sober is trying to tell me something. That I don't know this man. But the part that's drunk doesn't care.

I know how this evening's going to end, and despite the riskiness, the reckless way I'm behaving, it feels like I've been waiting for this moment for a very long time.

TEN

It's dark. So dark I can barely make out anything in the room. I'm lying on my back on a low bed, a futon maybe, but I'm alone. My mouth's dry, my stomach nauseous, and as I lay there, I try desperately to remember what happened the night before.

My memory is sketchy. I remember hanging on to Malik's arm as we walked along the towpath, trying not to trip on the weed-covered path. I remember the dark shapes of the canal boats at their moorings, the moonlight snagging on the brass cleats. I remember how we'd ducked under the shadows of the bridge, the rough stone grazing my back as we'd kissed. And how I'd wanted him.

Nothing more. Not how I got to be here in this room or what we did in the hours between then and now. Running a hand down my side, I realise I'm wearing the strappy top I had underneath my blouse last night and my underwear. Reaching out a hand, I feel beside me on the floor, relieved when my fingertips come into contact with my clothes and bag. I roll onto my side with the intention of looking inside it, but I haven't even found the zip when another wave of nausea floods through me and I roll back with a soft groan.

As my eyes become more accustomed to the dark, I start to make out shapes in the room: something tall and rectangular and some low square shapes, the nearest one an old packing case that's been made into a makeshift bedside table.

'Malik?'

When there's no answer, I pat the sheet beside me just to be completely certain he's not there. He isn't. The sheet on that side is cold. Gingerly, I try and sit up, managing this time to unzip my bag and find my phone before the next wave of sickness. It's only three thirty. Earlier than I'd thought. Where am I? And where's Malik?

The floor is just bare boards covered in thin rugs. Wrapping the duvet around me, I get up and make my way to the grey square of window to my left. The glass is covered with a sheet that's been tacked to the window, its bottom dragging on the floor. Lifting it, I'm surprised to see a slope of worn grass then the canal, moonlight rippling its surface. I try to get my bearings. When we came out of the pub, we turned left, away from the lock. On the opposite side of the canal, I can see the shape of dark buildings, offices probably, or maybe flats. If I'm right, we can't be that far from the radio station.

I shiver and go back to the bed, sitting cross-legged, the duvet wrapped around me. I press the cotton material to my nose, breathing in the scent of Malik. Beneath the soft fabric, my lips feel tender and I'm back in the darkness of the bridge. Remembering the feel of his fingers in my hair. The weight of his body as he'd pressed me back against the hard brick. The memory makes me take a sharp intake of breath. Makes me want more.

Presuming he's gone to the bathroom, or to the kitchen for water, I'm surprised to hear what sounds like the front door closing. I kneel up on the bed, my eyes straining to see better in the darkened room. The door is opposite, a thin thread of light shining under it. I fix my eyes on it. My heart racing. There are footsteps then silence and I wait, hoping it's him.

The next sound I hear is a small metallic scrape like a key turning in a lock.

The bedroom door moves. It's opening, and someone is coming in.

I say his name into the dark space between us.

'Malik?'

'Shush.'

There's the sound of trousers being unzipped, a soft thud as they fall to the floor. He moves closer and I feel the mattress give as he sits heavily. Unwrapping myself from the duvet, I lift it so he can get under, my body relaxing as he lies back on the pillow.

As he turns towards me, his breath soft on my cheek, I feel a need in me just as great as before. Moving closer, I press the length of my body against his, his skin warm through the soft fabric of my thin top.

It feels right.

Unable to stop myself, I reach out for him, but he catches my wrist and holds my hand against his leg.

'Where have you been?' I ask to mask my disappointment.

'Nowhere.' He releases my wrist and moves his hand to my hair, his fingers cold as they draw through the short strands. As his fingertips graze my neck, making me catch my breath, I lean into him.

Time passes. I feel the rhythmic rise and fall of his chest. Hear his heavy breathing. He's asleep. I close my eyes and lie with my fingertips touching his, remembering the sound of the key in the door. Had he locked the door to the bedroom? Locked me in?

I lie awake for what feels like an age until, finally, I manage to persuade myself I must have imagined it and sleep.

ELEVEN

By the time I wake again, it's morning, weak sunlight leaking through the gaps at the edges of the sheet hung at the window. Malik's arm is across my body, the weight of it making me feel at the same time secure and trapped. Lifting his hand, I ease myself out of the bed and find my jeans. As I pull them on, he stirs but doesn't wake, and I take the opportunity to look at him properly. Searching his sleeping face for something that might help me understand him better.

He's lying on his front, his arms crooked above his head, and I lean across the bed and hold my hand next to his cheek, being careful not to touch and wake him. How beautiful he is. The tops of his arms smooth and muscular. The sensitive bow of his upper lip making me want to kiss him again.

Who is this man that I'm so attracted to? Who makes me want to bend and press my lips to the smooth, exposed part of his back? My memory is hazy and the only thing I remember him telling me is that he moved to the area a couple of years ago and works in security. If he told me more, I've forgotten.

I wasn't looking for anyone. Yet he's here. Scared I'll wake him, I move away and button up my blouse. As I tuck it into my jeans, I hear my phone ping. I look at Malik, scared it will have woken him, but he doesn't stir. Reaching to my bag, I fish the phone out and read the name on the screen. Simon.

Are you okay?

I smile in the half-light. Of course I'm okay.
He's still typing, and I wait.

Chris and I shouldn't have left you.

Putting the strap of my bag over my shoulder, I tiptoe to the door and open it. It leads out into a dark hallway, but to my left is a small kitchen, light from the curtainless window spilling through. The space is cramped, just one stool up against the worktop that serves as a breakfast bar, a toaster, microwave and kettle the only items on display. I reach up and open a cupboard. There are two glasses and two mugs in there along with some mismatched plates. Taking out a glass, I go over to the tap and fill it, gulping down the water before refilling it and swallowing down the paracetamol that I've taken from my bag. Hoping it will cure my pounding head.

I search the cupboards for coffee, pleased when my eyes alight on a jar of Nescafé at the back of one of them. The fridge is empty of anything except a carton of orange, but we can drink it black.

As I wait for the kettle to boil, I type back a message to Simon.

I'm fine. You don't need to worry about me.

He doesn't reply at once and I unscrew the lid of the jar and place a large spoonful of coffee into each mug before topping it with boiling water from the kettle.

A message pings back. *Sorry, Mel. You might not want us to but we do!*

I can't help smiling. Although at times it can be annoying, I like that they look out for me.

Though I seem to remember waking up and thinking he'd locked
me in his room... He's nice, Si. A good choice. Chris did well!

This time the reply comes back immediately.

Locked you in his room? WTF?

It was just my imagination. There's no need to overreact.

Chris might know this guy but I don't. Just be careful.

Don't be silly.

But even as I'm writing this, I'm looking at the tatty melamine
worktops, the fridge that sticks out further than the units as it
doesn't quite fit, the patch of damp in the corner of the ceiling by
the window. The place is sad and neglected and I'm seeing it now
as Simon would. It's little more than a squat.

Last night I was drunker than I've been in a long while. I'd
thought I'd known exactly what I was doing, but now doubt is
burrowing into me. In the pub, and again on the towpath when
Malik had kissed me, I'd wanted more... I'd let my emotions take
over.

I'd planned to take our drinks back to the bedroom, take off my
clothes and wake Malik, but Simon's message has unsettled me.
Now I'm not so sure it's the right thing to do. The sensible, sober
Melanie has returned, and with her has come a new, heightened
awareness of how spontaneous I've been. How dangerous that can
be. He might be a friend of Chris's, but he's never been a particularly good judge of character.

Had I imagined the metallic rasp of a key in a lock earlier this
morning? I'm no longer sure.

Picking up the mugs, I cross the dark hallway and go back into
the bedroom. As I push open the door, the light from the hall illuminating Malik's sleeping form, I glance down at the keyhole,
seeing nothing but an empty black space where a key would go.

Reassured, I walk over to the bed and place Malik's mug on the floor beside him, hoping he won't knock it over when he wakes. Then I go back to the kitchen and drink a few mouthfuls of the hot liquid before pouring what's left into the sink.

By the time I've let myself out of the front door, the sun has risen properly. Instead of walking down to the towpath, I follow a side alley to the street in front of the building and search my phone for the number of a taxi. As I wait for it to answer, I turn and look at the squat seventies housing block that I've just left, wondering what Malik will do when he wakes to find me gone. My guilt grows... What I've done is cowardly, something Chris would do. I want to turn back, to ring the bell and get back into Malik's bed, but I fight the urge. I have to because, in the cold light of day, I know Simon's right.

When I arrive home, it's still early and as soon as the taxi drops me off, I realise how stupid I've been when I spot Fiona's white Fiat parked in front of the house. My heart sinks. I'd been so wrapped up in my own situation that I'd completely forgotten she'd be here. Now, as I stand outside my house, my key in my hand, steeling myself to go in, the truth dawns on me. This is how it's going to be from now on. Fiona in my house. Fiona lying in the bed that I used to share with Niall. Fiona doing the things that I once did. And if not Fiona, then someone else.

I screw up my eyes to stop myself from thinking about it. Niall and I are over. Have been for months and we have the divorce certificate to prove it. I couldn't expect things to have continued as they were.

The house is quiet when I go in. Too quiet. I would have preferred to have found Fiona in the kitchen making toast or the sound of a shower running. This silence brings with it a picture of Fiona's head on Niall's chest, his fingers tangled in her hair.

I'm shattered. What I want to do is go upstairs and have a shower, then make myself some breakfast and take it up to my room. I want to change into my baggy jogging bottoms and the T-shirt the boys bought me last Christmas, the one with the Breakfast Show logo on it, and curl up on my bed to digest the evening. But how can I when I'll have to pass Niall's door? How can I contemplate lying on my bed in the room next to theirs, my eyes sliding to the wall with every squeak of the bed? Every murmur of voices?

This house no longer feels like my home. It's as if it's trying to expel me, and for the first time since the divorce was finalized, I don't try to fight it. Instead, I stay downstairs in the clothes I was wearing the evening before and make myself a strong coffee... one I'll finish this time. I sit at the table by the window and open my laptop. Trying not to think of Niall and Fiona above me, I click onto Rightmove.

It's what I should have done a long time ago. It's time I stopped living in the past.

TWELVE

When I arrive at the radio station the next evening, there is only one car in the car park. It belongs to Phil Steel, the presenter of the show before mine. I'm glad as all day I've been feeling on edge, the thought of going into the empty building weighing on my mind.

The sky seems darker than usual tonight and I'm feeling fraught, but it's the thought of sitting on my own in the studio, surrounded by empty rooms that's unnerving me. I'm used to seeing Simon sitting across from me, his face animated as he talks about the song he's just played, the weather or the latest charity project he's involved in. I'm used to Chris's feet on the desk. His heckling.

I'm used to company.

When I've done the morning show, it's been with the knowledge that outside the brick walls, the sun will be rising. That when I've finished, I'll step out into the daylight and a world full of life. Tonight, after Phil has gone home, it will be just me. My only companion, after I've hung up my headphones at 2 a.m. and locked the front door, the moonlit canal.

The security light clicks on as I reach the door, making me feel strangely exposed. I quickly punch in the numbers on the keypad and enter the building, grateful for the warmth and the light of the reception.

The kitchen is in darkness and so is the meeting room, but down the corridor I see a light on in Studio One. Feeling the need to see another living person, even if only through the glass panel, I'm about to head that way when the board with our photographs on makes me stop.

Where my picture used to be, Charl's face now smiles out, flanked by the boys. Her hair in the photo is not the blonde I remember but is now candyfloss pink, cut straight around her jawline like Cleopatra. The full red lips are the same though and the stud in her nose. She looks young. Confident. How I used to feel. My eyes slide over to my own photograph. It's at the opposite end of the board. Not grouped with other team members but alone.

With a last look at the board, I swallow back my self-pity and continue along the corridor until I reach Studio One. Phil is staring at his monitor but when he looks away from it to adjust his microphone, he sees me and raises his hand in greeting. I return his smile, wishing he could stay. That he won't be leaving in an hour to go home to his wife and his warm bed.

I walk on to Studio Two and push open the door. I turn on the overhead light, then the brighter one by the mixing desk, sitting in the seat that Simon uses for the Breakfast Show. Propped up against the monitor is a white envelope with my name on it. Recognising Simon's handwriting, I pick it up and tear it open. The card has a picture of the three of us printed on the front, taken when we were guests at a summer fete, and I smile when I see what's written inside.

Good luck for tonight. You go, girl!

It's signed by both Simon and Chris. I know it's a lovely thought, but it only makes me feel more adrift. Without the boys and Dan, the studio seems bigger, emptier, starker. I can't work like this; I'll need to do something to change the atmosphere. Alan had told me that to succeed on the late-night programme, I'd need to embrace the hour. Settle into the slower rhythm. Learn to love the freedom and the mellower mood.

Getting up again, I twist the dimmer switch on the wall, just a small amount at first, then more until the room is almost in darkness, just the area where I'll be sitting illuminated. Despite the shadows, it already feels cosier. More intimate.

I smile to myself as I return to my seat and check everything's working okay. Ever since I joined the Breakfast Show, it's been Simon who's been the anchor. The one who's controlled the fader, managed the music tracks and decided what caller to put on air. Chris and I have been bridesmaids to his bride, but from here on in, there will be no one telling me what to do. I will be my own boss.

In front of me, I've a list of topics I'll be talking about tonight, but I'm prepared to be flexible. With no traffic news or weather interruptions, I can afford to be creative. The only part of the show that's not moveable is the hour between midnight and one when the listeners are invited to call up and confess to their misdemeanours. The True Confessions slot. I glance at the screen where the incoming calls on the six phone lines will be shown. It's the part of the show I've been looking forward to the most.

Checking the playlist, I see that the music I'll be playing tonight will be nothing like what I'm used to. Instead, it will be smoother, more soulful. Chill-out music rather than something that will have the listeners up and dancing. It's different but I like it.

Through the speakers I can hear Phil in the other studio. He's talking about a new gym that's opening in town and asking his listeners for tips on how to lose weight. It's good to hear him, his cheery voice helping me get back into work mode. Closing my eyes, I block him out and try to concentrate on what's important – the different ideas I've had for tonight. Arranging and rearranging. It's hard to stay focused though when Malik's face keeps entering my head. His cool, direct gaze. The way he kissed me as though certain I wouldn't object.

Like he knew what I wanted without me having to say it.

A glance at the clock tells me I'll need to be more professional if I'm going to have any chance of making my mark on this show. I can't let my fascination with a man I've only just met come between me and my work.

Feeling like the new girl, I try to firm up my ideas for the night's show. When I was eleven or maybe twelve, I'd had to move school halfway through a term. I'd worried that I'd never get to know anyone, but my form tutor had set aside half an hour after registration so the class could tell me something about themselves. At first no one had wanted to speak, but with gentle encouragement from the tutor, they'd eventually found their tongues. It hadn't taken long to find like-minded students to befriend, and I hadn't looked back.

I've been thinking I might do something along the same lines tonight. Alan had said his listeners love talking about themselves, so why not?

As always when I'm prepping, time passes quickly and, before I know it, Phil's show is coming to an end, and I hear him tell the listeners that the next two songs will be the last. He puts on the first track and, five minutes later, appears at the door with a mug of coffee.

'Thank God "Stairway to Heaven" is eight minutes long. The next is only four but that should be long enough to drink this.' He grins. 'I didn't know what you liked but I thought you could probably do with something. All set?'

'As I'll ever be.'

He puts the mug down beside me. 'Just be yourself. The audience will love you.'

'You think so?'

'Why wouldn't they?'

'Because I'm not Alan.'

He laughs. 'I'd say that's a good thing. He wasn't exactly the life and soul of the party, was he?'

'Maybe that's what the audience wanted.'

Phil shrugs. 'Who knows? They're a strange lot. Anyway,

you'll be fine. Just make the show your own. I'll be around for fifteen minutes or so after I've finished so give me a shout if you need me. Anyway, got to get back as the song's about to finish. I'll do the introductions then she's all yours.'

'Thanks, but I'll be fine.' I can't tell him that I feel anything but. 'Oh, Phil. No one ever told me the reason why Alan's leaving. Do you know?'

His face that had, up until now, been animated, becomes serious. 'Di didn't tell you?'

'No, it's all been very hush-hush. Did he do something wrong?'

'Wrong?' He scratches his chin. 'No, nothing like that. The reason Alan's leaving is he's dying. He has cancer.'

The shock is so great I can't answer – I just stare at him. I know I should ask more but there's no time. Phil is already walking to the door. As it closes behind him, I sit in the empty studio thinking about Alan and how alone he must feel living by himself in his flat with no wife or partner to help him through his illness.

The song that's been playing comes to an end and I can hear Phil's voice saying goodnight to his listeners. I sit in a daze while he says he'll be with them again tomorrow evening at seven, pulling myself up sharply when I hear him say my name.

'It's good to have you here on the Late-Night Show, Mel. So what have you got planned for your listeners tonight?'

I force myself to concentrate. Rubbing my cheeks with the flats of my hands to help me relax. Focusing on my voice. Not rushing.

'Tonight is all about us.' I make sure the pitch of my voice doesn't rise too high. 'You, my dear listeners... and me. A chance for us to get to know each other better. Sit back, relax and together we'll make the small hours something to look forward to.'

There's a movement to my left and through the glass panel of the door, I see Phil leaving Studio One, his coat over his shoulder. I wave to him through the glass then settle the headphones more comfortably on my head.

I feel Alan's presence in the dark room. See his thin face. The small hawk eyes. Phil's words are in my head. *He's dying.*

Is Alan out there listening to me? Is he rooting for me or hoping I'll fall at the first hurdle? I push the thought aside. Of course he'd want me to succeed... Why wouldn't he?

I remember something Alan told me. He said I should speak *to* my audience not *at* them. Imagine it's just one person I'm speaking to rather than tens of thousands. An image of Malik comes into my head, but he doesn't feel the right person. It's not just because he said he never listened to the radio but because I want to keep him to myself. Keep him separate from my work.

No, it needs to be someone else. Someone who understands what it's like to be me, sitting here alone. Pushing thoughts of Malik to one side, I think of Alan alone and ill in his apartment. Leaning closer to the microphone, the soft foam grazing my lip, it's him I talk to.

'I'll be your companion, on this cold and windy night. Welcome, my friend. Welcome to the Late-Night Show.'

THIRTEEN

The first two hours go quickly, and I'm surprised how much I'm enjoying myself. There's certainly been no shortage of listeners wanting to talk about themselves: I've heard about Colin's recent shift at the hospital, Maggie's ailing mother and the problem Keith's been having with cats that have been defecating on his vegetable patch.

I'd thought I'd just be going along with it, riding the surface of their talk, giving them space to leave their anecdotes before moving on to the next caller. This isn't what had happened though. Instead, as I'd sat in my darkened studio with the spotlight on me, I'd been drawn in. Had really listened to these people who had allowed me to part the curtains of their lives and peek in. I'd found myself asking them questions, encouraging them to open up more, given my opinions. Instead of being strangers, we might have been friends sitting in a front room with a glass of wine or a mug of coffee, having a chat at the end of the day.

One poor woman had been up for two hours trying to get her baby to feed. Between his shrill yells, she'd told me about the caesarean she'd had and her hopes that one day she'd marry the baby's father. After she'd rung off, others had called in to wish her well and offer suggestions as to how she might get her young one to suckle.

Rest him on a cushion.

Try feeding him from the other side first.

Put on some music to soothe you both.

Try him on formula.

I put on a song and take off my headphones. This couldn't be further from the Breakfast Show. The callers there are bright, faceless people who I forget the minute they've hung up. The late-night callers are still faceless but they're more fleshed out... an almost finished portrait rather than a sketch. They have substance. Emotions. They interact. Behind their different voices, their different accents, they're real people to me. What has surprised me is how welcoming everyone has been... even the regulars. As well as talking about themselves, they've asked me questions about my own life, and I've found myself answering honestly. For how can I expect to reach out to my listeners if I'm a closed book?

It's nearly midnight and the song is coming to an end. In a few moments it will be time for True Confessions and, although I'm not sure why, I've butterflies of excitement in my stomach. I tell myself it's because I'm naturally nosy but, deep down, I know the reason I'm interested in their secrets is because there's a skeleton in my own cupboard. As I think this, something starts to niggle at me. Might it be why I was moved from the Breakfast Show? Does someone here know?

Pushing the thought away, I fade out the song. I'm just being paranoid.

'It's time for True Confessions. Your chance to tell me that secret you've been keeping to yourself. However big, however small, I'm here to listen and absolve you. Come on, don't be shy... I'm waiting for your call.'

I put on another track and wait, my eyes glued to the screen, my stomach knotted with anticipation.

One line flashes. Then another. Followed by a third.

It's not until the song has ended that I click on the first number and the computer software system automatically puts the caller through to the desk and my headphones.

'You're through to Late-Night Radio and True Confessions. Do you have a secret to tell me?'

Me not *us*. It's important I maintain the feeling of a confessional at all times. Allow the caller to talk as though I am the only one listening.

The caller clears their throat. 'My name is Owen and I want to confess to something I did when I was at school.'

I settle back in my chair, my fingers steepled to my lips, and listen to him talk about the time he'd graffitied the inside of the lavatory door with the name of his science teacher. Miss Hill her name was, and he'd had a serious crush on her.

'I told the head teacher I'd seen my friend Adam do it and he had to spend the break time cleaning it off.'

I smile into the microphone. 'I guess you're not still friends with this Adam then.'

'Oh, yeah I am. He was best man at my wedding. Fucking good bloke.'

The calls come in thick and fast, and I settle into my role. Most of the confessions are amusing. Some are odd.

Line three lights up and I click on it.

'You're through to Late-Night Radio and True Confessions. Why don't you tell me your secret?'

There's a pause and I think that maybe the caller has hung up but then they start to speak. A woman's voice with a soft Irish accent.

'Yes, I have a confession.'

I smile. We haven't had many women phoning in. It seems that more men have secrets... or maybe it's just that more men choose to confess to them.

'What's your name?'

'Natalie.'

'And what would you like to share?' It's nearly one o'clock. A time when most people will be tucked up in their beds. It feels cold in the studio, and I wonder whether someone's altered the time when the heating's set to go off. I pull my coat from the back of the chair and place it over my knees. 'Natalie?'

'I have feelings for someone.'

There's a pause and I guess that maybe this someone is in some way unsuitable. Married maybe?

'Do they know about these feelings, Natalie?'

'Yes.'

'And do they share them... these feelings?'

Her voice drops and I hear the vulnerability in it. 'I don't know.'

'Tell me, is he married? Is that the secret?'

'There is someone.'

'And are you scared he's still in love with them?' I'm clutching at straws, but straws are all I have; she's not giving me much to go on.

'Maybe.' There's a heartbeat of a pause. 'He's damaged. He's not good for me.'

It feels as if the conversation is going nowhere. The listeners will be wanting something funny or disgusting or shocking. Natalie's confession to having feelings for someone unsuitable is going to have them switching off their radios or flicking to another station.

I glance at the clock. There's only ten minutes before the end of this part of the show, then it will be back to music and chat. There's something in Natalie's halting voice that makes me suspect there's more to it than she's saying. She doesn't sound like the type of caller I've had so far. Wanting to brag or amuse.

No, this girl sounds nervous.

I think about how I can connect with her. How to draw her out. Make her trust me.

'I know what it's like to have strong feelings for someone. It's not something you have control over. Your body... your emotions... sometimes take over and make you do things you shouldn't.' I wait, hoping I've struck a chord. 'Am I right, Natalie? Is this how you're feeling?'

I hold my breath waiting for her reply. Wondering why I think it's so important.

The air in the studio alters. Grows heavy with expectation. I'm just beginning to think I've lost her when her voice comes again through my earphones.

'This man...'

I hear the crack in her voice, and she tails off, but I mustn't let her lose the thread.

'Go on, Natalie. I'm listening.'

'This man,' she says, her words barely more than a whisper. 'I know he killed someone.'

FOURTEEN

Her words catch me off guard and for a moment I say nothing. Then I remember where I am, what I'm doing, and force myself to react. To respond to the terrible thing I've just heard.

'That's a serious accusation, Natalie. Can you tell me what you mean?'

Through my headphones, there's nothing but silence.

'Natalie?'

But when I look at the monitor, I see that she's no longer on the line. My heart's racing. What should I do? Instinct kicks in and I slide the fader, allowing the next piece of music from the playlist to go out through the airwaves. Buying me time.

What is the protocol for a situation like this? Should I call the police? Should I ring her back?

On the monitor to my right, the phone lines are flashing. Of course, it's not only me who will have heard, for despite the illusion the programme gives that it's only me and the voice at the end of the phone who are party to callers' confessions, tens of thousands of people will be listening... in houses up and down the county, on their way to work, in their vans and taxis.

They'll be wanting to talk about what they've just heard. They'll want answers. But she's gone. What she's said is so shocking that the professional side of me knows that listeners' hypotheses shouldn't be discussed on air. So, instead of taking more callers, I leave the lines flashing, putting on track after track while I think about what to do. Deciding, eventually, that my best option is to go on as if nothing has happened. To start a new topic and only take calls from listeners that relate to it.

Somehow, I muddle through and by the time it gets to 2 a.m. I've managed to convince myself that I imagined it... or misheard. And if I haven't, then the obvious conclusion is that it was nothing more than a crank call. Either that or Natalie was off her head on something.

Yet, some instinct tells me she wasn't.

I take off my headphones then lift my coat from my lap and put it on, tiredness pressing against my temples and not just because it's going to take a while to get used to this new pattern of working.

Picking up my bag, I leave the studio. The light on its sensor clicks on, and I walk down the corridor towards reception, passing Studio One, the meeting room, the kitchen... their interiors black behind the glass panels. The radio station is eerily quiet as I walk through it, and I'm so conscious of the sound of my shoes on the hard floor that I have to stop myself from walking on tiptoe.

I switch off the reception lights and go out, locking the door behind me. As I step into the car park, the security light comes on, throwing its stark beam across the area, picking out my lonely car. I hurry to it, my pace quickening as I get nearer and it's only when I'm safely inside that I realise how fast my heart had been beating. What's the matter with me? I'll be doing the same thing tomorrow and the day after and the day after that. But it's not the time – it's what I've just heard.

Turning my head, I look at the radio station. Until Simon and Chris show up for the Breakfast Show in less than three hours, the studios won't be manned. From now until then, the insomniacs and night workers' only company will be pre-programmed music.

I've decided that I'll go home and sleep on it, then later tomorrow morning, I'll come back and speak to Di. Ask her what I should have done. Natalie's call was an eventuality that Alan hadn't warned me about. At least her number will have been stored on our system if we need it. That's one good thing.

Wondering whether I'm doing the right thing or whether I should have called the police, I start the engine and begin to reverse, but as the car moves, I feel it shudder and pull. Cutting the engine, I get out and walk around the car to check what the problem is, swearing under my breath as I see that the back wheel is completely flat. I squat next to it and with the torch on my phone try to see the cause, but it's impossible to tell. The stony parking area is pocked with rain-filled potholes. Any manner of sharp things could be lurking beneath their surface. The boys and I have mentioned it time and again but nothing ever gets done.

'Damn.' Even though I know it won't help, I kick the tyre. Now I'll have to phone the AA and wait until they arrive. I could change it myself, but at nearly a quarter past two in the morning, the prospect doesn't appeal. I get back in the car and resign myself to a long wait. The security lights that had come on when I'd got out of the car click off, leaving me in darkness.

Unseen, beyond the car park, the canal lies motionless under a moonless sky. The thought of it doesn't help to lift my mood.

With a shiver, I press the central locking button and wait. Aware of how alone I am.

FIFTEEN

I feel the hairs on the back of my neck prickle. Something's not right but I don't know what it is. Twisting round in my seat, I crane my neck to see better. There it is again. A movement over by the entrance to the car park.

Cold fingers of unease play along my spine. Is someone there or am I imagining it? Might it just be the wind in the bushes playing tricks on me? I force my eyes to focus then I see it again. Where the movement was, a shape has materialised. Is it a person?

I wait, my heart hammering in my chest. Yes, it's definitely a person; I can see that now. Moving across the car park towards me. It's too early for it to be any of the breakfast crew, so if not them then who?

Keeping my eyes on them, I reach down to my bag for my phone. But as I take it out, it slips from my fingers into the recess of the footwell. Fighting panic, I reach down to retrieve it and when I sit back up, a cry escapes me. There's a face at the window. A hand cupping the glass to see me better.

When they lower their hand again, I think I'll cry with relief. Because the security light has snapped on and I see who it is.

'Malik.' The name is sweet on my tongue. Leaning across, I open the door. 'What are you doing here?'

'We arranged to meet after the show.' He smiles. 'Or have you forgotten?'

I force my mind to remember. Did we?

'I'm sorry, Malik. There's a lot I don't remember about Saturday night.' I smile at him.

He looks at me, an odd expression on his face. 'Then it's a good job I remembered for the both of us. It's not safe for you to be out here alone.' He frowns. 'Why did you leave?'

'I'm sorry.' I look down, embarrassed. It seems so long ago now. 'It's just that I'd drunk a lot and probably shouldn't have gone back with you in the first place. I don't usually...' I look away, hoping he'll understand what I'm saying.

The security light has gone off again and I can't see his face. Is he angry?

'We didn't sleep together, if that's what you think.'

I close my eyes briefly. 'We didn't?'

'No.' His voice is soft like the darkness that enfolds us. 'I wouldn't do that, Melanie. I would never sleep with someone who has been drinking.'

His features are in shadow. It's hard to read his expression, but I can tell by his voice that what I've suggested has saddened him.

'Remember we had only just met,' I say quickly. 'I didn't know you. *Don't* know you.'

He smiles ruefully. 'It sounds like you've already decided the sort of man I am. You've already condemned me.'

'No, of course I haven't. But it's nearly two thirty in the morning and I don't remember arranging to meet you. You can't blame me for being surprised to see you.'

I try and think back to what I told him, whether I mentioned what time I'd be leaving the studio, but it's like a fog has descended over the evening I met him. A confusing gin-induced fog.

'It's late, Malik. Even if I suggested it when I was drunk, why would you want to meet me at this hour?'

'I don't mind. Sometimes I find it hard to sleep.' Without asking if I mind, he slides into the passenger seat. 'Walking helps.'

'I was just about to go home but I've got a puncture.'

He frowns. 'That's too bad. Maybe I could fix it.'

Even though it's impractical, I love that he's asked. 'It's too dark to be able to see. Besides, I've already called the AA.'

In the confines of the car, I'm aware of his nearness. Just the handbrake between his thigh and mine. His head close enough that I wouldn't have to move far to touch a hand to his stubble. He smells of cigarettes and some sort of aftershave, and I feel my body ache with desire.

Over the last two days, I'd thought I'd rationalised my feelings for him, that what we'd had was something and nothing. A fleeting attraction. But now he's here next to me, the pull is as strong as it was in the pub. Despite the late hour and my tiredness, I'm conscious of him in a way I can't explain.

A few moments ago, I'd wanted the AA van to arrive, but now I'm grateful that it hasn't. It's as if this meeting has been pre-ordained. As if someone has been looking down on us. Given us this second chance.

I want him to take my hand. To place his own against the flushed skin of my cheek. To lean in and graze his lips against my collarbone. When he does none of these things, the disappointment is visceral.

'You don't have to wait with me,' I say, staring straight ahead of me, even though there's nothing to see except the blur of a hedge.

'No, and you do not need to wait either.'

I turn to face him. 'What do you mean?'

'Phone them and ask them to come in the morning instead.'

I frown. 'But it will take forever to get a taxi.'

'Come back with me,' he says without actually asking. 'You shouldn't be here alone. It is not safe.'

It's the second time he's said this.

When I don't answer, he opens his door and gets out, comes around to my side of the car and opens mine.

'Well?' He holds the car door open, waiting. I smile at his manners. The question has come at last, but it's unnecessary because my hand is already searching for my bag. My mind already going where I know it shouldn't.

'Yes.' The word is out before I can think it through. 'All right.'

It's starting to rain, white rivulets slanting down the windscreen. Malik holds out his hand and I get out. My coat is not waterproof as I hadn't expected to be going anywhere except to the car. Noticing, Malik takes off his own and puts it around my shoulders.

As we walk, I phone the AA and tell them that I won't be needing them tonight after all. That I'll ring again in the morning. 'Yes, I'm safe,' I say in answer to their question. 'Yes, there is someone with me.'

Malik is walking ahead. When I've made the call, he takes my hand again, his fingers wrapping around my own. I look at him, long tendrils of his hair plastered to his face, raindrops dripping from his lashes. Things are even more electric this time. This time as he leads me down to the towpath, I've no alcohol inside me, but I'm intoxicated with the idea of what might happen next.

SIXTEEN

Sun is streaming in through the blinds in the meeting room, casting bright ribbons across the table. Di is saying something but I'm finding it hard to concentrate. Even though it was me who made the appointment, I can't stop my mind from going back to earlier this morning. The feel of Malik's body. The smell of him. The things we did. At times he was gentle, at others passionate. When he made love to me, the intensity of his expression made me feel that nothing else mattered to him except that moment. So different from Niall, whose light-hearted banter as his fingers moved across my body would sometimes make me feel as though he were somewhere else.

'You say her name was Natalie?'

'What?' I tear my thoughts away from the touch of Malik's fingers and look at her. Today, Di's wearing smart black trousers and a jacket. She must be going to a more important meeting than this one after we've finished. 'Yes, that's what she said.'

'And she didn't withhold her number?'

'No. We have it.'

Di taps the tips of each finger in turn against her lips. 'And her exact words were?'

I think for a moment. Wanting to get it right. 'She said that she knew he had killed someone... this man she was having a *thing* with.' I make quotation marks in the air.

Di looks thoughtful. 'And how did she sound?'

I sift my memory for clues. 'I don't know really. If I had to say anything it would be anxious.'

'I see.'

I lean forward. 'Do you think we should do something? Tell the police?'

Di meets my eyes. 'No, I don't think that's necessary. If we informed the police every time we had an odd call, we wouldn't have time to broadcast.'

'But she accused him of killing someone, Di. In my book, that's a bit more than *odd*.'

She sighs. 'It was your first time presenting the Late-Night Show, Mel. You have to remember that it's a whole different ball game to what you've been used to. You can't come to me every time something like this crops up. By not making a huge meal of it, you did the right thing. It's what I would have done myself... Alan, maybe not. I expect he wouldn't have let it get that far. He had a knack of spotting problem callers early and would talk to them off air before anything contentious could be said.'

I think of Natalie. How normal she sounded. Nothing to make me suspect she'd drop that bombshell. 'How would I have known though?'

'You develop a sixth sense. That's what Alan used to say. But that will come with time. I have faith in you, Mel.' She smiles.

'I know but—'

'Think about it.' Di's voice is consoling. Patronising even. 'If you thought your boyfriend or husband had killed someone, would you really choose the radio to let everyone know?'

She has a point. 'I suppose not, no.'

'There you are then. Put it down to experience. Next time something like this happens, you'll be more prepared.'

'And what if she calls again?' The thought has only just occurred to me. 'What if she says something else?'

'Then let her. As long as she doesn't make any other accusations that could scare our listeners, it won't do any harm.' She looks at her watch, then stands and lifts her smart raincoat from the back of her chair. 'I've another meeting in fifteen. Was that all?'

'I suppose so.' I should feel reassured, but I don't.

I follow her out and as I pass the kitchen see the familiar figure of Simon through the glass panel of the door. He's making himself some toast. Moving from early to late has made me feel jetlagged, my body clock all over the place. Not only that but I've been so caught up in my own show, with Natalie's call and my night with Malik, that I've barely given the Breakfast Show a thought.

Chris is there too, sitting at the table nursing a mug of coffee. I miss all this. I miss them.

I stick my head around the door. 'Well, fancy meeting you two.'

Simon puts down his toast and smiles. 'This is a nice surprise. I wasn't expecting to see you here. I thought you'd be tucked up in your bed until at least midday.'

'Couldn't sleep.' An image comes to me. Malik's hand on my hip. The tangled sheets. Our discarded clothes on the floor. I hope he doesn't notice the blush that's heating my cheeks. 'And, besides, I needed to speak to Di.'

Chris looks up from his phone. 'Fucking hell. That's a first. You usually try to avoid her.'

Going over to him, I slap him on the arm. 'That's not true and you know it.'

Simon lifts my mug from the cup hook and raises his eyebrows.

'No, not for me, thanks.' Despite my tiredness, the last thing I want is caffeine. I'm jittery enough as it is through lack of sleep and the adrenaline that's coursing through my veins.

'So,' Simon says, sitting down next to Chris. 'Why the sudden need to see the big honcho?'

I'd been planning to tell them but, suddenly, I realise I don't want to. 'Oh, nothing exciting,' I lie. 'I just wanted to talk through my first show with her, that's all.'

Chris swallows a mouthful of his coffee. He's made it in the

Breakfast Show mug I gave him for his Secret Santa last Christmas and our faces smile back at me from the white china.

'So how did it go?' he asks.

'I enjoyed it actually... more than I thought I would. It feels more...' I look for the word. 'Real.'

'Surely you're not telling us you don't miss Sing for the Bling or Guess the Celebrity Voice?'

I shake my head. For some reason, these staples of our Breakfast Show, designed to help us connect with our audience, now seen trivial.

'I miss you guys though.' I think of the empty building and my solitary car in the car park. In daylight, it seems a totally different place. 'It's odd being here on my own... no one to spar off. Speaking of which, where is the lovely Charl?'

Chris shrugs. 'Not sure. She dashed off after our post-show meeting with the fat controller.'

I stifle a laugh. 'Hush. One of these days she'll hear you.'

'No, we're quite safe. I saw Di leave, dressed up like a dog's dinner. Maybe she has a lunch date.' He pulls a face. 'I pity the guy.'

Simon points a finger at him. 'She's not that bad, and if you don't reel it in, you'll be the next one shunted off to the graveyard shift.' Realising what he's said, he looks at me. 'Sorry, I didn't mean it to come out like that, Mel.'

'It doesn't matter. It's what everyone's thinking after all.' It's the truth. I've seen it in their eyes.

'Still,' Simon says, with an apologetic smile. 'It was thoughtless of me. Changing the subject, we were confused when we came in this morning. Your car was still in the car park, but the lights were off in the building.'

Chris chuckles. 'Yeah, we thought you'd been kidnapped.'

I feel wrong-footed. I'd forgotten that they would see the car. That I'd have to explain myself. While I was in the meeting with Di, I'd had a message from the AA to say they'd arrived. They'll have finished by now and I ought to go out and see them.

'I had a puncture.' Hoping the boys will leave it at that, I get out my phone and look at it, wondering if there's a message from Malik. There isn't.

'How did you get home?' Simon scratches at his stubble. 'Taxis are a devil to get at that time in the morning.'

I bite the inside of my cheek, thinking about what to say. 'I stayed at a friend's.'

Simon picks his plate up and takes it to the sink. 'What friend? I didn't know you knew anyone around here?'

'Look, if you must know, I stayed with Malik. All right? Your plan worked, Chris. I like him. Happy now?'

Chris holds his mug out for Simon to take then looks back at me. 'Who the hell is Malik?'

'What do you mean, who is he? He's your friend. The guy you were talking to in The Junction Saturday night.'

Chris frowns. 'What? The one you went off with? Whoever he is, he's no friend of mine.'

'But it was your idea. You set me up with him. In fact, you were talking to him for half the night before he came over to me.'

'That wasn't the guy. The one I wanted to set you up with cried off.' He shrugs. 'Sorry.'

Simon looks at Chris and shakes his head. 'You could have said, you idiot.'

I feel uneasy. 'So you're telling me you don't know him, Chris?'

'I've seen him at The Junction before so I suppose I know him in a sense, but I wouldn't call him a friend. Seemed like an okay bloke though... from what I can remember anyway. Not that he says much. Anyway, he gave me the impression he knew you.'

'Si?' I turn to him, hoping that he'll say something that will be a salve to the unease I'm feeling.

'No, sorry. Never spoken to him.'

I close my eyes a second. 'Jesus.'

Simon shifts in his seat. 'You're saying that after you found out about the puncture you phoned this Malik?'

'Yes.'

I realise how odd it would sound if I told them he'd just appeared out of nowhere. They'd say it was weird. *I* would say it was weird too if it had happened to anyone else. Arranging for him to meet me after the show, at two in the morning, something I still can't remember doing, sounds just as crazy.

Simon looks at me doubtfully.

'I knew he lived close,' I hurry on. 'It seemed the sensible thing to do.'

He narrows his eyes. 'If you say so. Look, Mel, I know it's none of my business, but I think you need to be careful. You don't know this guy. None of us do.'

'There are only so many times you can say the same thing, Simon.' I'm angry now, hating the way he's making me feel. 'And for your information it *is* none of your business. I'm a grown woman. I'm divorced. And I certainly don't need you to tell me who I can and can't see.'

Chris lets out a guffaw. 'That told you, Mr Holier Than Thou Winner.'

I glare at the two of them, glad that I don't have to put up with their idiocy any longer on the Breakfast Show. Charl's welcome to them.

'Why don't you piss off, the both of you.'

Leaving them to it, I go out to my car. The AA mechanic is leaning against the bonnet, filling out some paperwork. He looks up when he sees me.

'All done but you need to be more careful about where you park your car at night. Could I suggest you park it closer to the building where the security camera will pick it up?'

'It's not working.'

He frowns. 'What?'

'The camera. It's been out of order for months. Anyway, why does it matter? I could have got the puncture anywhere.'

He looks at me, his brows pulled together. 'I'm afraid that's not true. It wasn't a puncture. Not an ordinary one anyway.'

'It wasn't?'

'No,' he says, shaking his head. 'It was deliberate. That tyre was slashed.'

SEVENTEEN

My phone pings a message as I'm driving home and I hope it's Malik, but when I park the car outside the house and look at it, I see it's from Simon.

Sorry. I'm an idiot. Why don't you come over later and we can talk properly? Anne would like to see you.

I've had time to cool off, so I message him back. *Okay but are you sure she's up to it?*

He replies straight away. *Yes, she's been feeling a bit better the last couple of days. Not so sick.*

We arrange that I'll come over at six and it's a relief, as I realise the car I've just parked behind is Fiona's and the thought of spending the next few hours with her isn't the most appealing. Already, as I look at the red-brick semi, it's as if my house no longer belongs to me. That things are moving on and leaving me behind. What I *do* know is I'll have to find somewhere else to live soon. I can't go on like this. But it's hard when my Rightmove searches have come up with nothing better than studio flats miles from the radio station or places in the town centre with no parking.

When I let myself in, I hear the two of them in the kitchen. Niall's wearing the apron I bought him one Christmas with *Niall*

Head Chef on the front. It makes me feel sad when I see it. Not because I want to be with him but for everything it reminds me of. Happier times. Companionship. Friendship. Security. Now it's Fiona who has those things. She's leaning against the worktop, flicking through one of my recipe books. When she sees me, she closes it and slides it back into position on the shelf with my others.

'I was looking for a recipe for a chicken traybake to have later.' Her cheeks are tinged pink.

'You could join us,' Niall says awkwardly.

I ignore what he's said, knowing it's the last thing they'd want. 'I didn't expect you to be home.'

Niall looks sheepish. 'Fi has a half day on a Tuesday, so I thought I'd take one too. Anyway, where were you last night? We decided it must be some guy.' He pulls Fiona to him and kisses the side of her head.

I stare at them, unsure what to say. What is it with everyone interfering in my life all of a sudden? Feeling the need to comment? It's no more their business than it is Simon and Chris's. Suddenly, the house is making me feel claustrophobic.

I pick up my coat again. 'I'm going to have a shower and then I'm going out. I might or might not be back tonight.'

I mentally cross my fingers then, as I climb the stairs, I message Malik. *Can I come over later? Before or after the show?* He hasn't told me what shifts he's working so I'm hoping he'll be there. It's only been a few hours since I last saw him, but it's been the longest three hours of my life.

The answer is short. Abrupt.

No. It is not convenient.

Simon and Anne live only a fifteen-minute walk from me and it's Anne who answers my knock on the door.

She's dressed in a loose T-shirt and jogging bottoms, her fine brown hair pulled into a ponytail. It's been a while since I've seen her. I'd been worrying that it might be awkward, but when her face breaks into a smile, I know it's not going to be.

'I'm so glad you came. We shouldn't have left it so long. Come in.'

She holds the door wide, and I step inside. 'I know. It's my fault. I should have made more of an effort after...'

'You can say it, Mel. It's not a dirty word. *Miscarriage.* There – it's done.' Anne takes my coat from me and hangs it over the banister. 'While I don't agree with those who say time heals, it goes some way to dulling the edges of the pain.'

I feel myself colour. 'Yes, I know. I'm sorry. I should have been more supportive.'

'Don't be sorry. You had your own problems. Break-ups are never easy.'

Niall and I split up several months after Anne's miscarriage. In the months after I'd found out, I'd been caught up in my own little world with little emotional energy left for anyone else. I'd been selfish.

Wanting to change the subject, I hand her the potted plant I bought at the florist's on the corner. 'I hope you like orchids.'

She takes it from me. 'It's beautiful, thank you. But you needn't have.'

'They're about the only thing I've managed not to kill.' I can hear clattering in the kitchen at the other end of the hall. 'Sounds like Simon's doing something useful.'

'Yes, I've put him on tea duty, or coffee in your case... unless you'd prefer something stronger?'

'No, coffee will be fine. I've got my show tonight.'

'Of course – I'd forgotten. Anyway, come in and make yourself at home.'

Make yourself at home. It sounds so formal. There was a time when I'd been a regular visitor to Simon and Anne's house. Chris too. We'd pop round for coffee after the show to chat about ideas or complain about Di. Sometimes, Simon would cook us a brunch of poached egg and avocado on sourdough toast, and if Anne was on a late shift, she'd join us too.

What a difference a year can make.

I take a seat on the settee and watch Anne as she plumps the cushions on the one opposite and sits. Although I'd told myself I wouldn't, I let my eyes slide to her stomach. The looseness of the T-shirt means there's nothing to give away she's having a baby. But then I remember that Simon had said she's no more than a few weeks into the pregnancy.

I wish again that Simon hadn't shared his secret with me. How will I be able to get through the next couple of hours without letting on I know?

The door opens and Simon comes into the room, a big grin on his face. He's carrying a tray of drinks, which he sets down on the low table in between the two settees. He hands Anne her mug then sits next to her.

'I hope you don't mind but I told Anne what an idiot I was back at the studio. I've been feeling awful about it ever since. I think Chris and I are finding it hard to get used to you not being on the show.'

I shift in my seat, unsure how to reply to this, but Anne saves me.

'Stop it, Simon. Can't you see you're making Mel uncomfortable.' She tucks her feet under her and takes a sip of her drink. 'Anyway, how have you been? Considering Si's a radio presenter, getting any information out of him is like getting blood from a stone sometimes.'

'I've been okay.' I look away from her, taking a mug of coffee from the tray. 'Actually, that's not quite true. I was okay until recently. I don't know if Simon's mentioned it, but this thing with Niall and Fiona. It's getting pretty serious.'

Anne looks at me over the top of her mug. 'But that's okay, isn't it? You're divorced.'

'I know and I'm not bothered about that. It's just that things have moved on so quickly.' I put my mug down too heavily on the table so the coffee slops over the side. Taking a clean tissue from my bag, I wipe the bottom of the mug and then the mat. 'Can you believe Niall had the cheek to ask me if I'd like to have dinner with them? As if I was a visitor or a charity case.' I close my eyes for a second at the thought of it. 'Christ, I really do need to move.'

Anne looks at me with sympathy. 'It's not that you still have feelings for him?'

'Anne!' Simon frowns at her but she shushes him.

'I'm not being nosy. I just want to understand. You don't mind me asking do you, Mel?'

'No, I don't mind. He fell out of love with me, that's all. It happens.' I know my outburst has done little to disprove it, but it's true. 'I'm honestly fine about Fiona now, but I need my own space. It's living in the house, you see.'

'Have you still not managed to find anything?' Simon asks me.

I shake my head. 'Nothing suitable. Niall's going to buy me out of my share of the house, but that won't give me a huge amount of money.'

'I hope you don't mind me asking.' Anne looks at me kindly. 'But why isn't it Niall who's moving out? Does it have to be you? I can't believe how selfless you're being, especially after everything that happened...'

I tell her that Niall did offer but that my conscience wouldn't allow me to let him leave the house that had been his before we were married.

'Anyway, I don't want to live there anymore. I want a fresh start. Even if it's only somewhere short-term while I get a better idea of where I want to live. I'm planning on renting for a bit.'

'Fair enough.' Simon stretches out his legs. 'Let us know if we can do anything to help.'

'Thank you, but I'm not sure there is anything.'

Anne looks thoughtful. She looks out of the window and then back at Simon. 'What about Tina's place?'

His Adam's apple lifts as he swallows his coffee. 'What about it?'

'You must remember. Her boyfriend lives down south and she said she wants to move in with him but can't as she's mid-tenancy. From what I remember, the rent is quite low. If you took over the tenancy, it might be advantageous for you both. I could have a word with her if you like.'

'Would you?'

'Of course. You've got nothing to lose, and as long as the landlord agrees, I can't see a problem.'

As she speaks, I notice how her hand rests on her stomach as though hiding her secret. I really hope things go okay this time. She's had a tough year and I want the best for her.

Seeing me looking, Anne moves her hand away, her fingers worrying at the band that's securing her hair. 'I really must get this cut. I think your new hairstyle really suits you, Mel.'

My hand rises to the short, feathered ends of my hair. 'Thank you. For the first couple of days after I'd had it done, I'd thought I'd made a huge mistake, but I'm getting used to it now.'

'Well, I'm clearly not the only one who thinks so. Simon tells me there's a new man on the scene.'

I glance at Simon. Did he also tell her how he'd tried to warn me off him?

'Well, I don't know if I'd call him that. To be honest, I've only met him a couple of times. It's very early days.'

Simon finishes his drink and puts his mug down. 'We thought Chris brought him to the pub to set them up. Turns out they don't know one another. They were just drinking together.'

'Malik hardly drinks,' I say quickly, in case Anne gets the wrong impression.

'Ignore my husband.' Anne looks pointedly at him. 'He's an old stick-in-the-mud and doesn't like to see anyone having fun. Where does he work, your Malik?'

I hesitate, realising how little I know about him. 'I'm not really sure. We haven't talked about it.'

Anne laughs. 'Looks like you were too busy with other things. I don't blame you.'

I smile, remembering, but then I think of the abrupt message he'd sent when I'd asked if I could see him later. Does it mean he's changed his mind about me? That it's not just today he's talking about but always?

Anne links her arm through Simon's. 'Well, I think he sounds like a tonic. Just what you need at the moment. It doesn't have to be anything heavy. Just have fun. Mystery in a relationship can add a bit of spice. Don't you agree, Si?'

Simon shrugs. 'If you say so.'

I have a sudden need to tell someone. 'I know I've only just met him, but I really like him.'

Out of the corner of my eye, I see Simon slowly shake his head. 'Mel—'

I want to tell him that it's nothing to do with him, but Anne gets there first.

'Jesus, Simon. Let her be. It's not really any of your business.'

He looks awkward. 'I'm sorry. I know it's not. It's just that I don't get a very good feeling about him.'

'You don't know him. You said so yourself.' I feel my frustration rising. 'The problem is you and Chris have acted like my overprotective big brothers ever since I started on the show with you eight years ago. But I'm thirty-eight and you really don't need to keep doing it.'

Simon looks hurt. 'It's not like that.'

'It's *exactly* like that. Anyway, you've got Charl now. She's just a kid so maybe you should transfer some of your unwanted gallantry to her. Not that she looks like she needs looking after.'

This at least makes Simon smile. 'No, she's pretty feisty.'

Anne raises her eyebrows at him. 'I thought you said she was annoying.'

'Boy, you really do remember everything I say.'

She looks at him sharply. 'Only the important things.'

The exchange has come so out of the blue that I forget what I'm about to say. I look from one to the other, my bottom lip caught between my teeth, hoping they're not going to argue. It's something they do from time to time, and I wish they'd save it for when I've gone. To my relief, Simon's face breaks into a smile.

'Okay, you've got me. We've only done one show with the girl and already she's irritating me.'

Part of me is pleased, the other puzzled. 'But why?'

'I don't know. She's just so confident. It's like she's been doing the show for years and we're her lackeys. It's... well, it's just different.'

'What does Di think?'

'She thinks the sun shines out of her arse. Says that she's bright and new and the listeners clearly love her.'

I feel a twist of envy in my chest. 'She knows that already?'

Simon rubs the side of his face. 'You forget, Di makes it her job to know everything about everybody. I'd consider leaving if it wasn't for all this.' He sweeps a hand to indicate the beautifully decorated house. He and Anne have never done things by halves.

Anne gets up. She goes over to the table lamps in the alcoves either side of the fireplace and switches them on, before closing the slats of the expensive-looking white shutters that cover the windows. 'Anyway, what about you, Mel? Is the new show going well?'

'Actually, it is. It's early days but I think I'm going to like it.'

'I'm glad.' She comes back to the settee and sits down again. 'Simon said you'd been worried about it.'

'I was but it's fine. Just different.' They can't have heard about Natalie's call yet. If they had, they would have said something. I don't mention it either. 'It would have been even better if I hadn't come out to find someone had slashed my tyre.'

Anne stares. 'Really?' She turns to Simon. 'You never said.'

'I didn't know.' He turns to me. 'Why the hell didn't you say something? I thought it was just a puncture.'

'Me too, but by the time I'd spoken to the mechanic and found out the truth, you'd left for home. I told Di though and she's contacted the police, but I know the car was out of sight of the security camera – which isn't working anyway – so there won't be anything to see. It'll just be kids.' I push down the kernel of doubt.

But Simon isn't so easily mollified. 'At that time in the morning? I don't like the sound of it. It's a long time since anything like that's happened. There used to be a spate of vandalism but nothing in the last couple of years.'

'Let's not talk about it anymore. Being worried about what's going on outside the building isn't going to help me get to grips with the show. Talking of which, I really should go.'

I start to get up, but Simon puts a hand on my arm to stop me. 'Why don't you stay for supper? We've plenty.'

Anne smiles. 'Yes, do. I should have suggested it earlier.'

'That's kind of you but I really need to get back and give some thought to what I'm doing tonight. I'll grab a pizza on the way home.'

Anne stands and starts to collect up the cups. 'You always were the practical one of the three. I'm sure Simon makes half of it up as he goes along.'

I laugh, knowing that Simon puts as much thought into his show as I do. 'I just like to be prepared, that's all... especially as it's a new show. I don't like surprises.'

'I don't blame you. I'm the same.' Anne puts the cups on the tray then straightens. 'Would you like one of us to give you a lift home?'

'Thank you, but no. I do my best thinking while I'm walking.' I want to say that I need to work out what to say to Natalie if she calls again, but of course I can't.

I say goodbye to Simon, and Anne walks me to the front door. 'It was nice to see you, even if for a short time.' Her hand slides down to the waistband of her jeans, the flat of her hand resting against her stomach. 'He's told you, hasn't he?'

There's no vexation in her voice, just acceptance.

I think about denying it, asking her what she means, but what's the point? 'Yes, he did. I'm sorry – he shouldn't have. It's been so hard not to say anything.'

'It doesn't matter. I'd hoped to keep it a secret a bit longer, but Simon's never been very good with those.' She looks away, but not before I've seen the tears that have pooled in her eyes.

I reach out and touch her arm. 'It will be different this time. I know it will.'

She nods. 'Yes. That's what the doctor said.'

'There you are then.' I don't know what else to say. If I could will her a healthy child I would, but I have no influence over the miraculous workings of a human body. Nature will be the one to decide.

I'm relieved when she draws herself up and musters a smile. 'You're right. Just because something went wrong before doesn't mean it will happen again.' Her fingertips move in a slow circle, making the fabric of her blouse ripple. 'Simon and I are ready to be parents and this little guy or girl will know that.'

'Yes, they will, and you'll be great, Anne. You both will.'

'Thank you.' Anne opens the front door. 'Before I forget, do you still want me to see about the flat? What I forgot to mention was that you'd be sharing. His name's Nathan, but I don't think that should be a problem. Tina says he works at the hospital and does a lot of nights. As far as I know, she doesn't see much of him.'

'Yes, I'd like you to if you don't mind.' Sharing a flat with a stranger wasn't something I'd considered but if he's not around much, it has to be preferable to watching Niall and Fiona all loved up.

'Great. I'll ring her tonight then. I presume you'd like to see the place first?'

'That would probably be a good idea. Just to be sure.'

With a parting wave, I walk away, but Anne calls out to me. 'Just do me a favour, Mel, and take care tonight. If you see anything suspicious, tell the police immediately. Simon's stressing isn't good for my blood pressure!'

I laugh. 'Will do.'

But as I walk back to my house, along the dark streets, I'm starting to feel nervous. Not just at the thought that someone has been creeping about the radio station car park but about Natalie. Are the butterflies in my stomach because I'm afraid she'll call again? Or because I'm afraid she won't?

I walk back down through the town in the direction of my house, the streetlights pooling in front of me. I'm so deep in thought that when my phone pings a message I nearly don't answer it. Shoving my hand into my pocket, I pull my mobile out and look at the screen, my heart giving a jolt when I see whose name it is.

Malik.

Come round now.

EIGHTEEN

The studio is dark except for the spotlight illuminating my position at the mixing desk. With linked fingers, I stretch my arms to the ceiling, feeling the tension between my shoulder blades ease. I really should stretch my legs.

Checking the computer screen, I fade in the next song from my playlist and take off my headphones, surprised to see it's coming up for midnight. It doesn't feel like two hours have passed since I waved goodbye to Phil through the glass door panel.

I leave the studio and walk down the corridor towards the reception. It's only when I reach the shiny curved desk that I realise I hadn't allowed my eyes to stray to the rooms on either side as I passed them. Not wanting to dwell on why that might be, I push open the front door and peer out into the car park. It's silent. No sign that anyone's been here. When Phil had heard about what happened last night, he'd kindly parked further away, allowing me to have the coveted spot near the door. I step out further, holding the door so it doesn't close and wave my hand at the security light. It flashes on, lighting up my car.

As far as I can see, it looks fine. There must be a rational explanation for my tyre being cut – broken glass on the road, the remnants of a crash unnoticed near the house. Only a fool would tamper with a car so brightly lit, but then I realise how stupid I'm being. There would be no one here to see except me, and I've been in my windowless studio ever since I arrived. I let my eyes scan the bushes at the side of the car park and the gate that leads out onto the towpath, but there's nothing to be seen. Relieved, I go back inside, checking the door is secure before returning to my studio.

I've timed it well, as the song is just coming to an end. I glance at the clock. Midnight. Time for True Confessions. I put on the theme tune, 'Tell Me Your Secret' by Tiga, and settle back, my eyes on the monitor, bringing my own voice in as I fade the tune out again.

'It's midnight and True Confessions. The time you've been waiting for. A chance to tell me that one thing no one else knows.'

As if my words have conjured up a magic spell, the phone lines start flashing. In front of me on the desk, I have Natalie's number. I glance at it then at the numbers on the screen, feeling a kick of disappointment when none of them match.

I pick a line at random. 'Who's calling and what would you like to confess to me tonight?'

'It's Natalie.'

I sit bolt upright in my chair and press my headphones closer to my ears, trying to ignore the thumping of my heart in my chest. Imagining the late-night audience doing the same and wondering what new revelations she'll offer our collective ears.

'Hello, Natalie. It's good to hear from you.'

She doesn't answer. There's a rhythmic shushing sound like material on material and I wonder if she's walking.

'Natalie?'

'Yes, I'm still here.'

I wipe the palms of my hands on my jeans. 'Is there something you'd like to confess?'

The soft Irish lilt to her voice is strangely beautiful. Hypnotic. 'I lied. I'm sorry.'

All my senses are on high alert. What can she mean? 'Lied?'

'What I said about the guy I'm seeing.' She pauses. 'I made it up.'

I breathe in deeply. 'So there is no man. No infatuation.'

Even though she's on the end of a phone line, I can imagine the shake of her head as she replies. 'No, that part's true. I mean the other thing.'

'That you thought he'd killed someone.'

'Yes.'

I press my fingers to my forehead. 'But why?'

'I'd been drinking. I didn't know what I was saying. Haven't you ever lied when you're drunk?'

Of course I have. Everyone has... but I'm not going to say that on air. Instead, I lower my voice. Making it more personal. Intimate.

'This isn't about me, Natalie. It's about you.'

I hear her sigh down the phone line. 'I don't know what he wants. Sometimes it's as if I mean the whole world to him, then he'll turn cold.'

'And that's why you said what you did. To punish him?'

'Yes.'

It makes sense, yet still I feel uneasy. She'd sounded so genuine last night. I'd heard the emotion in her voice. Raw. Like a wound laid open.

As she talks, my thoughts turn to Malik. The way he'd brushed me off when I'd asked if I could come over. How I hadn't questioned when, later, he'd changed his mind and demanded that I come. I think of how he'd made love to me in the tiny kitchen, my back pressed against the cold door of the refrigerator.

I force myself to concentrate. 'Infatuation can be all-consuming. It makes us feel alive.' I imagine Malik tracing a path down my cheek and neck, grazing the curve of my breast.

'What should I do?'

The chair squeaks as I turn to get a closer look at the number on the screen she's calling from. Scribbling it down on the pad in front of me, I frown at it – it definitely doesn't match the one from the night before.

Something's not right but my head's not in the right space to think what it might be. The skin of my chin smarts from Malik's stubble and I touch a finger to it.

'What I would do, Natalie, is take that feeling you get when you're with him and treat it as you would a precious object. One day, it might be gone and the memory of it will be all that's left.'

She doesn't answer and the line goes dead. I fade in some music and push my chair back, linking my fingers behind my head. Remembering.

The beginning of this relationship feels so different to the first weeks with Niall, who didn't blow hot and cold or make me feel on edge. I knew from the start that my future husband was reliable and dependable. It made me too comfortable and was what eventually made our marriage stale.

Simon wouldn't understand what I see in Malik. Neither would Chris or Anne. Some men have their weaknesses, but it doesn't make them bad. They'd say that Malik was using me. That he should treat me better. They'd say my feelings for him were obsessive and that I should know better at my age.

They'd be wrong. They haven't seen him when he strokes my hair from my face and says my name as though it's something to be cherished. They don't know him.

No, they wouldn't understand.

But maybe Natalie would.

NINETEEN

I see Chris as soon as I open the radio-station door to go home. He's slumped against the brick wall, his eyes closed, his face puffy.

'Jesus!' I let the door swing closed and crouch next to him. 'Chris, are you all right? Are you hurt?'

When he doesn't answer, I shake his shoulder. 'Wake up, Chris. Can you hear me?'

Slowly, as though it's taking a lot of effort, his eyes open. They're unfocused. Bloodshot. I'd been scared he'd been attacked, mugged outside the radio station, but I can smell it now, the sour scent of stale drink.

'What are you doing here?'

Chris spreads his fingers wide and turns his palms one way then the other as though expecting to see something – the answer to my question maybe. He drops his hands to his sides and looks up at me, his eyes struggling to focus.

He tries to speak but his words are so slurred, the only ones I catch are *promised him*. I've seen Chris drunk before but never as bad as this. I stay crouched beside him, wondering what I should do.

I look at my watch. It's ten past two. I could phone Simon, but it doesn't seem right when he'll be getting up himself in two hours' time to get ready for the morning show. It wouldn't be fair on him. Besides, it might wake Anne, and with a baby on the way, she needs all the sleep she can get.

I put my lips close to Chris's face, repulsed by the sour smell of his breath, but it's the only way I can get him to concentrate on what I'm saying. 'Put your arm around me, Chris. I'm going to try to stand you up, but you need to help me. Put your other hand on the wall to steady yourself.'

Chris looks at me blearily through bloodshot eyes and I fear it isn't going to work, but he does what I ask, the weight of his arm on my shoulder pushing me down. It takes a while but eventually he's on his feet, swaying dangerously.

'Okay. I'm going to get you to the car then I'm going to drive you home. Do you think you can walk?'

Chris's head lolls to one side but together we shuffle forward, the weight of him causing my left shoulder to stoop. The car isn't far away but it seems to take an age to get there. Eventually, we reach it. I prop Chris up against the passenger door and open the one at the back.

'Come on. You have to help.' With difficulty, I manage to wedge him into the back seat, praying that he won't throw up on the drive home. I watch, helplessly, as he falls sideways, sprawling across both the seats. There's no way I'll get him up again, or get the seat belt around him, so I don't bother. It will be quiet on the roads at this time of night, and I'll have to take my chances.

I've been to Chris's house a few times, so I don't need him to tell me where to go. I'm going to get him home and then message Simon. He and Charl will just have to do the show without him as there's no way he'll be sober enough to join them.

Parking in Chris's road is a nightmare at the best of times and there are no parking bays free, so I stop on the yellow lines in front of his house. When I've managed to get him out of the car and up to the front door. I hold out my hand.

'Keys?' I hope I'm not going to have to fish in his pocket for them.

Thankfully, the short sleep Chris has had on the back seat has sobered him a bit. Leaning his back against the wall, he manages to pull them out, bringing the lining of his pocket with them. Before he can drop them, I take them from him and unlock the door, then help him into the house. The living room is closest, and I guide him in there, watching as he slumps onto the settee.

'Don't move.'

I leave him and go to the kitchen, trying not to look at the unwashed plates and cups in the sink. The empty beer bottles standing next to the kitchen bin. After a search of the cupboards elicits nothing suitable, I take the plastic washing-up bowl from the sink and carry it back.

'In case you're sick,' I say, with a frown.

I kneel on the floor beside him and unlace first one trainer then the other, slipping them off his feet and dropping them onto the carpet. The soles are caked in mud. The bottom of his trousers too. There's a tartan blanket on the back of the settee and I drape it over him.

'You smell good.' Chris reaches out a hand towards me. 'Good enough to eat.'

I bat his hand away. 'Cut it out, Chris. You're pissed.'

With difficulty, he struggles into a sitting position, then leans forward until his forehead is resting on my shoulder. 'Hold me.'

'What?' I move away a fraction.

'Please, Mel.'

He sounds so sad that I do as he asks. I slip my arms around his big frame and hug him. Like a sister would. His hair is damp against my cheek; it smells like it could do with a wash.

'What were you doing at the radio station, Chris? What made you get into this state?'

He doesn't answer, just slides his arms around my back, leaning heavily into me. We stay like this until I feel his large hand slide up my back until its cupping my neck, his fingers stroking the fine hairs at the nape. Before I can do anything, he turns his head and tries to kiss me.

Pressing my hand to his chest, I push him away. 'Stop it! You don't know what you're doing.'

I get off the settee and Chris lies back down, closing his eyes with a groan. I want him to say something but equally I don't. It would take just one wrong word from him to spoil our friendship.

There's an empty whisky glass on the ring-marked coffee table. Picking it up, I go to the kitchen again, rinse it out and refill it with water from the tap. I give it to him, seeing how the shivering water mirrors the tremble of his hand.

'Just don't spill it.'

He lifts it to his lips and takes a mouthful then gives it back to me before sinking his head back on the cushion and closing his eyes. 'Thanks.'

I put the glass on the coffee table. 'I've got to go now. I need to get some sleep. I'll makes sure Simon knows that you won't be in this morning.'

Chris mumbles something unintelligible. Soon, he's snoring, his mouth slack. I look at him, worried he might be sick. Wondering at the likelihood of him choking after I've gone. Not wanting to risk it, I reach both hands to his side and roll him over so he's facing the room.

As I shut the front door behind me, I realise how tired I am. Earlier, I'd considered going back to Malik's but it's too late now. What I really need is sleep.

Before I drive home, I message Simon. He'll be awake soon.

Chris is pissed. There's no way he'll be doing the show today. Will tell you about it later x

A message comes back. *This is Anne. I couldn't sleep. What an idiot he is. I'll let Si know when he wakes up.*

I type quickly. *Thanks, Anne. Glad I didn't wake you. Just thought Simon should know.*

You did the right thing x

I look at the phone then put it into my bag. With a last glance at the house, I release the handbrake and drive away. Wondering if she's right.

TWENTY

A week later, I go to look at the flat Anne has recommended. It's actually in a better position for the radio station than my house, in a road of similar three-storey houses. It's only a twenty-minute walk away from work, and as soon as I see the Victorian red-brick front with its bay window and shiny front door, I know I'm going to like it. I lift the brass knocker and release it, feeling the stir of anticipation in my stomach.

After a couple of minutes, the door opens and a woman in jeans and a stripy T-shirt smiles out at me. 'Hi, you must be Melanie.'

'Yes, I hope I'm not too early.'

'Not at all. Come in. The flat's on the first floor.'

I follow her up the stairs to a small first-floor landing and wait while she fishes a key out of her pocket.

'There are three flats in the building,' she says, fitting it into the keyhole. 'The one on the ground floor is empty at the moment as the guy's working abroad.' She points to the stairs that continue up to the second floor. 'Jean's in her seventies. I never hear her.'

'That's good. I'm not used to a flat and, if I'm honest, my biggest fear is being woken up by loud music from the person above.' I hurry on, feeling the need to offer an explanation. 'My hours of work are pretty unsociable, and I need my beauty sleep.'

Tina laughs. 'Don't worry. There'll be nothing like that.'

'That's good to know. What about your flat share? Has that been working out okay?' Even if it hasn't, she's unlikely to tell me but I'm still glad when she shakes her head.

'It's pretty difficult to have problems with someone you never see. Our paths hardly ever cross. He's a bit of a neat freak too. Never leaves his dirty crockery in the sink or anything like that, and I don't think I've had to empty a bin since I've been here.'

I smile. Relieved. 'That sounds like my sort of person.'

She lets me in and stands back so I can see. The door opens onto a small hallway with four doors opening off it, one of them closed. 'Shall we start with my room?'

'Whatever you like.'

Tina pushes open the door to my left and beckons me in. The bedroom is at the front of the house, its large bay window looking out onto the street. It's furnished with a double bed, a mahogany wardrobe and a matching dressing table. I walk to the window and push aside the net. 'It certainly would be good to be nearer to work.'

I also realize that it's nearer to Malik too.

'It's the bigger of the two bedrooms,' Tina says, folding her arms and looking around her. 'But I was the first to move in. First come first served is my motto.'

When I've seen everything I want to see, I follow Tina back along the hall and into the room opposite. It's long and narrow with a living room at one end and a kitchen at the other. There's a bookcase overflowing with books, and the settee is covered with a colourful throw and cushions in a variety of shapes and patterns. A tall green houseplant stands in the corner, looking like it could do with a good water.

'I'm guessing this is all yours,' I say, gesturing at the photographs on the one shelf not covered in books and the bright prints on the walls.

'How did you guess? Nathan doesn't seem to mind... not that he's said anything.'

'If he's anything like my ex-husband, he won't care what a room looks like as long as it has a TV.'

Tina looks at me, her hand on her hip. 'Anne told me about your situation. She said you'd be happy to move in as soon as you could. To be honest that would be great for me.'

'Yes, the sooner the better. My situation is' – I look for the best word to describe it – 'complicated.'

She smiles sympathetically. 'Anything involving men usually is. I love your radio show by the way. I listened to it when I couldn't sleep last night, and, to be honest, I think you're better than Alan Calder. He always came over as rather creepy. You just sound like the girl next door you want to confide in.'

I open one of the kitchen cupboards and close it again. 'I'll take that as a compliment.'

'You should. Anne said you were gutted when you had to leave the Breakfast Show but, to be honest, I much prefer the Late Show. It has more' – she pauses – 'heart. How you handled that caller with the crazy lover was genius. It's better than a soap. God knows why anyone would stay with someone like that when it's obvious he doesn't give a shit about her. Probably married too.'

I turn and part the blinds at the window, peering down at the small garden, not wanting her to see my expression. When I'd been talking to Natalie, I'd almost forgotten that it wasn't just the two of us. That all across Greater Manchester thousands of people would be listening too. The atmosphere on the night shift is so intimate it can be deceiving.

'I doubt she'll ring again,' I say abruptly, bringing an end to the subject.

When I turn back, I see Tina's surprise in the slight raising of her eyebrows, but I don't want to discuss Natalie with her. I don't want to discuss her with anyone.

'Is Nathan likely to be back soon?' I say, forcing my tone back to conversational.

'No, I'm afraid not. He's been hard to pin down recently, but I could leave a message for him if you want. See if there's a time the two of you could meet before you make a decision.' She looks doubtful. 'The landlord's breathing down my neck to get this sorted though.'

'Don't worry. I'll take it.'

Tina looks relieved. 'You will? That's great. I haven't shown you the bathroom yet though.'

She leads me out of the living room and holds open one of the two remaining doors to reveal a rather old-fashioned bathroom. Just a white sink and a bath with a shower attachment. A limp plastic shower curtain with a pattern of large sunflowers hangs from the rail that runs above it.

Tina shrugs apologetically. 'Not quite hotel standard but it does the job.'

'It's fine.' In fact, it's a whole lot better than the bathroom at Malik's with its water-stained avocado suite. The toilet seat that doesn't fit properly. 'When can I move in?'

We decide on two days' time, which will give Tina time to pack, and immediately I feel my shoulders drop. I close my eyes and imagine lying in the bedroom with its big windows. No Niall on the other side of the wall. No Fiona. A new start.

Tina opens the door and we arrange a time for her to hand over the keys. 'Anne's done us both a favour,' she says, then pauses. 'How do you think she seems at the moment? She's had such a hard time the last year or so.'

It's clear that Anne hasn't told her about the pregnancy and it's not my place to mention it. 'Actually, she seemed on pretty good form when I saw her.'

The concern on her face melts into a smile. 'That's good to hear. I've been worried.'

'We all have.'

I know none of us will be able to relax though until she's had her twelve-week scan. Simon hasn't said as much but it's obvious in the way he's been recently. When I've spoken to him on the phone, he's been abrupt with me; not his usual calm self. Maybe I'll try him again tonight.

'So you'll let Nathan know I'll be moving my things in in a couple of days?'

'I will.' She leans her back against the door frame. 'Then it won't come as a surprise when he sees a different toothbrush in the holder or a different towel on the radiator.'

'Yes, we don't want to give the poor guy too much of a shock.'

I say goodbye and walk back to my car. I should feel happy – after all, a new start in a new place is what I wanted – but deep down inside there's a nagging doubt. I know little if anything about Nathan.

Am I being too hasty moving in with someone I've never met?

TWENTY-ONE

I'm lying in Malik's bed, my head on his chest, the sheets tangled around us. His arm is across my body like it was the first morning, the weight of it pinning me down. Slipping out from under it, I get out of bed and search for my clothes.

He raises his head and looks at me. 'Where are you going?'

I find my jeans and pull them on. 'To the radio station. The show starts in an hour.'

Reaching across, he catches my wrist and pulls me back onto the bed. 'Stay with me.'

'I can't, Malik.' I laugh and try to pull my hand away, but his grip is strong.

'You can.' Lifting my wrist to his lips, he kisses it, his eyes not leaving mine.

I shiver, remembering what we did earlier, and despite myself, my body starts to respond again. His hand releases mine and I close my eyes, feeling his fingers trace my cheek, my jaw. They hover for a moment on my shoulder before moving lower and circling my breast. The fingertips grazing my nipple.

'Stay.' His voice is raw. Wanting.

But he's not the only one who feels this way. My need for his touch is startling. Primal.

I tip my head back and his lips follow the path his fingers

took. When he lowers his body onto mine, his hand reaching to push down the jeans I've just put on, I don't stop him. Even though I'm going to be late. Even though it could cost me my job.

He's just pressing his lips to mine when a shrill ring shatters the quiet.

Malik raises himself onto his elbows and reaches across me to his jeans. He pulls his mobile from his pocket, reads the message then throws the phone onto the floor.

His face freezes into a frown. 'I'll see you out. You don't want to be late.'

'But, Malik...' I'm confused. It was only a moment ago he was begging me to stay. But he moves away from me and gets out of the bed, the cold air of the room replacing the warmth of his skin. Reluctantly, I drag my jeans back over my hips.

He's at the window now, his forehead pressed against the cold glass. His hands either side of his face, fingers spread as if wanting to push through. Then he turns and comes back to me, placing a kiss on my head before holding out his hand.

'Come.' There's an urgency in his voice that stops me from arguing.

As I take his offered hand and let him help me off the bed, I see how the muscles of his shoulders are bunched, tension radiating from him.

'Is everything okay?'

He smiles awkwardly. 'Of course. It's nothing for you to worry about. I'll call you.'

My stomach tightens.

'Who was it, Malik?' I do up my bra and pull on my top. 'Maybe I could...'

I leave the sentence hanging, my heart beating into the silence of the room. But already his attention has shifted from me to something else. With no other choice, I pick up my coat and bag and walk to the door. 'There's no need to see me out.'

Looking back at him, I muster up a smile, but as the door closes behind me, my throat burns with the effort it takes to stop myself from crying.

For the first time since I met Malik, I see myself as others would see me... a thirty-eight-year-old woman acting like a teenager. Worse than a teenager. Someone who should know better.

The night is grey and damp as I step out into the fresh air. It suits my mood.

Finding my phone, I message Simon. *I've been an idiot. Malik's weird and I should have listened to you. One minute he was trying to convince me to stay and skip work, the next he practically threw me out. I'm well out of it.*

His reply comes back as I'm driving away, leaving behind the dismal street with its depressing blocks of social housing. I glance at the phone on the passenger seat, Simon's words still lit on the screen. Despite my hurt and humiliation, they make me smile.

Don't beat yourself up about it. It happens. We're here for you.

I'm out of breath by the time I pull open the door to the radio station. It's nine thirty and I've only half an hour to get myself ready for the show. As I pass Studio One, Phil looks up and raises his eyebrows at me.

Don't ask, I mouth, unwinding my scarf.

Once I'm inside my own studio, I take off my coat and sit down at the mixer desk. My lips are sore and bruised, and I run my tongue across them, remembering Malik's kisses. I push the thought away. I've already invested too much time on him.

Yet, as I study the notes I've written and consider how I'll lead into tonight's discussion topic, as I introduce my show, even as I'm talking to the callers, my treacherous thoughts keep turning back to him. I have no control over them.

I try to concentrate on what the man on the end of line five is saying. Something about his daughter and drugs. I formulate an answer that will hopefully fit in with what he's said and am relieved when he thanks me for understanding. I bang my forehead with the heel of my hand. I've got to get a grip or it won't just be a new flat I'll be needing.

For the first time since I started the Late-Night Show, the hours drag and I'm relieved when, finally, the digits on the wall clock click their way to midnight. Almost time for True Confessions. Instantly, I feel a flutter of anticipation in my stomach. It's welcome, pushing thoughts of Malik into the background. I can't help wondering if he's hiding something from me... a relationship perhaps? Why else would he always want to meet me at his flat rather than taking me out?

Tonight, when the lines start flashing, there are two numbers I'm searching for. I'm not interested in what any of the other callers have to say – it's Natalie I'm waiting for. Natalie with her soft Irish accent. The girl who wants me to listen. To help.

But that's not the only reason I'm holding my breath, hoping that she'll phone in.

It's because we're kindred spirits. She's the only one who understands what it's like to play with fire. The only one who knows what it's like to be with a man like Malik.

TWENTY-TWO

I'd hoped that Malik might help me move my things to the new flat, but he'd said he was too busy and in the end it's Chris who lumbers up the stairs behind me, a large cardboard box in his arms. Halfway up, he rests his shoulder against the wall to steady himself and I'm worried that he might drop something. There's a smell of beer on his breath; it's clear he's been drinking despite it being only twelve. The smell reminds me of the night I found him slumped outside the radio station. We still haven't talked about what happened and a part of me doesn't want to. With a bit of luck, he won't remember anything anyway.

When he reaches the first-floor landing, he dumps the box on the floor and leans against the frame of the open door, catching his breath.

'Fuck me. What did your last slave die of?'

I pick the box up and carry it into the living area. 'Think yourself lucky I'm only taking the bare essentials... anyway, you didn't have to say you'd do it.'

'Yeah, I was a mug.' He stands with his hands on his hips, taking in the room. 'It's not bad though, is it?'

I take a frying pan out of the box and add it to the other kitchen items I've already unpacked. 'No, it's not. Though I can't help feeling like a student again. It's years since I've rented and years since I've shared my space with someone. Not counting Niall.'

Chris walks round the room, picking things up and putting them down, opening and closing cupboards.

'It's pretty bare though – not that it would bother me.'

I take in what he's seeing: the pictureless walls, the bookless shelves, the settee with no cushions. All the things that had made the place homely had been Tina's and she's taken them with her.

'It's like no one else is living here.' Chris points to the open door. 'Have you met him yet... this Nathan guy? We could always take a peek in his room.'

I shake my head. 'No, I haven't met him but I'm sure I will soon. And don't even think about snooping.'

Chris sniffs. 'He could be an axe murderer for all you know. Don't you think you should have checked him out first?'

I start to laugh, thinking he's joking, but his face is deadly serious. 'Oh, come on, Chris. You really think Tina would have continued to live with someone she wasn't happy with?'

'Maybe that's why she's moved out. Maybe he gives her the creeps?' He throws himself onto the settee and puts his feet up on the coffee table, looking pleased with himself.

I slap his feet to get him to move them and continue unpacking the box. The kitchen cupboards are almost empty and there's plenty of room for what I've brought.

As I work, I think about what Chris has said. Yes, it's odd there's so little evidence of the guy who's my flatmate, but welcoming sunlight is shining through the kitchen window, and I've been looking forward to this move ever since Anne first suggested it. I'll be dammed if I'm going to let Chris spoil it for me with his idiotic comments.

'For your information, Tina is moving in with her boyfriend, otherwise she'd still be here, and I wouldn't have to be listening to your drunken ravings.'

Chris looks hurt. 'I'm not fucking drunk. I had a pint after work. What are you, the alcohol police? I'm only saying that you should take with a pinch of salt what people tell you. You don't even know the woman. You're too bloody trusting, that's your problem.'

I want to tell him to shut up, tell him that normal people have coffee at eleven in the morning, not beer. But I don't. I know Chris is only trying to be a good friend and also know that what he does in his free time is his business not mine. It was good of him to agree to help today, and I don't want to appear ungrateful.

Chris scratches at his neck. 'The Breakfast Show isn't the same without you, you know.'

His comment surprises me. I continue putting cutlery into a drawer. 'That's what Simon said.'

'That's because it's true.'

I look at him, my head on one side. I've never heard him say anything like that before. 'Are you all right, Chris?'

'Sure. Why wouldn't I be?'

He pinches the soft skin between his eyes with a thumb and index finger. 'To be honest, when the alarm goes off at 4 a.m. I want to just put my pillow over my head. Either that or smash it. The alarm clock, not my head.' He gives a tight smile. 'Christ, listen to me. I'm in danger of turning into a miserable old sod.'

'Too late.' I put the empty box on the floor and walk over to where Chris is sitting, taking the seat next to him on the settee. 'Go home, Chris. Get some sleep or at least have something to eat. It might help you sober up.'

'I will in a minute.' He folds his arms. 'Why didn't you tell me about the slashed tyre?' Seeing my expression, he answers before I can ask. 'Simon told me.'

'I didn't say anything because it's not something I particularly want to dwell on. It will just be kids.'

'At that time of night? I don't like the sound of it.'

'Please, Chris. This is exactly what I knew you'd say which is why I didn't tell you. It's nothing.'

Yet, despite my words, what happened *has* unsettled me. If it wasn't for my connection to Natalie, I might consider asking Di to move me on to something else. But I can't desert her. Not until I know what's going on. She keeps ringing in, and last night she was crying so hard it was impossible to hear what she was saying. I'd tried to soothe her, persuade her to tell me what had happened, but she'd rung off. As a last resort, I'd gone back on air, given a list of numbers she could call if she needed to talk to someone. Whether she was listening, I have no idea. I can only hope she was, as I want to help her. For some reason it's important to me.

Chris gives an audible yawn, bringing me back to the moment.

'Do you want me to give you a lift back?' I ask him.

He studies the baggy knees of his jeans. 'No, I've got legs and I suppose I ought to use them occasionally.'

Although I'd have been happy to drive him home, I'm glad. The walk will do him good. I smile at him. 'Thanks for helping me this morning. I'm sorry I had to ask at short notice, but Malik let me down.'

I hadn't wanted to let my frustration show but I can't help it.

Chris sees it. 'Stick with your friends, I say.'

I take in the pink-tinged whites of his eyes, the brewery smell of the alcohol on his breath. 'Yeah, right... says the man who tried to set me up on a blind date. But, seriously though, I *am* grateful. Come on. Time for you to go home.'

I pull Chris to his feet, and he leans on me a second, getting his balance. 'You're still seeing him then.' The sentence drops at the end, a statement rather than a question. It clearly bothers him.

'Yes.' My smile drops. 'Was that something else Simon told you?'

He doesn't answer that, but he doesn't need to. We both know they tell each other everything.

'I'm not saying you shouldn't see him but just be careful. Have you found out any more about him? What he does? His family? His friends? I've met guys like him before. Unreliable. Thinking only of their own needs.'

Not wanting to admit I've wondered about these things myself, I turn defensive. 'You've said it yourself: you don't know him.'

'I know enough about him to know I don't trust him. You should be with someone stable. Reliable. It's the reason I suggested a blind date in the first place. I thought Calvin would be just the person. If only the bastard had turned up.'

I sigh heavily. 'Well, he didn't. And you should have been more specific at the time. You're the reason I left with Malik.'

'There's someone else I—'

'No, Chris. Enough. Stop trying to run my life for me.'

The reproach in his eyes makes me feel guilty for snapping. I soften my voice. 'Look, I know why you're doing it, but there's no need. I'm fine. Let's leave it there while we're still friends.'

I lead him to the door and say goodbye. When he's safely at the turn of the stairs, I wave then go back into the flat. Only then do I allow myself to feel angry.

I'd decided I wasn't going to see Malik again but Chris's words, instead of making me wary, have had the opposite effect. I won't be told what to do.

I haven't contacted Malik for a couple of days, and he hasn't messaged me either, even though he said he would. After his odd behaviour, I'd thought I'd be relieved, but now I feel again the pull of him. Call it love. Call it lust. Call it what you want. My need to see him is greater than my need not to.

I go back to the settee and sit down. I think for a minute then take my phone out of my pocket.

Do you want to see me? I type.

TWENTY-THREE

Natalie's voice comes to me over the headphones. 'I have something new to confess.'

I close my eyes and focus, not wanting the relief I'm feeling that she's phoned to be relayed over the airwaves. 'Take your time, Natalie. I'm here to listen.'

The studio is dark as usual, just the one light pooling around me, leaving the rest of the room in shadow. Being here is starting to make me feel strong. In control. With just the flick of a switch or the slide of a lever, I have the power to choose whose voice will be heard over the airwaves.

Each night when midnight approaches, I find myself waiting for Natalie's call. Desperate to hear her story. Praying that the woefully inadequate words I utter after she's confessed, might help her in some way. When I'd last seen Di, she'd praised me for how well I'd been doing. Called me a proper agony aunt. I'd been surprised at her unexpected praise and don't want to let her down.

'I'm scared,' Natalie whispers, and I feel the hairs on the back of my neck stir. I raise my hand to the cool skin. With the headphones on, it's as though Natalie's words are for me alone.

'What are you scared of, Natalie?' I'm desperate to hear what she has to tell me. Worried for her too.

'That he'll hurt me. That he'll leave me.' I hear her breathing turn ragged. 'Most of all I'm scared that I won't be able to leave *him*.'

Knowing it's what Di would suggest I do, I take her off air and put on a music track. It's the first time I've done it.

'It's just you and me now, Natalie.' Now we're off air, I can almost feel her presence in the studio. 'You're safe and anything you say will stay between the two of us. I just want to help.'

She doesn't speak to start with, and I wonder if it's because she's trying to decide whether she can trust me.

'Please. Don't be afraid.'

She speaks at last, her voice hesitant. 'I need to talk to you.'

When she's phoned the show before, it's been on her own terms, not on mine. I've had the sense she's been using the programme as a confessional. That by telling her secrets, she's been hoping to be absolved... though of what, I've not been sure.

Tonight, off-air, I get a different feeling. She's asking for help.

'Why don't you tell me what's happened,' I say gently.

'Last time I saw him he didn't want me to leave. He tried to keep me there. We were in his flat. He locked me in his room.'

I lean closer to the microphone. 'Did he use force to keep you there? Did he hurt you? If he did, it's important you say. I have another number you can call if you'd like me to give it to you. Someone trained to help with things like this.'

I close my eyes and wait for her reply.

'I waited until he came back and let me out. I didn't question him, but when I got home, I wouldn't answer his calls. I thought he might be ringing to explain, but when he eventually left a message on my phone, it was to say he didn't want to see me again.' She speaks so softly the words slip into the darkness around me. They're full of pain. Of hurt. 'I'm scared of him, but I can't let go.'

'You have to. How he's behaved isn't normal.' It's the rational thing to say. How most people would think. Yet, even as I say it, my chest is tightening. My words are making a hypocrite of me, and I know it. When I'd heard the turn of a key in the door on the first night I'd spent with Malik, it hadn't made me want to stop seeing

him. Far from it. And when I think of the two agonising days I
spent waiting for him to message me after his strange behaviour the
last time I'd seen him, the pain of his rejection hits me afresh.

Looking back, I wonder why I never asked her more. Questioned the coincidence of our situations and the similarities
between the men we were seeing. That must be why they say love
is blind.

Natalie's voice comes back to me through my headphones.

'What if he doesn't want me anymore, Melanie?'

I massage my temples with my fingers. 'Then we have to learn
to live with it.'

We, not *you*... as if we're in it together.

I'm just about to say something else when I hear a distant bang.
I turn my head towards the studio door, wondering where the
sound has come from. Whether it was from inside the building
or out?

When I look back, Natalie's line is no longer lit.

'Natalie?' There's no answer. The line has gone dead.

Swearing under my breath, I glance back out at the dark
corridor again then put on some more music, my hand running
nervously over my short hair. I'm trying to think whether I closed
the front door properly behind me when I came in earlier. It had
been raining and I'd been distracted, trying to get out of the deluge
before I got soaked. Yes, I definitely remember pulling the door
closed, but of course Phil would have gone out since then. Maybe
he didn't close it properly and it's banged shut in the wind.

Getting out of my chair, I walk to the door and open it, peering
out into the passageway with its darkened rooms either side. I
listen, straining my ears for the slightest noise, but there's nothing.
The open space at the end with the reception desk is brightly lit as
it always is, and I can just see the back of Dawn's computer screen
and a vase of lilies, their over-sweet scent reaching me even back
here. On the wall, the TV flashes up images of the latest news.

I'm just about to shut the door again when my eye is caught by
something. Scattered across the floor are pieces of brightly

coloured paper. Making sure I have enough time before the song ends, I go to investigate and when I pick one up, I see it's one of the leaflets the police gave us for the anniversary appeal. I pick the rest up and put them neatly back on the shiny surface of the desk. The skin below my scalp prickles.

My eyes move to the front door, as I remember the wind that had clawed at my coat as I'd come in. It must have happened when Phil left the building, the draft from the open door lifting and scattering the paper. But earlier I'd nipped out to the kitchen during a song to make myself some coffee. It had been after he'd gone, and the leaflets hadn't been on the floor then.

Remembering the bang that had made me look up from my conversation with Natalie, I feel my heartbeat quicken. Pounding against my ribs. And that's when I see what I hadn't noticed before.

The security light in the car park is on.

TWENTY-FOUR

It's almost two thirty by the time I let myself into my flat. As I step into the hallway, I glance at Nathan's door. It's closed but that doesn't mean anything as I've never seen it open. Never actually seen into his room at all.

Unsure whether he's in or out, I walk as quietly as I can to the bathroom to use the toilet and clean my teeth, then back to my own room, closing the door behind me. I don't want to wake him if he's in. It's only as I put on my night things and get into bed that I think how strange it is to be sharing a flat with someone I've never actually seen, let alone met. How quiet he is. How very tidy.

Tina had given me Nathan's mobile number, and on the day I'd moved in, after Chris had gone home, I'd messaged him before going to work, unsure of when I might see him. In case Tina had forgotten to tell him, I'd explained what job I did, what time I left for work and what time I'd be home on weeknights when I was hosting the Late Show. I'd told him I'd used the top shelf of the fridge for my chilled food and the upper and lower cupboards to the right of the cooker for the rest of my food and for my cooking utensils and crockery. Said I hoped that was okay. They were the emptiest ones, and I assumed those were the ones Tina left. Not that it would have made much difference to him as there was little evidence that he ate at the flat. I'd ended the message by saying how much I was looking forward to meeting him. There had been no reply, but the next morning the message had shown it had been read.

It always takes me a while to wind down after I get home, and tonight sleep is evading me as I can't get Natalie's voice out of my head. I turn onto one side then the other, trying to get comfortable. Trying to push her out of my mind. When that doesn't work, I lie on my back and force myself to think of something else instead, and my thoughts turn to Nathan. Wondering what he's like. Trying to imagine the man who might be lying in his own bed. Just one wall between us.

It's been a while since I shared a house with someone other than my ex-husband. It feels strange, but it also feels like the beginning of a new chapter. Niall and I had thought we were good for each other, but it turns out friendship isn't enough to keep a marriage together after an affair. I should have left straight away, but something had stopped me.

Now I've done it.

I burrow down lower in my bed and pull the duvet closer around me. The room still feels alien, not yet my own, and I've yet to get used to its unique sounds: the click of the radiator, the rattle of the sash window.

After minutes of restlessness, I get up again and find my way to the door in the half-light. Feeling for the key in the lock, I turn it, telling myself it's just a sensible precaution.

I go back to bed and lie on my too-hard mattress, eyes wide open. There's a full moon tonight and I can see its glow through the thin curtains. At this hour of the morning, the bedroom that had seemed so large and welcoming the morning Tina had shown it to me feels too big. Too empty. It brings home to me how lonely I've felt recently and that I'm strangely missing Niall.

My eyes feel sore, the eyelids heavy. Knowing that what I need is sleep, I reach across to the bedside table, take out an eye mask and put it on. It does the trick and, despite thinking I won't, it isn't long before I'm sinking into the darkness.

A noise wakes me from a dream where Natalie had been knocking at my window, begging me for help. I sit up, trying to tamp down my beating heart, disorientated for a moment. Is it my old house I'm in or Malik's? I take off my eye mask, and as my eyes slowly adjust, the room comes into charcoal focus, the wardrobe looming from the far wall. Of course – I'm in my new flat.

I lay down again, on my side, my eyes fixed on my bedroom door. The sound I'd heard was the front door closing, I'm sure of it. Is Nathan coming in or going out? After what seems like an age, I hear the toilet flush then muffled sounds behind the wall that separates our two bedrooms. When all is quiet again, I put my eye mask back on and turn over, not sure why I'm feeling so uneasy. It should be a relief to no longer be alone in the flat.

I think I won't get back to sleep again but I'm so tired it's impossible to stay awake, and by the time my eyes open again, it's morning, the sun pushing through the curtains. A look at the clock shows me it's nearly ten. Pushing back my duvet, I get up and go to the door. Normally, I walk around the house in just my pyjamas, but with someone I don't know in the flat, it doesn't feel right, so I lift my dressing gown off the hook and put it on. I push down on the handle, feeling a moment's panic when it won't open. But then I remember how I'd locked the door when I'd gone to bed.

I turn the key, the sound it makes bringing back memories of my first night at Malik's flat when I'd woken to find myself alone. He's never told me why he locked the door behind him when he went out and I haven't asked. Now I wonder why I haven't. It was, after all, me who'd told Natalie that locking someone in a room isn't normal. Maybe it's because I don't want to know the answer.

Not wanting to dwell on it, I go through to the kitchen to make myself some coffee, trying not to look at Nathan's door as I cross the hall. I'm not sure of the etiquette of sharing with a stranger. Should I offer to make him a drink? Should I knock on his door?

Deciding to do neither, I make myself a quick breakfast and

take it back to bed. Relieved that it's Saturday and that I don't have to go to the studio tonight.

I sit cross-legged on my bed and take a bite of my toast. My phone is on the table beside me and I see there's a message on my screen. I grab it up, hoping it's from Malik. When I'd told Chris I was still seeing him, it hadn't been strictly true. In truth I've heard nothing from him since the night he sent me away. The message isn't from Malik though – it's from Simon asking if I want to meet him later for a walk along the towpath. A chance to catch up now we no longer work on the show together.

I try not to be disappointed but I am. My need to be with Malik is like a drug, the absence of him throwing me into a state of disarray. Like I'm being forced to go cold turkey.

Instead of messaging Simon back, I click on Malik's name and start typing. *I need to see you. Please talk to me.*

I finish my toast and coffee, then take my clothes to the bathroom where I have a quick shower behind the plastic sunflower curtain. I towel myself dry so quickly that my skin is still damp when I pull on my clothes, my jeans clinging uncomfortably to my thighs. Not bothering with make-up, I hurry back to my room, a towel wrapped around my head and snatch up the phone in case Malik's replied.

He has... but it's not the response I'd been wanting.

I'm busy. I'll call you soon.

The second wave of disappointment is more crushing than the first and I don't message back. Instead, I change into my running clothes and my trainers and let myself out of the flat. Without a proper plan, I run through the backstreets behind my house, my head down, until I reach the canal. It's like my body's on autopilot and I turn left, in the direction of the radio station, knowing that if I keep running, I'll eventually come to the area where Malik lives.

It's warm today and it isn't long before I have to stop to take off my sweatshirt. As I tie it around my waist, I take in the narrowboats that are moored up against the canal side. They're the brightly coloured ones the holidaymakers rent, their green sides painted with blood-red castles and flowers, but as I start to run again and enter the run-down industrial area further along, they become more functional, the barges duller in colour, with rust-pitted hulls, their roofs cluttered with necessities: dirty wheelbarrows, bikes, tubs of herbs waving in the breeze.

On the fraying canal bank, a dog lifts its head from its paws and watches me as I walk past. I think it's going to bark but it doesn't. Instead, it lays its head back down on its paws and goes back to sleep.

The area has become wilder now, the towpath choked with weeds and broken glass that I have to step around. The mirror-flat surface of the water that had earlier been filled with cloud and tree canopies now reflects nothing but the buildings on the opposite bank. A long narrowboat motors by and the buildings in the water ripple. Become distorted. Reminding me of my thoughts. I've no idea what I'm going to do or say when I get to Malik's flat. I'd had a mad notion that if he saw me standing on the doorstep, he'd change his mind. Want to be with me again. But now, as I watch the shimmering outline of the buildings settle into clarity, I'm not so sure.

Just when I'm wondering if I've missed it and gone too far, I see something I recognise up ahead. It's the patchy scrap of grass leading down to the towpath that I'd seen from Malik's bedroom window. I only have to walk a bit further before his block of flats comes into view.

I leave the path and climb up the steps beside the muddy bank. As I approach the building, I'm still thinking about what I'm going to say if Malik answers the door. Tenting my hand to the glass of the small kitchen window, I see nothing but a cracked mug on the draining board. The next window along is Malik's combined bedroom and living area, but with the sheet at the window, it's impossible to see in.

I go round to the side where the entrance door is and hesitate, wondering if what I'm doing is right. What if Malik's been working all night and is sleeping? He hasn't told me what companies he works for, and I haven't asked. Maybe it's the not knowing that's part of the attraction for me, keeping him elusive. Mysterious. If I knew the ins and outs of his everyday life, the spell could be broken.

But I'm here now and I want more than anything for him to be here too. To prove to me that he still wants me in the way that I want him.

Lifting my finger to the buzzer, I press it and wait, but as I hear it reverberate inside the entrance hall, a small, insistent voice nags in my head.

You're no better than Natalie.

TWENTY-FIVE

Minutes pass but Malik doesn't come to the door. A woman walks by, pushing a pram. She stares at me as though I shouldn't be there, but I ignore her. *Come on, Malik. Where are you?* When I push the buzzer again and there's still no answer, I step away. Either he's not in or he doesn't want to see me.

I get out my phone and type a message *Are you in?* but that too remains unanswered. I'm clearly wasting my time.

I feel aimless. Not myself at all. The sky above my head is blue, combed through with white clouds. It's been a while since we've had such a nice day and I have no plans. What I do know is I don't want to go back to my flat. In fact, I'm beginning to wonder if I made a mistake taking the tenancy over from Tina as I feel as much a stranger there as I had in my own home when Fiona was there.

I tap the screen of my phone with my nail, wondering what to do, before remembering Simon's message earlier this morning. The one I never replied to. Is it too late to contact him? Might he have made other plans? With nothing to lose and nothing else to do, I find his number and ring it. He answers straight away.

'Mel.'

'Hi, Simon. Still up for that walk?'

'Of course. You hadn't replied to my message, so I thought

maybe you hadn't seen it. Where do you want to meet? Shall I come by the flat?'

'No, I'm not there.'

'Oh, where are you?'

I don't want to tell him as I know what he'll say and don't need to hear it right now. I step back from Malik's door and look around me. The street has a sad air about it. It's a mix of shabby modern apartment blocks and older terraced houses – leaking drainpipes staining their greying pebble-dashed fronts. The round metal ears of satellite dishes that protrude from every wall gives them a cartoonish appearance. The thought of living here is depressing.

'Nowhere interesting. I've just been out for a run. I'll head back and meet you at Kenning Bridge. Fifteen minutes?'

I hear the smile in his voice. 'Sure. See you there.'

With a last look at Malik's building, I turn and walk back down the slope, retracing my steps along the towpath until I'm almost back to the area where my flat is. Ahead of me is Kenning Bridge, a magnificent arc of ironwork linking the two sides of the canal. Simon has got here before me. He's standing on the bridge, his elbows resting on the white iron rail, watching a swan and her cygnets as they disappear into the darkness beneath.

When he sees me coming towards him, he smiles. 'Glad you could make it.'

I join him on the bridge. 'It's not like I've got anything better to do.'

'Thanks.'

I punch him on the arm. 'Don't be like that. You know what I mean. Weirdly, I can't remember what I used to do with myself at a weekend when Niall and I were married.'

Simon smiles. 'You slobbed around like the rest of us I expect. Trying to get over a week of bloody hellish early mornings.' He turns from the canal and rests his back against the iron rails. 'Bet you don't miss those.'

'No, I don't, but the late nights take a lot of getting used to as well.'

'I suppose.' He looks at me, his expression serious. 'I couldn't sleep the other night and tuned in to your show. I heard that girl, the one with the crazy lover.'

I frown. For some reason having Simon listen into the show makes me feel the same way I did as a teenager if one of my parents overheard a conversation between me and my best friend. It hadn't crossed my mind that he'd ever be listening.

'Her name is Natalie.' The words come out stiffly as if I'm defending her.

'Right...'

He sounds like he doesn't think her name is important. I turn and walk back across the bridge to the towpath, then wait for Simon to catch up with me before following the path under the bridge. 'These people are real, Simon. Real people with real problems.'

'I didn't say they weren't.' Simon's voice echoes off the cool brick. 'It's just—'

'Just what?' I stop walking and Simon nearly bumps into me. In the gloom, his pale face looks almost white. The water under here smells mossy. Faintly stagnant.

'Nothing.'

'No, go on. You don't normally hold back when it comes to my life.'

He gives a small shake of his head. 'Don't be like this. You don't even know what I was going to say.'

I carry on walking until I break out into the daylight. 'You don't have to. You think I'm getting too involved.'

'You said it, not me.' Simon runs a hand through his hair. 'I just know what you're like, Mel. You care about people too much. Think it's your responsibility to fix them. Tell me I'm wrong.'

I want to but I can't because he's right. 'I'm worried about her.'

Simon's beside me now, his hands in his pockets. 'She's unstable, Mel. You must see that. You encouraging her isn't going to help her.'

'It's called engaging, Simon. You should try it sometime.' I know I'm being unfair, but I feel like a child whose favourite toy had been dropped into the mud. This walk was a bad idea.

'I'm sorry.' Simon reaches out a hand and gives my sleeve a small tug. 'Still friends?'

I can't help smiling. 'Yes, still friends. But you have to let me do the show *my* way, Si. I need to make my own mark.'

'You like it then? Better than the Breakfast Show?'

I think for a moment, realising I do. 'Yes. It's like I'm a part of it... not just on the outside looking in.' I look at him. 'Do you know what I'm saying?'

Simon nods.

A heron flies out from the reeds beside us, making me jump. The thump of my heart reminds me of something.

'Last night, when I was doing the show, I heard something.'

I look ahead but can feel Simon's eyes on me.

'What do you mean?'

'I heard a bang, like the front door slamming. When I went to look, there were leaflets all over the floor of the reception, as though the wind had blown them.'

'So you didn't close the door properly... or Phil didn't.'

In the bright sunshine, what I'm saying sounds trivial. I hear it with Simon's ears. Hear how silly it sounds. Yet, if it was nothing, why had I double-checked the lock then spent the final hour of the programme glancing at the glass panel of the door, my stomach churning?

'I think someone was in the radio station, Simon. Maybe the same person who slashed my tyre.' The thought has only just occurred to me, and I don't like it.

'You should tell Di,' he replies, and I nod.

We walk in silence for a while, and I can see Simon's deep in thought.

'What is it?' I ask.

'You're not going to like what I'm about to say.'

'Say it anyway.'

He rubs at his stubble, falling back to let me go on ahead when the path narrows. 'I've got a bad feeling about this. Have done ever since you messaged me the other day.'

He's talking about Malik. My heart sinks as I remember tapping out my message, standing outside Malik's house on the day he'd summoned me and then cast me aside. I'd been confused, angry at having been mucked about. I'd made Malik out to be something he isn't.

I try to remember what I told him. I know I'd mentioned the way he hadn't wanted to let me go to work. Had tried to make me stay. My fingers move to the soft skin of my wrist, remembering the press of his fingers. What I hadn't told him was how tenderly he'd kissed my wrist after. Now, I get that horrible uncomfortable feeling you get when you've told someone too much. I should never have said anything to Simon. But I'd been angry, and anger makes you do things you shouldn't... I should know.

'Have you ever wondered who that phone call was from? The one that made him chuck you out of his flat?'

I feel my face redden. I'd forgotten I'd told him that in one of the conversations we'd had since. 'No, I haven't wondered. It's none of my business who phones him.'

Simon draws in a breath. 'I never had you down as a fool, Mel. Niall's a bit of an idiot but at least he was sane.' He falls into step beside me once more, stepping over a rope wound around a metal stake that's been hammered into the canal bank. The boat it's securing moves in the sluggish water, nudging the one in front. 'There's something going on with this guy and you should be careful. I know you don't want to hear it, but Anne and I have been talking about this.'

I can hardly believe what I'm hearing. I picture the two of them sitting in their tasteful living room in their expensive house talking about me. *Poor Mel. She never makes good choices.* They mean well, but with Chris on my back as well, it feels as though the three of them are my minders rather than my friends.

'And what did you and your lovely wife come up with?' I know I sound petulant but that's how he makes me feel.

'Don't be like that.'

'I'd have thought you'd have had enough to think about with Anne's pregnancy without wasting your time on my love life.'

Simon grabs my arm, making me stop. He puts his other hand on my shoulder and turns me round to face him. A canal boat chugs by, sending ripples across the water. Simon waits until it's gone past before speaking again.

'That slashed tyre of yours. Chris and I had talked about the fact that it might have been done by somebody you know but had dismissed it as unlikely. Now, though, after what you've told me, I'm thinking that it wasn't such a ridiculous hypothesis after all. It could well be Malik.'

With the narrowboat gone, a stillness has settled on the canal again. Neat houses with picture windows follow this stretch of the canal but, on the opposite bank, it's more rural, white willows reaching down to the water, searching for their reflections.

I can hardly believe what Simon's just said. 'Why on earth would Malik do something like that? What would he gain from it?'

'It was your first night doing the show. He knew that. He knew you'd be there.'

Frustration is gripping me. 'You haven't answered my question, Simon. What would Malik have had to gain?'

'He might have thought it was just a one-night stand. Persuading you to let the AA wait until morning to look at the car was his way of getting you to go back to his squalid little place.'

'Squalid? Jesus, Simon. You really can be a snob when you want to be.' I walk quicker, not wanting to be near him, then a thought occurs to me as I picture Malik's road with its sad houses and scruffy gardens. The car on bricks I'd seen in one of the drive-ways. The toys that had been left out to rust and mould in another. The Mickey Mouse ears of the satellite dishes. I stop, pressing a finger to his chest.

'How do you know what it's like?'

He chews at his lip. 'I just do.'

'Oh, Christ. Don't tell me you've been there. Please don't tell me that.'

An image comes to me of Simon in his SUV, trawling the streets looking for the right block. Sitting in his raised seat, looking down on the people walking by on the pavement. People who aren't as lucky as him. People who, through the lottery of birth or bad luck, have no choice but to live in a terrace where the neighbour's TV or fists can be heard through the thin walls. Or a block of flats where a tacked-up sheet takes the place of a curtain.

'Please don't get mad. I haven't been there.'

I don't believe him. 'Then how could you possibly know?'

Simon looks at the sky then back at me. 'All right. *All right.* It wasn't me – it was Chris. He was the one who went snooping. Happy now? But it was done with the best of intentions. He was worried. We both were. He thought if he did a scout, he'd be able to find out a bit more about the guy, okay? He feels guilty.'

'Why on earth would he feel guilty?'

'Because if he hadn't suggested the blind date to you in the first place, then none of this would have happened. You wouldn't have thought that Malik was his friend, and you wouldn't have gone off with him that night.'

I can't tell him that it would have made little difference. That the minute I'd set eyes on Malik I'd been under his spell. 'You should have told him not to... or at the very least you should have told me. How did he even know Malik's address?'

Simon shrugs. 'I don't know. Maybe he told him in the pub. Anyway, we're getting off the point. Don't you think it odd that Malik just turned up at the radio station on the night someone knifed the tyre? What was he doing there at that time of night if it wasn't to lure you back? It's bad enough him sleeping with you when you were drunk let alone—'

'He didn't sleep with me.'

Simon shoves his hands into his pockets. 'He didn't?'

'No. He's decent. He wouldn't do that.' I push to one side the inconvenient fact that the following morning I'd been afraid he had. That I hadn't trusted him enough.

'That's something then but it doesn't let him off the hook. Why was he hanging around there at that time of night? There's not exactly a lot to do at two o'clock in the morning in that part of town.'

'He was walking. He has trouble sleeping and we'd arranged to meet up.'

'So he thought he'd turn up at the place where you were working and scare the living daylights out of you?'

'It wasn't like that.'

I want to tell him that it didn't happen the way he imagines. That I hadn't been scared... but that would be lying. I think of how I'd turned round in the driver's seat. Knowing I'd seen something at the entrance to that dark car park. A movement that formed into a man's shape, a silhouette against the moonlit canal. There's no denying my fear when I'd looked up after retrieving my phone from the footwell, a phone that had dropped through shaking fingers. Or how I'd nearly screamed when I'd seen the man's face pressed against the passenger window.

But that doesn't mean anything. It doesn't make Malik a tyre slasher or a trespasser. No one had forced me to do anything. I'd gone back to Malik's house because I'd wanted to, not because he'd made me. I could have stayed and waited for the AA van, but I hadn't. Instead, I'd rung them and asked them to come in the morning instead. It had been my decision. No one else's.

'I've been thinking, Simon. It might be as well to have some space from each other. You and Chris have got so used to playing the big brothers, my protectors, that you forget I'm a grown woman.'

Simon rocks back and forth on his feet. With his windswept fair hair and preppy scarf, he looks like a schoolboy who's just been given detention. 'We have each other's backs. You know that. We're The Three Musketeers.'

I shake my head sadly. 'No. We *were* The Three Musketeers. It was a game, nothing more. We're grown-ups not kids. I told you before: I don't need someone to have my back. No one's ever made me feel the way Malik does, and it will be my decision whether he's good for me or not.'

Simon looks down. What I've said has hit him hard but I'm not sorry. We've been in each other's pockets for too long and it's time we broke away from one another, allowed to make our own mistakes and learn from them, however hard that might be.

We've come to a large stone bridge. Veering away from the towpath, I climb the steps that lead to the road that will eventually take me back to where I now live.

'Mel, wait!' Simon is following me. He grabs my hand. 'Don't do this.'

'Go home, Simon. You can't always be a superhero. Anne needs you... I don't. We all just need a bit of space.'

Simon sighs and runs his hand down his chin. 'Just don't do anything stupid...' He stops, seeing my expression. 'I'm sorry. It's habit, that's all. But you won't, will you?'

'No, I won't.' I give him a reassuring smile. 'I promise.'

But I know he'll find it hard not to look out for me. Like he says, it's become a habit, but it's one he needs to break. I feel sad leaving him there on the towpath but there's something I know that makes it easier for me.

Simon hasn't always been able to save me from making stupid mistakes.

TWENTY-SIX

I run my hand down Malik's chest, feeling the soft hairs move under my touch. I think he's asleep as his breathing is slow and even, but I can't be sure. What I do know is my heart is bursting with the knowledge that he still wants me. Still needs me, despite everything.

His message had come just as I'd been resigning myself to a lazy Sunday afternoon in front of the TV.

Come over tonight.

I hadn't questioned where he'd been the day before or even why he'd dismissed me the way he had when I'd seen him last. Instead, I'd sat in my room and counted down the hours until I'd be seeing him again, stubbornly ignoring Simon's worries – the one's he'd shared with Chris. I push down the insistent nag of his last words to me when I'd left him on the canal bank.

Don't do anything stupid.

I feel Malik's heart beating against my palm. How can this be stupid when it feels so right? My lips feel sore. Chapped. The insides of my thighs tender. I hadn't been lying when I'd said it to Simon... No man has ever made me feel the way Malik does. Not used or embarrassed or guilty. No, the feeling is more powerful than that. I smile to myself, thinking that I sound like someone in a bad romantic movie. Except that in a film like that, they wouldn't have done what we've just done.

'Malik, are you awake?'

Lying in the darkened room with its furniture made from old packing cases, I have a sudden need to know more about him. Where he works. Who he sees when he's not with me. I've told myself that I won't ask, that he'll tell me in his own good time, but surely knowing these things will make us closer.

I lean up on my elbow and brush his damp hair from his forehead. 'Malik?'

He sits up, the duvet falling to his waist. He's looking at me, but his eyes are blank and staring. It's as if he can't see me.

I lean away from him, my heart thudding inside my ribcage.

'What's wrong?'

He doesn't speak but fights with the duvet to get it off him. He's still asleep – I can see that now. Dreaming some terrible dream.

'It's me, Melanie,' I say, trying to soothe him. 'It's just a dream.'

When I reach a hand to his face, he knocks it away, his fist clenched. He's saying words I can't understand. It's a language I don't know.

I move back, rubbing at my arm, scared at the force with which he struck it. 'You're safe, Malik. You're okay.'

His eyes move rapidly from my face to the door then back again. He looks different, as though he's someone else. Anxiety tightens my chest, making it hard to breathe.

'You're okay,' I say again.

But he doesn't look okay – he looks terrified. He's shouting now, rapid words that I have no hope of understanding. I want to put my arms around him, but I'm scared to. This isn't the man I know.

He's standing now, a dark shape at the side of the bed, looking wildly around him. Then, as quickly as it began, it's over. He presses the heels of his hands against his eyes and a low moan escapes him.

'Malik?'

He lowers his hands and when he looks at me this time, I know he's seeing me.

I reach across and take his hand. 'You've had a bad dream. Come back to bed.'

He pulls his hand away. 'I need to walk.'

In the faint light that's coming through the sheet at the window, I see how his forehead shines with sweat.

'Then I'll come too.'

'No.' He sits on the edge of the bed and searches for the jeans he discarded earlier. I don't want him to go. Not in this state.

I place the flat of my hand against his back, feeling the muscles taut beneath his hot, sweaty skin. His breath comes loud and heavy. Unsure if it's the right thing to do, I lean forward and press my lips to his damp skin.

'Lie down with me.'

For a moment, he doesn't move. Then, reluctantly, he drops his jeans to the floor and gets back into bed. He pulls me to him and kisses my forehead, his long hair trailing my face. I think he'll make love to me again, but he doesn't. Instead, he lies on his side facing me, my hand pressed against his chest, his breathing ragged.

'I'm sorry,' he whispers into my hair. 'I have these nightmares sometimes...'

'It's all right. I'm here.'

He leans forward and kisses my forehead again. 'I'm glad. Talk to me. It might help.'

'What do you want me to talk about?'

'Your job... anything. Just the sound of your voice will help.'

As we lie face to face, my fingers stroking his hair in the darkness, I talk. About the Breakfast Show. About the fun I'd had on it and how hurt I'd been when Di had moved me to the Late-Night Show. I show him a part of myself I've hidden from my friends: the part that's resentful someone could so easily step into my shoes.

Then, later, I tell him about Niall and my disappointment that our marriage failed. On and on into the night.

It's me who sleeps first, and when I wake again it's still dark. Malik isn't beside me; I sense rather than see it. The flat is silent, no sound to be heard through the thin walls. Sometime between me falling asleep and waking again, he's got up and put on his clothes. Left the place as he did that first time, leaving me alone.

At first, I wait, hoping that I'll hear the bang of the front door. The sound of his shoes in the hallway signalling he's come back to me. But there's nothing. Somewhere above me a baby cries, faint but insistent, breaking the silence. I listen to it until it quietens again. The darkness is oppressive, so I switch on the light that stands on the floor beside my bed – just a bare bulb in a second-hand lamp base. It casts shadows across the stark room, and I see it as others would. The packing-crate tables, the linoleum floor that's lifted in places to expose dirty wooden floorboards, the water stain on the ceiling.

I feel uneasy.

Hoping a coffee might help me think more clearly, I throw back the covers, get off the bed and pull on my clothes. If we're to have a relationship, I need Malik to talk to me. Tell me where he goes at night when he can't sleep.

In the harsh light of the bare bulb, I walk to the door. The handle is a cheap metal lever and I press down on it. It doesn't open. Even though I know it's futile, I press down again, pushing the door with my shoulder. Still it won't give.

I hadn't been imagining it before... Malik has locked me in.

My throat tightens as I step away from the door. Why would he do that?

Suddenly, it's as if the scales have been lifted.

I feel myself panic.

What on earth am I doing here? What could I have been thinking? I'd been desperate for him to return but now I don't want him to. I just want to go home.

It's windy outside; I can hear it buffeting against the single-glazed window. Picking up my bag from beside the bed, I hurry over to it and lift the sheet before edging myself under the fabric. The mould-streaked casement is damp under my fingers as I feel for the handle. I lift it up and push, relief surging through me when the window cracks open, bringing with it a blast of chilly air. Leaving the window, I drag over one of the wooden crates and stand on it, using it to climb onto the windowsill. Below the window is a patch of muddy grass. Grateful that the flat is on the ground floor, I sit on the ledge and jump to the ground.

I glance back at Malik's room. The sheet is flapping at the open window, and I push it closed, then stand on the muddy slope deciding what to do. I didn't bring my car so I'm going to have to walk home. The streets are better lit than the towpath but following the canal would get me back sooner.

I make my decision and run down the steps to the narrow, over-grown path beside the water. Thankfully, it's a clear night, the sky swept with stars, the wind blowing rags of cloud across the moon then away again. Keeping as close to the grassed edge of the path as I can, I use my phone to light the way, its beam picking out the glint of a mooring ring, the white twist of a tow rope.

I've only been walking ten minutes or so when I hear something. I stop and look back, wondering if the sound I heard has come from one of the barges lying low in the water. A gust of wind sends ripples of moonlight towards the bank.

Telling myself it was just the wind, I walk on, relieved when I see the black arc of Kenning Bridge ahead of me.

But the noise is there again. Closer now.

I whip round. 'Who is it? If you come any closer, I'll scream.'

I hear it clearly now, footsteps on the stony path, the owner not trying to disguise them.

With rising panic, I flash my torch from one side of the path to the other. 'I know you're there.'

I stand, rooted to the spot, petrified of what will happen. I should never have come this way. Only a few months ago Simon and I had seen a homeless man asleep under the stone womb of one of the bridges and teenagers have been known to come here to score drugs. Only a mile or so away, that poor woman disappeared from the tunnel, never to be seen again. What had I been thinking?

A shadow looms and I think I'll die of fright, but when I hear my name and recognise the voice, I sink to my haunches in relief.

'Jesus, Chris! What are you doing out here?'

I shine the torch on him. He looks down at me, his face an apology.

'I was worried.'

The dark, sluggish water laps at the stone edge of the canal. Now that the wind has dropped, I see how beautiful the night is, but I'm too wound up to appreciate it, my anger bubbling close to the surface.

'You've been following me. What the hell?'

If I've been expecting an apology, it's clear from his face that I'm not going to get one. Chris stands his ground, his legs astride. 'Of course I've been fucking following you. Jesus, Mel. I sometimes think you must be off your head. Do you get off on putting yourself in danger?'

I stare at him, wondering if I'm hearing him correctly. 'It's the middle of the night. You've been acting like a goddamn stalker and you have the cheek to say *I'm* off my head? I thought Simon was bad enough... but you?' I stop, remembering the night I'd found him slumped outside the recording studio. The drunken pass he'd made at me. I don't want to think of what it could mean. 'For God's sake, Chris, can't you see how creepy what you did is? I could report you to Di for harassment.'

His laugh is harsh. 'You think Di would care? She's too busy acting like Big Brother to give a fuck.' He steps closer, holds his hand out in supplication. 'Look, I didn't mean to frighten you, Mel. I just...' He stares down at the water. 'I just don't trust him.'

He doesn't need to say who he's talking about.

Chris looks tired, the torchlight showing up thread veins in his full cheeks that I haven't noticed before. He doesn't look drunk but that doesn't mean he hasn't been drinking. My anger melts away and I feel suddenly sorry for this big man whose only crime is to care for me a bit too much.

I straighten up and take his arm. 'I'm not saying what you did was right... in fact, it's crazy. But I appreciate the sentiment behind it. Where's your car?' I move closer and give a surreptitious sniff but can't smell alcohol on him. That's something, I suppose.

He jerks his thumb in the direction we've both come from. 'Left it in the road outside his flat.'

I think about it. 'How did you even know I was there?'

'How do you think?'

'Don't tell me... Simon.'

An expression shifts across his face, gone again before I can catch what it is. 'When he told me about the conversation you'd had earlier today, the things he'd said to you about Malik, I could've decked him. Not because I don't agree – I wouldn't have put it past him to have slashed your tyre – but because you're stubborn. So fucking stubborn.' He looks at me meaningfully. 'If someone warns you off something, you just go and do the bloody opposite.'

I stare at him. My instinct is to disagree but what would be the point when we both know it's true.

'Even so. I could have been anywhere.'

'But you weren't. You were exactly where we thought you'd be. Sunday night's your last free night before the show starts again and it was an educated guess you'd be spending it with him.' He unhooks my arm from his and walks to the canal edge. Stares down at the dark water. 'So bloody predictable.'

'And what were you planning to do?' I ask. 'Run into the flat in your Superman outfit and rescue me from his evil clutches? We're not five-year-olds, Chris.'

He turns his head. 'No, of course I wasn't. When I think about it now, I can see how what I did would seem odd, but my plan had just been to drive by the place. I don't really know what I was expecting to see or do, but as it happened, I couldn't have timed it better. You can see the steps that lead down to the canal from the street and when I saw you run from the building towards them, my first thought was that something was wrong.' He comes back to me and places a hand either side of my shoulders. 'He didn't do anything, did he?'

I shake my head and move away from him. 'Not really. He gets nightmares. Really bad ones where he doesn't know where he is or what he's doing. It freaked me out a bit when it happened tonight. I thought I'd managed to persuade him to go back to sleep, but when I woke again, he'd gone.'

In the moonlight, I see Chris raise his eyebrows. 'Gone where?'

'I don't know.' I close my eyes a second wondering whether to tell him about the locked door and how I'd had to climb out the window as Chris wouldn't have been able to see it from the road. For some reason I decide not to. Maybe it's because a small part of me still wants to believe in Malik. 'You don't need to worry. I've decided I won't be seeing him again. I'll message him when I get back and explain.'

Even as I say it, I'm experiencing the gut-wrenching ache of loss. Breaking up with Malik is what I *should* do but it's not what I want. Far from it.

Chris takes my arm again. 'I'm glad. Come on – I'll walk you the rest of the way.'

'No, it's fine. It's not far from here.' I look at my watch, realising something. 'You've only an hour before you have to be at the radio station. You should have been getting your beauty sleep rather than running around after me. You'll be shattered.'

Chris shrugs. 'I'll survive.'

He releases my arm and points back along the canal path. 'But if you're sure you're okay, I'd better get going or Di will be on the warpath.'

'Yes, you had.'

I think he's going to leave but he doesn't. He's waiting for me to go. Clearly, he isn't going to be happy until he's seen me climb the steps at Kenning Bridge.

'You don't have to wait. I'm fine, Chris, honestly.'

'Okay, but, Mel?'

'Yeah?'

'Best not to tell anyone what I did tonight.' He shifts his feet awkwardly. 'They might not understand.'

I give him a half-smile. 'No, I won't say anything.'

'Good.' His relief is evident in the slight sag of his shoulders. 'I'll maybe catch you tomorrow then.'

'Sure.'

I leave him on the towpath and head towards the bridge. The rail is cold as I climb up to the road. When I reach the welcoming streetlight, I look back down. I'd expected to see Chris's back disappearing into the darkness. What I hadn't expected was to see him still standing there watching me.

When I get home, I make myself a camomile tea and take it to bed with me. I prop myself on my elbow and, in the light of the bedside lamp, type out a message to Malik. *I'm sorry. It's been fun but I don't think it's a good idea we see each other again.*

I stare at the words, my finger hovering over the send button. It's what I know I must do, what I should have done a long time ago. Even so, bringing myself to press that button is so much harder than I'd thought it would be.

How Malik was tonight has made me scared. It's not just his unpredictability but the nightmare he had. It makes me suspect something bad has happened to him in the past. Something he won't share but which resurfaces at night when he's at his most vulnerable. I fear he needs help that I'm not trained to give him. Especially if he refuses to open up.

I'm no longer able to hide from the truth. At first, being with Malik had been exciting, but there's a fine line between excitement and fear and I may have just crossed it. It's time to put a stop to whatever this thing is between us.

Pressing send quickly, I place my phone face down on the bedside table, not wanting to see his reply. I switch off the bedside light and lie back against the pillow before sitting up again and reaching for the phone. I switch it to silent. If he tries to call me, I won't answer, and if he sends me a message, I can delete it in the morning when I'm feeling stronger.

I thought that sending the message would be an end to it, that I'd be relieved, but I'm not. If anything, I'm more anxious. As I lie awake, listening to the silence, I wonder if he's seen it. Whether he's asleep or whether he's still out there somewhere walking the streets.

As I close my eyes and wait for sleep to come, another thought occurs to me. I've never told him my new address, but it wouldn't be hard for him to find it.

Fear flutters in my stomach and I pull the duvet up higher. That's not something I want to think about.

TWENTY-SEVEN

I sleep late, and when I wake the sun is shining through my window. The noise that woke me is the front door buzzer in the hall. I swing my feet over the side of the bed and lift my dressing gown from the hook on the door, wondering whether the visitor is for me or for Nathan.

Rubbing the sleep from my eyes, I press the button of the intercom. 'Yes?'

'Hi, Mel. It's me. Anne.'

I look down at my cheap high-street pyjamas and grimace. 'Oh, hi, Anne. This is a surprise.'

'I hope you don't mind me turning up unannounced, but I was at a bit of a loose end and thought I'd come over and see you. I have a belated housewarming present for you from me and Si.'

'That's nice of you, thank you.'

Anne gives a laugh. 'To be honest, it wasn't the only reason. I wanted to check that I hadn't made a huge mistake in recommending Tina's place to you.'

I stifle a yawn. 'Well, whatever, it will be nice to have some company. Though I must warn you, I'm still in my pyjamas.'

'Don't worry about that. Soon the tables will be turned, and it'll be me issuing the warning before turning up with baby sick on my shoulder and leaking boobs.'

I laugh. 'Heaven forbid!'

Five minutes later, we're sitting on the settee, the large green houseplant that Anne's brought on the coffee table in front of us.

'So how have you settled in?' Anne takes a sip of peppermint tea, made with the sachet she brought with her. She looks fragile, and as she reaches forward to put her mug back on the table, the row of silver bangles she's wearing jangle on her slim wrist.

'It seems strange to be living somewhere else after all these years but it's okay. I just have to get used to it.' I take a sip of my coffee. 'I'm still waiting to meet my housemate though. You were right about him keeping unsociable hours. We're ships in the night. Sometimes he wakes me when he comes in and I leave the occasional note for him, to remind him it's bin day... stuff like that. But it's obvious he likes to keep himself to himself.'

Anne smiles. 'That's what Tina said. Sounds ideal to me. In fact, I'm quite jealous.'

She leans her head back against the cushion and closes her eyes for a moment. She looks tired, her foundation not quite hiding the hint of dark shadow beneath her eyes.

'How are you, Anne? What are you now? Eleven weeks?'

'Nearly twelve.' She looks down, her hand moving to her stomach, smoothing the soft fabric of her jumper. It's very early still but she's so slim it's impossible not to notice the slight swelling. It warms my heart. I raise my eyes to hers.

'And the scan?'

'Next week. After last time, I'm making sure I eat well and get lots of rest. I'm doing everything in my power to make sure the same thing doesn't happen again.' She stretches her legs out in front of her. 'You know what though, Mel? I have a good feeling about it this time. I think it's going to be all right.'

I lean over and place my hand on top of hers, giving it a squeeze. 'I do too. But you know what happened before wasn't your fault. Sometimes these things just happen.'

Anne nods. 'I know that, but it doesn't hurt to do what I can. I want the very best for this baby.'

'Of course you do.'

Kicking off her shoes, Anne tucks her feet under her and surveys the room. Having her here makes the place feel comfortable. More like a home. It's only now that I realise how much I've missed having a female friend to talk to.

'Thank you for coming round – it's good to see you.'

'You're welcome. To be honest it was nice to escape the house. Simon's fussing can be a bit much sometimes. When he's home he treats me like an invalid.' She slides the silver bangles up her slim arm and down again. 'Not that he's home much. It's like he doesn't want to be with me at the moment.'

I look at her with pity, unsure of how to respond. 'I expect it's because he's worried. What happened was hard for him too, and I'm sure he'll be back to his usual self once you've had the scan.'

She smooths her hair back from her face. 'God, I hope so. Anyway, let's not talk about Simon. Tell me about the radio show. Are you still enjoying it?'

'I am. It's hard to explain but compared to the Breakfast Show it feels so intimate. So private. I'm more engaged than I ever was on the morning slot.' I look at her then away again. 'I don't think Simon can understand it.'

Anne pulls a face. 'He's probably jealous.'

'Jealous? What of?'

'Of you, of course... having the show to yourself.'

I think of Simon at the mixer desk, deciding which caller to put through, what topic will be discussed and who will introduce it. 'But he's the anchor. It's basically his show.'

'That's not how he sees it.'

And he's right of course. Chris and I might not have been in charge of the controls, but it was a definite case of teamwork. The way we sparred off each other was what made it work. What made it successful.

'Anyway, Simon would hate what I do.' I pick up the packet of digestives I've opened and offer them to her. 'Especially the True Confessions part. He'd probably turn everything into a joke or offer solutions. He wouldn't really *listen*. But I've been enjoying trying to understand what's going on inside someone's head and considering what I'd do in their situation. There's this girl called Natalie...'

I stop. I hadn't planned to mention her.

Anne takes a sip of her drink. 'Go on.'

'She's been ringing in to the show, and I can't really explain it but it's like we have a connection. That she's reaching out to me.' I lean forward, my elbows on my knees, my hands cupped around my mug. 'I think she's lonely. Scared too, and I'm worried I could be the only person she has to talk to. I'd like to help her if I can.'

Anne puts down her drink. 'It's a radio show, Mel. There's only so much you can do.'

I sit back, considering what she's just said. 'Simon thinks people who phone in to confession shows like mine are attention seekers. Is that what you think too?'

She shakes her head. 'No, of course not. But I'd be careful. It's not a good idea to get too close to your listeners. What's she been saying?'

'It doesn't matter.' I realise I don't want to talk about her anymore. 'You're right. I expect I'm worrying over nothing.' I get up and take our empty mugs to the sink, then go to the window and look down at the small garden below. 'She probably won't ring again anyway.'

Anne joins me at the window and puts an arm around me. 'Even if she does, I'm sure you'll handle it. The main thing is you're enjoying doing the show.' She gives my shoulder a squeeze. 'Don't listen to what anyone else says. Least of all Simon. What does he know?'

I laugh. 'Exactly.'

We stand in silence, watching a dog in next door's garden chase a ball. After a couple of minutes, Anne turns to me.

'You wouldn't know where he goes when he goes out, would you? Simon, I mean.'

I hadn't expected the question. 'No, he hasn't told me. My guess is he's probably with Chris. You know what they're like.'

She gives a rueful smile. 'Exactly. But if you knew something, Mel, you'd say, wouldn't you?'

I hear the hidden meaning behind her words, the ones she's too scared to say, and wonder if this was the real reason she came round. 'Yes, of course.'

But would I? Simon's been my friend longer than Anne.

'I'd better go.' Anne picks up her bag. 'I'm sorting out the baby's room which at the minute is full of Simon's junk. I know it's months away yet, but it gives me something to do. Stops me worrying.'

'I think it's a great idea.' We walk to the door, and I open it for her. 'Don't overdo it though.'

'I won't – I promise. Thank you for the tea.'

I shut the door behind her and sit back down on the settee, thinking about what we've talked about – Simon, my show, Natalie – glad that I didn't open up to her too much or tell her any more about Malik. She wouldn't have understood any more than Simon does.

I take out my phone and look at the message I wrote to him, relieved yet strangely disappointed that he hasn't replied.

If I'd told Anne about what he did last night and how I feel today, she would have spoken her mind. Said what everyone else would be thinking. There's only one person who would understand the thoughts that pull me one way and then another and that's Natalie. We both know what it's like to keep wanting someone even when it's obvious they're not good for us. Maybe it's something she sensed the first time she rang in. Maybe I gave it away in something I said. No, however much I want to, I can't distance myself from her as Anne suggested.

As I think this, two ticks appear against the message and my heart thuds. Malik's read it.

What will he think? Will he be disappointed? Upset? Angry?

I remember the unyielding wood of the bedroom door as I'd tried in vain to open it. I also remember Natalie's voice as she'd described a similar experience. I feel lightheaded as I allow the terrible possibility to percolate. Is it possible they could be the same person?

The screen of my phone goes black. He's not replying.

That's good as I don't want to see him again. I turn the phone over so I'm not tempted to check then go into my bedroom to get dressed.

The sun's streaming in through the large window, warming the room. I slide off my dressing gown and hang it on the door. As I do, I glance at the door handle and laugh at the way my imagination has been running overtime. I've no doubt that Malik locked me in his room but the other thing...

As I pull open my underwear drawer, I shake my head at my foolishness. There are many men out there who act strangely. Who walk the streets at night and treat their lovers badly.

Sharing the same experience with Natalie is pure coincidence. Nothing more.

TWENTY-EIGHT

The meeting room is full. We've all been summoned at short notice but we're not sure why. Di stands at the window looking out at the canal, waiting for the final people to arrive. Simon is sitting to my right, staring at his phone and I'm glad he isn't wanting to talk.

Dan catches my eye and smiles. It's clear he doesn't know what's going on either and I wonder what would have happened if he'd been the producer on my show. Would he have made me cut Natalie off? Would he have dismissed her and her fears as everyone else seems to have done?

I look around to see who's missing and nudge Simon's arm. 'Where's Charl?'

He looks up. 'I dunno. She wasn't in for the show this morning. Didn't leave a message or anything. Chris and I ended up having to do it on our own in the end. Between you and me, I don't think she has the stamina for the early mornings.'

The door bangs and two more people come in. Luke from Drive Time and one of the evening producers.

Di turns from the window. 'Thank you for coming in. It looks like we're all here now.' She comes to the long table where we're all gathered and sits down. 'You're probably wondering what this is all about.'

'Too right we are. Some of us have been up since four and need a kip.' Chris is sitting at the end of the table. He raises bloodshot eyes to her. 'How long is this going to take?'

I will Chris to be quiet. He's treading a thin tightrope with his attitude, and he's got a mortgage to pay.

Thankfully, Di doesn't rise to it. 'I won't keep you long.' She scans the room, her face serious. 'You've probably all noticed that Charl isn't in today.'

I look up. What has this meeting got to do with Charl? Beside me, Simon is flicking through his phone. His finger stops and his face goes pale.

'Shit,' he mutters under his breath. He looks as though he's going to say something else, but Di is speaking again.

'This morning, I had a phone call from her, and she's given permission for me to tell you what she said. Early this morning on her way to work, she was the victim of an assault. She believes someone was following her. I don't want to give any more details as the police will be wanting to speak to you all individually, but I thought it important that you know so you can take precautions.'

'Is she all right?' Chris sits up straighter. He looks sick, his fingers gripping the edge of the table.

'Yes, she had a rape alarm which was enough to scare them off but, not surprisingly, she's pretty shaken.'

I feel numb. 'Can you tell us where it happened?'

'I can't divulge that information, I'm afraid, but it was near here. That much I can say. And, because of that, I'm going to need you to think about your own personal safety.' She looks at me. 'You especially, Mel, being here late at night on your own. In fact, I'm wondering whether we maybe ought to have another reshuffle. Move you back to a daytime slot.'

'No,' I say too quickly. Simon is staring at me, and I moderate my voice. 'No, that won't be necessary.'

I never got round to telling her my suspicion that someone had been in the radio station the last time I'd been there, and I wonder if Simon's going to say something. He doesn't. Instead, he leans his elbows on the table and rakes his fingers through his hair.

'Why the hell didn't she tell us?' he mutters. 'We're supposed to be her friends.'

'When something bad happens, it's not always your friends you want to turn to,' I whisper back. I'm thinking of Anne, and I wonder if he is too.

I picture Charl with her wide blue eyes and her nose stud. So confident. So sure of herself. Poor girl. I hadn't liked her much, but this is a horrible thing to have happened.

Di is speaking again. 'Charl didn't want to make a fuss. In fact, she wasn't keen on notifying the police, but thankfully I managed to persuade her to see sense. If I could just ask you all to stay here until the police arrive, I'd be very grateful. Simon... Chris... I'll suggest they talk to you first so you can get home.'

Simon nods. 'Thanks.'

'For nothing,' Chris mutters.

Di picks up her jacket from the back of the chair and puts it on. 'This might be a good time to have a think about anything that might shed some light on what happened. She was probably just in the wrong place at the wrong time' – her eyes settle on mine – 'but just in case.'

She leaves the room, and the place falls silent. No one wants to say what we're all thinking. As radio presenters, we let a whole world of people into our lives. People we know nothing about.

What if she's wrong?

When I come back to the building later to do the show, I park as close as I can to the front door. With a quick look at the dark, empty car park, I hurry to the keypad, swearing when I get the numbers wrong and have to start over again. This time it works, and I breathe a sigh of relief when the door releases.

I check and check again that the door has closed properly behind me then hurry down the corridor, my nerves settling somewhat when I see Phil in his studio. When he sees me, he raises his hand and smiles. I give a half-smile back, remembering how he'd offered to stay for a bit longer than usual after his show finished and how I'd told him not to be so silly. When I'd spoken to the police, they'd confirmed what Di had said. Charl had probably just been unlucky.

I'd mentioned my suspicions of an intruder, but with the only evidence a loud bang that could have been anything and some scattered promotional material, I hadn't felt they'd taken it too seriously. They'd been more interested in my slashed tyre, but with the security camera not working, there wasn't much for them to go on. The only good outcome of all this is that Di has been shamed into looking into getting the camera fixed. About time.

As I sit down in my chair at the mixer desk, I'm on edge. I think of Charl, so young, just starting her career, and feel guilty for not having given her more encouragement. For blaming her for taking my job when it wasn't her fault. After all, if it hadn't been Charl, it would have been someone else. I think back to myself at her age – ambitious, determined. Yes, I would have done anything to have got that coveted breakfast slot.

It's then I have a horrible thought. Is it possible that Malik might have had something to do with this? Did he follow her and scare her? Would he do that for me? I know that I should tell the police, but the thought that I could have been taken in by someone capable of something like that is so abhorrent I push it away. Simon. Chris. It's their fault. They've been getting into my head.

I spend the next half hour going through my notes. Just before ten, Phil plays his last track. Soon he'll be gone, leaving me alone, and my anxiety returns. Quickly, I push it down. Phil has promised me he'll double-check the door on his way out. The building will be secure, but even if it isn't, the police are aware I'm here on my own. The thing that happened to Charl is dreadful, but it has nothing to do with me. I must remember that.

I pick up the headphones and fit them over my ears then lean in to the microphone. As always, I'm counting down the minutes until midnight and tonight, more than usual, it's as though the digits are stuck on the clock face, invisible fingers preventing them from changing. I'm no longer interested in Ray's poorly dog or Janet's meddling sister. I'm only interested in Natalie. Desperate to find out what's happened to her since she last phoned in.

When at last it's time for True Confessions, I'm sick with anticipation. My earlier fears have returned and I'm looking for a clue. Something that will tell me I got it wrong. For I'm not ready to believe the impossible idea that Natalie and I could share a lover.

Come on, Natalie. Ring in. I need to know she's all right.

The lines are flashing, and I run my eyes down them, looking for a number I recognise. Not seeing one, I feel a surge of panic as I pick a caller at random, my heart sinking when it isn't her. I cut someone off, pretending it's a fault on the line. Pick another line and let the caller speak for less than a minute. My replies fall from disinterested lips. My eyes search and fail. As the minutes pass and the end of the hour is in sight, I know it's hopeless.

Natalie isn't going to call.

Disappointment fills me, and it shocks me how great my need is to hear her voice. To know she's okay. I push back my chair and close my eyes in frustration. The lines are no longer flashing as the True Confessions hour is about to end. How I'm going to get through the next hour, I don't know.

I breathe in deeply and try to assess my feelings. Is it normal, wise even, to react this way to a caller I've never met? My brain says no but my heart says yes. For some of the lonely souls of the night, I'm all they have. I may be all Natalie has.

When I open my eyes again, one solitary line is flashing. A number I don't know.

It takes just seconds to connect.

'True Confessions... What would you like to tell me?'

I wait. All my senses on high alert.

Natalie's voice comes through the earphones. Her words are stilted. Dead. As though they are someone else's words, not her own. 'I can't phone you anymore.'

'No, please, Natalie. I appreciate that you might not want to tell me on air. Maybe you're worried about reprisals. If I'm right, I want you to know that you can ring me after the show has ended. We can speak privately. It's important you don't bottle this up.'

'No, it's too dangerous.' Her voice has lowered, and I imagine her looking over her shoulder, checking she's no longer being over-heard. 'For you too.'

'Natalie, please...'

But she's gone.

What does she mean for me too? What is she saying?

I sit staring into space then, slowly, I become aware of a change of light. I spin my chair to look at the door, but the glass panel shows just a rectangle of darkness. Getting up, I go to the door and open it, looking down the corridor to the silent reception.

Everything's as it should be – no open door to the car park, no leaflets on the floor. Closing the door again, I go back to the mixing desk to continue the programme.

But it's hard when Natalie's words are still in my head and, every so often, my eyes flick to the door. That shift from light to dark... it was as though the sensor in the corridor had timed out. And if the light had been on, that can mean only one thing.

Someone was in the corridor.

TWENTY-NINE

One day passes then another. Each evening, I drive to the studio. Do my show. Go through the motions. I try my best to be professional, hoping that I'll rekindle the spark I'd had when I'd first taken over Alan's late-night spot. Trying and failing. For now, everything I say sounds false, the listeners' calls to the show trite and banal – to my ears at least.

And all the time I'm waiting for a call that doesn't come, my anxiety growing until I can't stand it anymore. Knowing I should let it go. That Natalie's not my problem. I can't let it go though, and on the third day, I press my lips to the microphone and beg her to call in. To tell us she's okay.

But she doesn't.

I've heard nothing from Malik either. There's been no call. No message. No sign that he cares that I called it off. It's as if the two of them have abandoned me.

Each night I go home, burdened with the knowledge that Natalie hasn't rung. Wondering if something's happened to her. Becoming more and more certain, as the days pass, that it has. Is she out there somewhere? Is she lonely or afraid? I can't think about anything else.

If only I knew where she was when she made that call.

Whenever I play her words back in my head, my perception

changes. Sometimes I imagine her to have been alone. At other times, there's someone with her. Recently, I've been picturing Natalie alone in a locked room, the packing case furniture her only company. A sheet acting as a curtain. And when she ends the call to True Confessions, I imagine her trying the window, only to find it locked too.

Is it possible that we could have shared the same man?

The thought makes me shiver. Had his fingers, his lips, touched her skin? Had he made her feel how he'd made me feel? Alive. Wanted.

My overactive imagination moves from Natalie to Malik. Is he angry that I've left him? I think of him walking the streets. Trawling the canal path. Watching the radio station.

And what about Charl? Just a young girl on her way to work when this terrible thing happened. She's back on the Breakfast Show now. Simon says she's doing okay, thank God. The day after it had happened, I'd sent her a message of support and she'd thanked me politely. But I know the police are no nearer to discovering who it was who assaulted her in the early hours of that morning and I'm wondering if maybe I should contact them. But what would I say? Everything that's going through my head sounds fantastical with nothing concrete to support it.

It's the weekend again and once more I'm at a loose end. Deciding what I need is exercise, I change into my running gear and head for the kitchen to grab myself some breakfast. As I cross the landing, I notice Nathan's door is ajar. It's usually shut and, although I know I'm invading his privacy, I can't resist a peek. Last week, we bumped into each other for the first time. I don't know what I'd been expecting, but it certainly hadn't been the pale-faced youth in the Iron Maiden T-shirt who'd been sitting at the breakfast bar in the kitchen. He'd looked up when I'd come in and nodded but, other than that, he'd made it clear he had no desire to engage in conversation.

Not sure if he's in or out, I go quietly to his door and poke my head around it. The room is small, half the size of mine, and the first thing I notice is how dark it is, the curtains at the windows tightly closed, and how immaculate. The bed is neatly made and, unlike my room, there are no clothes on the floor or on the chair. I go back out and pull the door to, feeling guilty for having intruded into his private space.

Today, when I reach the towpath, instead of running in the direction of the radio station, I turn right towards the town centre. It's a nice morning and I'm not the only one who's taking advantage of the mild weather. As I run, I have to keep veering off the path onto the verge to avoid people: an elderly woman with a dog that strains on its lead, a couple trying to navigate their child's pushchair around the potholes and stones, a cyclist.

Running is good for me. It stops me from dwelling on everything that's been happening recently. I'm aware only of my breathing, the flex and contraction of my leg muscles, the burning sensation deep inside my chest. I run until my tired legs can go no further then bend double, my hands on my thighs, trying to catch my breath.

I've run further than I expected. Almost as far as the lock. I walk the rest of the way, one hand pressed against my waist where a stitch has started. A narrowboat is waiting to enter the lock, a woman holding tightly to the towrope as a teenage girl hurries to the lock gates, a windlass in her hands. Soon there's the metallic ratchet sound of sluice gates being lifted. A sound that sets my teeth on edge.

I reach her and watch as the deep chamber fills with water. When I ask if she'd like some help pushing the paddles, she gratefully accepts and the two of us lean our backs against the wooden beams, bracing our feet against the brick ridges on the ground to get them to move. It's as the narrowboat slides into the chamber and we're closing the gate behind it that I become aware of where I am. To my right is the flat, red-bricked frontage of The Junction. The place where I first met Malik. It seems so long ago now.

I look at its large, dark windows, the canal reflected in them, remembering the way Malik had taken my face in his hands and kissed me in a way nobody else had. As if he knew me. As if he owned me. The thought is disconcerting, and I turn away. Had I been the only one or had there been a string of women stupid enough to fall for his intense dark eyes? The way he had of making you feel like you were everything to him... yet nothing. I'm glad I made the break. Glad too that I now feel strong enough to resist the temptation of contacting him again.

It's then my phone buzzes, vibrating against my hip. I unzip the pocket of my sweatshirt and take it out. As I read what's written on the screen, my heart sinks. There are only three little words but the message they deliver has the same effect as if it had been a whole essay.

I miss you.

I close my eyes in frustration, everything I'd believed unravelling in front of me.

THIRTY

Of course, I wasn't to know that this simple message would be only the start. At first, it was just the odd one or two but now it's every day, sometimes more.

I sit in the studio and look at the latest one: *I thought I'd got over you but I haven't. We should be together.* I cover my face with my hands. Once this is exactly how I would have wanted him to react but not now. I think about messaging back but what if it just encourages him?

Placing the phone on the desk in front of me, I stare at the blank screen wondering how long he's going to keep this up. I'm tired and I want to go home to my bed. What I don't need is this.

I stand and press my hands into the small of my back, kneading the hollows at the base of my spine with my fingers. Tonight, I had a caller ask about Natalie. She'd sounded as concerned by her absence as I am, wondering if we ought to follow it up. Other calls had followed. Some saying the girl was nothing but an attention seeker, others sharing the first caller's worry. I'd found it hard to know how to respond when I wasn't even sure what I believed myself.

I stuff my notes from the show into my bag and pick up my coat. I've just got my arm into the sleeve when my phone pings again.

I need to see you. Please talk to me.

The groan I give sounds strange in the empty studio. Leave me alone. Just leave me alone. I'm angry but I'm worried too. I've read about people like this... ones who won't let go. After I told him it had to stop, he'd given no indication that he cared. What's prompted him to say these things now?

There's a loud bang and I stop, my hand on the door. This time, there's no imagining it. It's the sound of the front door closing. If I look out of the glass panel, I'll be able to see who it is but then they'll see me too. Quickly, I turn off the light and press myself against the wall. With any luck, whoever it is will think that the place is empty. Will take whatever it is they've come for and leave.

My first fear is that it could be Malik, but then I reason that there's no way he'd know the key code for the door. No, this is someone who works here or knows someone who does.

But what would they be doing inside the radio station at just after two in the morning? Whoever it is that's in the building knows what they want. Their footsteps are echoing in the corridor. Coming towards me.

Pulling my phone out of my pocket, I fumble to bring it to life, ready to phone the emergency services if I have to.

The footsteps stop.

The door opens.

I press myself against the wall. Willing myself not to cry out. Willing them not to see me. Then the room is flooded with light and I hear my name.

'Well, well. What have we here? Melanie Abbott, playing hide and seek in the dark.'

Alan stands just inside the door, his finger on the light switch, a look of amusement on his face. His thin hair is longer than when I saw him last, his face gaunter.

I stare at him as my heart struggles to return to normal. 'I thought you were an intruder.'

He turns his palms to the ceiling. 'Well, if you want to nit-pick, technically I am. I no longer work here. Or had you forgotten that?'

I suppose he's right, but he was with the radio station for so long that I doubt anyone would think anything of it, let alone mind.

'It's gone two in the morning, Alan. Why are you here?'

'Why are *you* here?'

I remember now, his disconcerting way of answering my questions with ones of his own. I move away from the wall, feeling foolish now. 'You know why I'm here. I'm doing my job.'

His thin smile is reptilian. 'Ah, yes. Your job.'

He walks slowly over to the desk and pulls out the chair by the mixing desk. He sits heavily, giving a grunt of pain as he makes contact with the seat.

'Are you all right? Can I get you something?'

He looks amused again. 'I'm dying, young lady. What do you think you could get me for that?'

I don't answer. Instead, I pull out the chair opposite, the one I used to occupy on the Breakfast Show. I sit and look at him, wondering again what he wants.

He doesn't wait for me to ask. 'I'm here to help you.'

I frown, puzzled. 'With what? I'm fine. The show's going great.'

Alan laces his fingers behind his head, reminding me of that first night I came to see him. The first time I talked to him about the job. *His* job.

'Is it?' He lets the question hang in the air. 'Is it really?'

I feel awkward under his gaze, the warmth of my skin giving away the blush that's spreading up my neck to my cheeks.

'Ratings are good,' I say quickly. 'Di's pleased.'

'Ah yes.' He nods. 'Of course.'

'What do you mean by that?'

'The radio station is a business like any other. Of course she's pleased. That's all that interests her. But you? You I think strive for something more. You have compassion. You have empathy. You want to make a difference.'

I stare at him. If only he knew the truth. If only he knew the secret that gnaws away at me.

'This girl. This Natalie,' he continues. 'There's something in her that calls to you. That you recognise. If you disagree, please feel free to say.'

My silence is his answer.

'Her voice lingers. Insinuates itself into your waking hours... the ones when you're asleep too. She hasn't called for days and you miss her, like a lover who has gone cold.'

I think of Malik and shiver. How does he know so much?

'I am dying, Melanie. I'm not afraid of it. It's God's will. But the presence of death makes me bold. It makes me inquisitive. I lie awake at night, the Grim Reaper's scythe threatening to sever the last ties between my body and my soul and listen to your show in the hope that the distraction will amuse him. Amuse *me*. Wondering what you'll say. How you'll react. It might sound strange, but I recognise some of myself in you. Oh, you might not think we're alike, but we are.'

I look at him, his skin tinged with yellow, his arms frail beneath the sleeves of his jacket. Wondering what quality of life he still has. How the human spirit can be so much stronger than the body. Despite his obvious discomfort, does he pray for more days of life or does he sometimes long for it all to end? If I was bold like him, it's a question I'd like to ask. But I'm not him. I'm me.

'So why *are* you here?'

He puts his head on one side. 'I told you. I'm here to help you.'

'And how are you proposing to do that?'

His lips stretch into a smile. 'By telling you to stop what you're doing.'

It wasn't what I'd been expecting him to say. 'But why?'

'Because, young lady, you're like a dog with a bone and if this Natalie calls again, I'd suggest you don't answer. Sometimes you need to be outside of a situation to know it, but you should be careful. I told you once not to take the job if you valued your sanity and I haven't changed my view. Being the object of someone's attention is powerful but also dangerous.'

He fixes me with his protruding eyes and waits. I feel sorry for him, but I don't need his help. It's not as though I asked for it. Alan's just jealous that it's me who's wearing the headphones and not him.

'Thank you for your advice, but it's not necessary. And you're wrong, you and I are not the same. We're different people. Very different.'

Alan presses heavily on the arms of his chair and levers himself up.

'No, not so very different, Melanie Abbott.' He walks to the door and then turns and looks back at me. 'We're both stubborn. I had to learn the hard way and it looks like you will too.'

He leaves the studio, and as the door closes behind him, I remain where I am, staring at the mixer desk, thinking about what he's said. It's only the ping of the phone that brings me back to the here and now. Another message.

Remember what we did. How it felt. How it tasted. I want that again.

I feel the colour leach from my face and grip the phone to still my racing thoughts. But when I feel ready to get up and leave, it's Alan's words that are in my head. Not his.

Being the object of someone's attention is powerful but also dangerous.

I just hope he's not right.

THIRTY-ONE

Chris and I are sitting beside the canal on a bench dedicated to a woman called Norma Chapman. Apparently, it used to be her favourite spot when she was alive, and it's mine too.

'Fucking bitch.' Chris thumps his forehead with the heel of his hand. 'Fucking, fucking bitch.'

A female runner who's just gone past turns her head and shoots him a look of disapproval but I'm used to his moods and know that the best thing is to ignore them.

'I don't think you can blame it all on Di, Chris. What on earth were you thinking of going into work drunk?'

He turns his head and looks at me, his cheeks ruddy, his chin in need of a shave. 'I wasn't drunk. I can show her drunk if she wants to see it.'

Further along the towpath, a man looks up from the lump of wood he's whittling on the roof of his canal boat. Clearly wondering who's disturbing the peace on this bright morning.

'Shush,' I hiss, tapping Chris's leg with the back of my hand. 'Getting angry isn't going to help anyone.'

'It helps me. Stupid woman's a control freak. Final warning? What the fuck!'

It's worse than I thought. All I know is what he told me on the phone earlier. That he made an inappropriate comment on air that some listeners had taken offence to. Complaints had come in and he'd been hauled up in front of the programme controller for a hand slapping.

That won't have gone down well.

'So, what happened exactly?'

'What happened is that some people just don't have a sense of humour. Everything's so PC. It didn't used to be like this in the good old days.'

I shake my head at what I'm hearing. Surely, he can't really mean it.

'People have become more aware of what they're saying, of course they have, and rightly so. It's time you did too.' Sometimes, on the Breakfast Show, I'd felt as though Chris forgot it wasn't just Simon and me he was talking to and his jokes were often close to the mark. 'There are thousands of people out there listening to you every morning, a lot of younger people too. You're supposed to be setting an example to them.'

He folds his arms defensively. 'Now who's the pot calling the kettle black?'

'Meaning?'

'You can't go around pretending to be holier than thou when you spend your nights buddying up with a woman who's clearly lost the plot.'

I sigh. 'You sound just like Alan. He came here last night.'

'What? To the studio? What on earth did he want?'

I think back over the things Alan said. 'Basically, he wants the same as everyone else... for me to back off. He thinks engaging with a listener to the extent I have is risky. In fact, he came right out and said it was dangerous.'

Chris lets out a breath, the sound whistling between his teeth. 'And I thought *I* had problems. Why is she dangerous?'

'Not her... the situation. I think what he was trying to say was that by getting too involved, I could be attracting unwanted attention. There are some odd people out there, especially in the early hours. That's not all though.' I stop, my attention snagged by a paper bag that's caught in the reeds on the other side of the canal bank. Eventually, the wind picks it up and carries it away. 'He thinks I'm feeding off other people's problems because it makes me feel powerful.'

'Jesus. The old guy doesn't pull his punches, does he?' Chris yawns, not bothering to cover his mouth. 'What do *you* think?'

I stop and think. Could Alan be right? Does it make me feel good to focus on other people's secrets?

'I honestly don't know. But, whatever the reason, I'm really worried about Natalie. She hasn't called in to the show for days. What if something's happened to her? This guy she was seeing... he had some sort of hold over her. She was scared. Do you know that when she first rang in, she said she thought he'd killed someone?'

I stop, seeing Chris's expression.

'You don't believe me.'

'Of course I believe you. If she said it in front of several thousands of listeners then you can't have made it up. The question is... did *she*?' He pats my hand. It's a brotherly gesture and I'm grateful. 'I just think this business with the guy you were seeing, this Malik, has skewed your judgement. I wish I'd never spoken to him at the pub.'

'Then why did you?' I get up, bored with the conversation.

From his vantage point on the roof of the canal boat, the woodcarver looks up and smiles at me. There are several carved animals lined up on the roof of his boat and he points to a sign with the prices on. When I don't respond, he shrugs and carries on with his carving, curls of pale wood covering his lap.

Chris stands and shoves his hands into the pockets of his trousers. 'There's no need to get shirty with me.'

I sigh heavily. Dealing with Chris is sometimes like dealing with a child. 'You don't need to worry. I've stopped seeing him. Didn't Simon tell you?'

Even though things are still strained between us, I'd messaged Simon to tell him – an olive branch of sorts.

Two lines form between his eyes. 'No, he didn't.'

'And there was me thinking you told each other everything.'

'No, not everything.' He looks away from me and I wonder if it's because he's thinking about the stupid drunken pass he made at me. A memory I've tried to bury.

'I'm glad though,' he continues. 'The guy's a creep.'

My phone pings a message. Before I can think what I'm doing, I've taken it out of my pocket and clicked on it.

I want to smell you. Taste you. Be inside you.

My stomach flips unpleasantly, and I shove the phone back in my pocket. I'm scared to look up in case Chris has seen. Surely he can't have; he was standing too far away. But as I raise my eyes, I can tell by the look of bewilderment on his face that he has. Slowly, his expression changes.

'Jesus fucking Christ.' With a snort of disgust, he strides away, leaving me alone, the back of my hand pressed to my burning cheek.

THIRTY-TWO

I can't let this go on. *Leave me alone,* I type.

The message comes back quickly. *You were wrong to have left me.*

My heart is thumping so hard that I'm afraid it will burst through my chest. There's no point in replying. I can sense that it will only make things worse. I clutch a hand to my stomach and sit back down on the bench, feeling sick.

Why now, after all this time?

'All right?' The woodcarver puts down his knife and shuffles to the edge of the roof. He swings his legs over the side, the heels of his boots banging against the glass of the small round windows. 'That guy been bothering you?' He jerks a thumb in the direction of Chris's disappearing back.

'No. No... nothing like that. I'm fine. Really.'

He doesn't look convinced. 'Okay, if you're sure.'

'I am.'

I'm tired too. Tired of everyone trying to control my life. I'm finally free of my domestic ties to Niall, have a new job where I'm able to make my own decisions and thought I'd sorted out my tangled relationships once and for all. But I've come to realise that life isn't as simple as that. It's as though everyone still has a little piece of me.

I run my fingers across the shiny brass plaque on the back of the bench wondering if Norma Chapman had as much bother in her life.

As I drive to the radio station, the knot that's been in my stomach since I received the text messages has tightened. I don't know what to do about them, whether to ignore them or reply. Something tells me it should be the former.

When I pull up outside the building, I'm surprised to see Phil's car isn't there. It's strange as he lives quite a long way from the station, too far to walk, so he must either have been given a lift or got a taxi. I let myself into the building and head straight to Studio One to find out whether Phil's had a problem with his car. Peering through the glass panel, I see that although the light is on, there's no sign of him, just his empty chair.

The light is off in Studio Two as it should be, so I go back down the corridor and into the kitchen, the only place I can think of where Phil might be. But it's not Phil who's at the worktop, a mug in his hand, leafing through a newspaper.

'Chris?'

He looks up and points to his baggy grey hoodie and jeans. 'There's no fooling you, even in this disguise.'

'What are you doing here?'

'I work here, or have you forgotten?'

Prickles of irritation make me rub at my arms. 'You don't work at this time of the night, and don't tell me you wanted to get in seven hours early to prepare for the Breakfast Show.'

'Okay, Sherlock.' He closes the paper and shoves it into the recycling bin under the worktop. 'If you must know, Phil is ill and I've taken over his slot.'

'Even though you'll be back here in a few hours?'

Chris shrugs. 'Phil put in an SOS and I volunteered. Thought it might be a good way of getting back into Di's good books. And sleep's overrated. You know me – I'm used to functioning on just a few hours' kip. This helps too. Thought I'd have myself a little something in the music break.'

He shoves the mug he's holding under my nose and I take a step back from it, the alcohol fumes stinging my nose.

'I don't know what you're trying to prove. You're crazy.'

He raises his mug in a mock toast and takes a drink, wiping his mouth on the back of his hand. 'That's your opinion and who am I to argue with someone with such a good track record in recognising dubious personality traits.'

'Don't be like that.' It's obvious what he's referring to and I feel again the burn of shame at what he saw written on my phone.

Chris doesn't answer. Instead, he walks past me, brushing my arm as he goes by, not bothering to apologise when my bag drops from my shoulder onto the floor. I make myself a coffee then follow him down the corridor, glancing into his studio on the way to my own. He's sitting with his feet propped on the desk, his mug of whisky beside him. There's only another half an hour before his programme ends and mine starts so I'm hopeful he'll manage to get through the final minutes without saying or doing anything too stupid. But you never know with Chris. Like me, he's only ever been part of a team and I'm surprised that Di agreed to him taking over Phil's show after his dressing down. Maybe there was no one else willing to do it at such short notice.

I'd not been expecting to see Chris again after my show started but, five minutes in, his face appears through the glass panel. He remains there a moment then comes in, the door swinging closed behind him. I smell the alcohol on him before he even reaches the desk. He sits opposite me, but I can't say anything as a phone line is flashing. I mouth at him, *What are you doing?* before clicking onto it. But Chris doesn't answer, just picks a paper clip from out of the blue plastic desk tidy and straightens it.

The caller is telling me about their new job as a night support worker in a care home. It's their break and they want to find out how other listeners with night jobs manage to cope with the tiredness. It's hard to concentrate with Chris sitting there and I wave him away, but he ignores me, taking sips from the mug he's brought in with him. I wouldn't put it past him to have refilled it.

It should feel like old times having Chris in the studio with me, but it doesn't. With someone else here, I don't feel like myself, and I'm aware of how I'm sounding as though hearing myself through his ears. Why is he even here?

I wait until the caller has finished then put on a music track and take off my headphones.

'You're putting me off.'

'It never bothered you before.'

I close my eyes for a beat. 'It was never my show before.'

He looks around. 'It looks different in here at night, don't you think? Creepy.'

'I suppose so.' I paste a bright smile on my face. For some reason I don't want him to know I agree. 'I like it. It's peaceful.'

'That's what they say about morgues.'

He says it as a joke but still I shiver. Is this his plan? It's like he wants me to feel nervous.

'Go home, Chris. Get some sleep or you'll be the one feeling dead when you get back here at five.'

'I'll stay. I don't like the idea of you going home by yourself. Things have been odd around here lately. Your tyre, Charl, not to mention the fact that you thought someone was in the building the other night.' Chris cradles his mug in his hands, studying my face. He hesitates a moment then nods at my phone on the desk. 'And there's that other thing.'

He's talking about the message again. He only saw one but, since then, there have been others. Each one more insistent. More uninhibited. As I'd walked to the studio, I'd heard my phone go again but had managed to resist the temptation to look. What might once have been exciting is now the opposite. The scales have fallen from my eyes, and I see him for what he is. Controlling. I want him to just leave me alone.

Even so, I don't need Chris's censorship. 'That's my business and no one else's.' I take the mobile off the desk and put it in my pocket then shove my headphones over my ears. 'I mean it, Chris. Go home. I know you mean well but I can't be myself with you sitting there staring at me.'

I swivel my chair so I'm no longer facing him and concentrate on my computer screen, relieved when I eventually hear him get up and walk to the door. The corridor lights up as he goes out and a few minutes later darkens again.

Relieved that he's gone, I settle into my chair and look at my notes. When someone calls in, I make sure that I really listen to what they're saying and that my reply is considered and empathetic. As I talk, I imagine that my headphones are a buffer between my own private life and the one created by my listeners. If I close my mind to everything else, I can slip into their world and forget all the things that have happened to me recently.

It works so well that the time slips by quicker than usual, and it's only when my eyes rise to the clock that I realise it's time for True Confessions. Quickly, I play the introductory music then lean forward and say my bit. It's been a while now since Natalie called in and I no longer feel so panicky about it. She must have sorted her life out. Maybe she's done the same as me – broken away from something toxic. As I watch the lines light up, I no longer feel the need to scan down to look for hers. It's like the two of us have moved on to a different place.

The two of us.

Even now, I'm linking us together and I have to stop.

I put the first caller through. It's a man called Dean who wants to confess to stealing money from his mum's purse when he was fifteen. The next caller doesn't want to give their name but says that three days ago she got the sack from her shelf-stacking job. She hasn't told her boyfriend yet and doesn't know how as they can barely make ends meet as it is.

I tell her she really must let her partner know and give her a number she can ring for debt advice. She thanks me and says she'll think about it, and I give a small smile of satisfaction. If I can help just one person, it's made sitting in a dark and empty building in the middle of the night worthwhile.

Another line flashes and I reach over and click on it before leaning back in my chair and closing my eyes. I wait for them to say something but all I can hear is the sound of them breathing. I open my eyes again. Don't say this is going to be one of those stupid prank calls Alan warned me about.

I'm going to end the call when they speak, taking me by surprise.

'I have a confession.'

There's something compelling about the voice. Strangely hypnotic. I sit up straight, some strange sixth sense telling me that what I'm about to hear will be important.

'What's your name?'

His voice sounds odd, distorted. 'My name isn't important.'

'That's no problem. Not all of my listeners like to give their name.' There's a strange feeling in my stomach, a tensing, and I realise I'm pressing the cushions of the headphones closer to my ears. 'What would you like to tell me?'

Silence again.

'Hello. Are you still there?'

When he speaks again, the strange robotic tone playing tricks with my mind, a nub of fear lodges in my throat.

'I know your secret, but you don't know mine,' he says. 'That's my confession.'

THIRTY-THREE

'You've gone silent, Melanie... Why's that? Is it because you're afraid of what I'll say? That this call will no longer be about me but about you? What would be the fun in that? It's enough that you know I know.'

It's like my blood has frozen in my veins. 'Who is this?'

I look wildly around the studio as though somehow it might help me find the answer to my question, but of course there's nothing. The voice is strange, unrecognisable, but the words chill me nonetheless.

'But that's not my only confession,' he carries on, as though he hasn't heard me. 'What I want to tell you tonight is that I hurt. Right deep inside my chest, the way it would feel if a knife was thrust into my heart to the hilt. Then further still. And all this because I've experienced the most perfect love. The purest love. Can you understand that?'

I have to keep him talking. Have to know who it is who's phoned in. Maybe he'll give something away if I ask the right question. I want to ask someone for advice but there's no one to ask... not at this time of night.

'Yes, I've felt that kind of love.' I try to keep my voice steady, even though my body is shaking.

'Of course you have. Then you'll also know that when you feel love like that, passion like that, madness like that, you will do anything to keep it. Anything to make sure that no one will ever stand between you and that perfect state. But what if that love is taken from you?'

I wrap my arms around me to still my shaking. It feels so cold in the studio now, the computer, the monitor and the microphone on its long arm casting dark shadows across the desk.

I feel suddenly very alone.

'I don't know.'

'Then let me tell you. Maybe you'll seek that person out or perhaps you'll seek out another. Always chasing. Always searching. And when you have them, you will make them understand they are yours, that you won't let them leave you as the other one did. You will cling to that love with fingers capable of tenderness but also capable of much worse.'

Phone lines are flashing; I'm not the only one hearing this. A voice in my head is telling me to cut the call. Cut it now. And yet I don't, for I have to know for sure who it is. This person who knows so much about me.

I know I should do something, but my mouth has gone dry and the words won't come out. I have no option but to let him continue.

I hear him sigh. 'And yet, even though you have someone new, you will never forget that first perfect love. How they left you empty. How can you forget when the space they left in your heart has become filled with something harder? Darker. When that darkness threatens to turn you into a monster you don't recognise, it's hard not to wonder if it really was your fault.'

'Okay, you've had your fun.' I give a nervous laugh, aware, suddenly, of the listeners. 'This isn't really the place—'

'Oh, I think it is.' He draws in a rasping breath. 'You are, after all, the one who would understand. What do you think, Melanie? Now you've heard my confession, my secret, does it surprise you that I might not be who people think I am? That I'm worse... so much worse. Maybe it does or maybe you knew all the time because, perhaps, we're not so different.'

There's a glass of water beside me and I take a sip, moistening my dry mouth. A terrible fear has come over me. A dread that has been growing all the time he's been speaking.

'Please. What about Natalie? If you've done something...?'

I'm drowning in regret. I should have told the police about my concerns.

There's a smile in his voice. 'You women. You're all the same. Liars. Whores.'

I don't know what to say.

The silence expands. The phone lines flash. In my pocket, I can feel my phone vibrating an urgent message. Ignoring them all, I hold my breath and wait.

At last, he speaks.

'And yet, something still bothers me. Something I wanted to ask. It's a question that comes to me when I walk the dark streets at night or see the cold moonlight reflected in the canal.'

I wait, rigid in my seat.

'What?' I say, my voice barely more than a whisper.

'I've made my confession, Melanie,' he says. 'When will you make yours?'

THIRTY-FOUR

The phone in my pocket is buzzing. Vibrating against my hip in a way that can't be ignored. It's Simon.

Cut the call, Mel!

I stare at the screen, seeing the words yet not fully understanding them – as though they're written in a different language. My fingers grip the plastic cover. I will them to move but I can't.

Through my earphones, I can hear the man breathing. He's waiting for me to say something. To confess.

The phone vibrates again in my hand, and I nearly drop it.

For God's sake. Are you mad? Do it now!

Simon's words begin to filter through my shock. Yes, he's right. I must cut the call. I think of the woman who was attacked in the tunnel. How Charl had been followed. My slashed tyre. Natalie. This man. This caller.

He's dangerous.

I end the call and throw my headphones onto the desk, the chair's casters scraping along the floor as I push away from it. Every fibre in my body is telling me to leave the studio, but just as

I'm about to grab my things and go, the professional side of me kicks in. Unless I do something, the people in their bedrooms, their cars, their staffrooms, will hear nothing but silence. The caller has left me numb but I can't leave the listeners hanging.

What I need is someone to talk to and there's only one person I know who's definitely awake. Reaching out a shaking hand, I fade in a song from the playlist then call Simon. He picks up straight away.

'Mel, are you all right?' His voice is barely more than a whisper.

I press my knuckles to my cheeks, making myself focus. Forcing my voice to be business-like. If it wasn't for the late hour, I'd have called someone else but there'd been no choice. 'What did he mean, Simon? Who was it?'

'Wait a minute.' There's a pause then the sound of a door being closed. He won't want to wake Anne in the room next door.

His voice is clearer now. 'You didn't recognise his voice?'

'No.'

'I don't like it. I think you should leave the building and go home now. I can come and pick you up if you like.'

I shake my head, even though he can't see. Irritation battles with my fear and wins. I don't need his help. 'You don't need to do that. I've got the car.'

'Yes, but—'

'Why are you awake anyway, Simon? Why were you listening in to the programme?'

'Anne's not been feeling too great. She had some pains earlier this evening and got herself into a bit of a state.'

My heart goes out to her. This is all she needs when she's already worried about the pregnancy. 'Is she all right?'

'We called the doctor out and he said the baby's heartbeat is strong and that there isn't anything to worry about, but it's easy for him to say. The twelve-week scan showed that everything was normal but of course we're still going to worry. We wouldn't be human if we didn't.'

'Is Anne with you now?' It's only just occurred to me that she might be.

'No, thankfully. The doctor gave her something to help her sleep but I'm wide awake. I always found Alan's late night voice soporific and had this mad idea that yours would do the same. I got more than I bargained for... Thank God I tuned in.'

I glance around the studio uneasily. 'Maybe I should call the police? But it's not as though he actually threatened me.'

'Yes, of course you must.' He pauses and his voice changes. It sounds as though he's pacing. 'If *you* don't, I'm sure one of your thousands of listeners will. Did a number come up for him?'

'Yes.'

'That's something. Should be all they need to find out who it was.'

I turn my head and look at the dark panel of the door. 'I thought it was a crank call but those things he said...' With a shock, I realise I'm crying.

'Mel... speak to me.'

'It's all right. I'm okay.' I breathe in for three then out again slowly. I don't want him to fuss. I can't take it. 'I'll phone the police in the morning.'

'And you're sure you don't want me to come over?'

'I said no.' It's come out too sharply. I take another breath and force my voice to remain even. 'No. Thank you, but I'm fine now.'

'All right but I'm not happy about it.'

I rub my forehead with the heel of my hand. 'The caller sounded bitter and resentful as though the person he was talking about had left him. What if he was Natalie's lover?'

'You were the one who mentioned Natalie. It was *you* he was talking about. About your secret. Like he knew something. What's going on, Mel?'

His voice is stern, but I ignore the question. It's impossible to stop my mind racing away from me.

'What if he *was* the man Natalie was seeing and he's moved on... to *me*.'

I picture my hand pushing back the sheet covering the window. Levering it open before jumping to the muddy patch of grass below. I've tried to ignore the link between me and Natalie, but now I can't deny it any longer. There's a possibility it was Malik who made that call. I think back to his voice. The flat, robotic timbre didn't sound like him but maybe that means nothing.

'Mel, are you okay?' Simon's voice is laced with concern. 'Answer me... *please.*'

His words bring me back to the present. I take my phone away from my ear and look at the screen, thinking of the messages written there. Just one click away. That's not something I can ignore so easily.

'Mel? I'm worried. What is it?'

I hear what he's saying but my mind is still on the messages. I can't put it off any longer – I have to show him.

'I need to speak to you about something important, Simon. Something I'm deeply concerned about.'

'Can you tell me now?'

'I'd rather not.' I fade in another track, not caring that I'm letting my listeners down. A glance at the monitor shows that the lines are still flashing. This is not going to go away. 'I'll tell you tomorrow after you've done your show. I'll meet you outside.'

'Okay. Chris too?'

I think of how Chris was this evening at the studio. His drinking. His bravado. Behind his jokey exterior, I know there is a different Chris. One with a short fuse that I have no wish to light. There's no reason for him to know about this.

'No,' I say. 'Just you.'

'Okay.' He sounds relieved. He knows Chris as well as I do. Better in fact. 'Put the last tracks on auto and go home, Mel. You sound done in. Di will understand when you explain it to her.'

I look at the clock. There's just under an hour to go until the end of my session but he's right – it's the best thing to do.

'Yeah, maybe. I'll see you tomorrow.'

I switch my phone off and move the microphone nearer to me to introduce the next track. As I do, I see how my hand's trembling. Alan was right. I'm not cut out for late-night radio. Not ready for the intensity. The seclusion. *The confessions.*

Maybe I'm no longer cut out for radio at all.

I collect my things up, picturing the walk to the front door. Imagining the reception area strewn with flyers as it was the other night. Then my mind turns to my car waiting for me in the dark car park, imagining its tyres slashed. It's as much as I can do to stop from phoning the police here and now... but I don't.

I can't. Not until I'm sure.

Wanting to be out of the building as quickly as possible, I throw on my jacket and run down the corridor. When I reach the front door, my phone pings a message. I stand rooted to the spot, my hand on the cold metal handle as I look at it. My breath catching in my throat when I see who it's from.

Malik.

Just four simple words. *I will never forget.*

I stare at them, trying to grasp their meaning. Are they words written with love?

Or malice?

THIRTY-FIVE

Simon is waiting for me outside the radio station. It's ten thirty but my eyes are still gritty with tiredness.

He looks at me with concern. 'God, you look terrible.'

'You don't look too good yourself.' It's true. Today, he looks more like the middle-aged man that he is. There are bags under his eyes and the designer stubble he's so proud of looks more like he's just forgotten to shave.

'There was something you wanted to tell me.' He holds the door open, expecting me to come in.

'Not here. What I want to say is private.'

'Where then?' He looks at his phone. 'I don't want to be long. Anne made me promise to come straight home after the show. She's on edge after her scare last night.'

'That's understandable but this won't take long. Let's go down to the canal.' I'm thinking that it might calm me as, rather than help matters, I'm worried that showing Simon the messages might make things worse.

'Okay, but it's nippy out here. Let me just get something to put on.' He disappears back inside and returns a few minutes later with his leather jacket. 'Come on then.'

As we walk, I don't look at him, knowing that I might change my mind if I do. 'I phoned the police this morning,' I say, knowing that I'm just putting off what I really want to tell him. 'They're going to come and talk to me. I said we could use Studio Two as it won't be in use.'

Out of the corner of my eye, I see him turn his head towards me then away again. 'Right. That's good.'

'Yes, it sounds like they're taking it seriously. There are so many things that have happened, I think they might be joining up the dots.'

We've reached the canal. A weak sunshine has turned the water golden. Simon points to a bench. 'Shall we sit?'

'No, let's walk.'

I turn left; it's the way we walked the morning Di told me I was leaving the Breakfast Show. It seems so long ago now. Months... not just a few short weeks. I need to keep moving if I'm to carry this through. My phone is in the pocket of my jacket and I clutch it tightly.

'Is Anne going to be okay?'

'I reckon so.' He walks with his head down. 'The pains have stopped and there's no bleeding. There's no reason to think she won't go to full term this time.'

The path takes us under a small bridge, and when I look back the radio building is out of sight. There are no people on this stretch of the canal... there hardly ever are. It's wild and pretty but untended, the weeds growing across the towpath a hazard for pushchairs and runners. And then there's the tunnel of course. The recent police appeal might not have brought forward any new witnesses but it's brought the horror back.

It's there ahead of us now, its dark mouth opening into a black yawn. Even with the terrible thing that happened there, it hasn't ever bothered me walking this way. It's probably because I've never walked this section of canal alone. Simon or Chris have always been with me.

Simon's still talking. Telling me something about Anne's next scan. When it will be and where. It's not what I want to talk about though. Not when there's so much else I need to say.

I can't stand it anymore.

Turning to him, I shove the phone into his face. 'How could you?'

Simon stops what he's saying, his mouth falling open. 'What?'

'You know what!'

We've both stopped walking. I pull my hand away, jabbing at the screen. 'This.'

I hold the phone up again so he can see. 'What the hell were you thinking?'

He looks at it and away again. 'It's nothing. Forget it.'

I stare at him in disbelief then back at the message. *Remember what we did. How it felt. How it tasted. I want that again.*

'How can you say it's nothing? Those things...' I stop, feeling sick. 'Please tell me you didn't mean them. That you were drunk when you wrote them, like you were all those months ago. Go on – read them... properly.'

He takes the phone, his eyes scanning the screen. His face pales and I know it's because he's realised there's nothing he can say in his defence.

The air is rich with a musky pollen scent. Sweet. Unpleasant. There's something else too, a dank smell that comes from the canal water. Rotting vegetation maybe. In the distance, the black tunnel's mouth gapes as if in horror.

I wish this was a dream and that I'd wake up. In my heart, I always knew this could happen, that he'd never let it lie, but I'd prayed it wouldn't. The warning signs have been there in the way he looked at me across the mixer desk and how he's acted in the last year. Overprotective. Overbearing. His wish for control masked by our long friendship.

'It was one night, Simon. One stupid, drunken, idiotic night and I've hated myself for it ever since.'

Simon brushes his fair hair from his face. 'You don't mean that, Mel. You felt it as much as I did.' He reaches out to me, but I push his hand away, shocked.

'No, you're wrong. It didn't mean anything to me. I was drunk.

You know I was. It should never have happened and it destroyed my marriage.'

'It didn't have to. It's not as if Niall ever knew.'

'That's not the point, Simon. *I* knew and I couldn't continue with our marriage with that on my conscience.'

It's like he isn't listening. 'I understand why you regretted it – you didn't want to hurt Niall. I get that and I left you alone. But now you're divorced. You don't live with him anymore. You're dating again. That was your choice and now there's nothing stopping us from being together.'

I stare at him aghast. This man, the friend I've known and worked with for so long, is suddenly like a stranger to me.

'What about Anne? She's pregnant with your child, for God's sake, and she needs you now more than ever. It's been over a year, Simon. I didn't leave you. How could I when we were never together? Anything more than that one night was simply your imagination running away with you.'

His hands are either side of my shoulders, his earnest face close to mine. 'You weren't ready then, but you are now. You've been more relaxed, more independent. You've let go of the house... embraced change. You proved it with your little fling.'

The weak sunshine that had been with us as we'd walked along the towpath has given up the struggle. A strong breeze has blown up – it stirs the reeds at the canal edge, and above us, grey clouds are gathering. I'm aware of how quiet it is. Just the two of us. The only boat moored up is a shabby barge lying low in the water, no owner in sight.

'Please take your hands off me, Simon,' I snap.

Simon drops his hands and looks at them as though they don't belong to him.

'I'm sorry, Mel, but you have to see I only stayed with Anne because of the baby. When she had the miscarriage, I waited for the sadness to come but it didn't. I never told you that, did I? How the only thing I felt was relief.'

I look at him with disgust. 'You don't mean that.'

'I do because it meant we could be together.' His face freezes into a frown. 'I would have left her then, but how could I when she was in such a state? I was trapped.'

I'm shocked at the venom in his voice. 'Please – you shouldn't be saying these things.'

'Why not?' He looks up at the sky as though it might offer him up some answer. 'It's been killing me not to be able to tell you, but now I can. This baby was a mistake and I need to leave. I can't go through it all again. It's you I want to be with.' He looks at me in desperation. 'If it's the baby you're worried about, I can still be part of its life. We both can.'

'Are you crazy?'

I stare at him in horror, just the sight of him filling me with disgust. I've never thought of Simon as a weak man but now I see him for what he really is. Uncaring. Cold. Duplicitous. What a fool I've been to believe we could still be friends after what happened; it's clear now that friendship was never on his mind.

It happened after one of our nights out. A drunken tryst around the back of the club like a couple of teenagers. Simon's trousers around his ankles. My skirt hiked up around my thighs. I'd been angry with Niall for not managing to tear his eyes from the football when I was trying to tell him about a problem at work and the drink I'd had that night had only fed my resentment. He wouldn't even care, I reasoned as Simon led me outside. But even before Simon had pressed me back against the cold bricks, and our lips had found each other's, I was starting to feel the hot creep of shame and guilt.

The next day at work we'd agreed it had been a mistake and that we would never speak of it again. It had taken a huge amount of effort to get our friendship back on track but we'd managed it. What else could we do when we worked so closely together?

I think of all the nights I'd lain in bed beside Niall, wracked with guilt at what I'd done. Our love was one that had grown out of a long friendship but, somehow, the passion had never sparked. It hadn't bothered us at first as a lot of what we had was good: we shared the same interests and could be ourselves without feeling like we were being judged. But it wasn't long before I knew something wasn't right. We'd grown too comfortable with each other – that was the problem. It was like Niall had forgotten I was his wife and if ever I needed his emotional support, he would make a joke of it in the same way he had before we were married.

Poor Niall. Making me feel like the invisible woman wasn't the greatest of crimes but it had been enough to push me into Simon's arms. Just that once. But once had been enough, and the guilt had finally driven a wedge between us.

I'd thought Simon had viewed it as a mistake as well but he clearly hadn't. He'd simply been biding his time.

I turn on him, white-hot anger making me reckless. 'We had sex once, Simon. When we'd both had too much to drink and should have known better. I've had to live with that guilt, and its consequences, every single day since, and so must you. This isn't about you and me. This isn't about you wanting to be with me. You're scared. This is about your wife and your unborn child and how you can make things right. You don't love me. That's just a fantasy. It's not about love; it's about fear.'

Simon's face, so full of certainty a second ago, falls.

'You've got to let it go.'

I'm chilled to the bone, but I don't know whether it's because of the cold wind or a reaction to what he's just told me. 'I'm going back now to talk to the police about last night. Don't message me again. This has to stop.'

He hangs his head and for a moment he looks like the Simon I recognise – his boyish face flushed, the stiff breeze blowing his hair – not the one I've glimpsed just now. I know what's happened here. I witnessed how cut up he was after Anne's miscarriage and he's trying to protect himself from the pain of being too invested in another child. When he pushes his fringe back from his face, it's a gesture so familiar that I'm filled with a great sadness. In the months since we slept together what we did has become a cancer, unseen but deadly nevertheless, spreading through our friendship. Exposing the fault line in both his character and mine.

'I'm sorry,' Simon says, a muscle working in his jaw.

He looks so dejected, I almost feel sorry for him. My anger creeps back into its cave a little. 'We need to stay away from each other, Simon. I've got enough on my plate. I can't cope with your...' I raise my hands in exasperation. 'Your whatever it is. It's for the best.'

'Who for?'

'For everyone.'

I brush past him and start running back in the direction of the radio station, my heart thumping out the rhythm of my feet. Words are in my head. A mantra keeping pace with my steps. *No one must ever know. No one must ever know.*

But as the radio building comes into sight, new words take their place. Those of last night's radio caller. It brings with it a chill realisation.

No one must ever know.

But it's too late. Someone already does.

THIRTY-SIX

Two uniformed officers are already at the radio station when I get back. I recognise the female officer from the day we were questioned about Charl's scare on the way to work. PC Lilley I think her name was. I don't know her younger male colleague. They're talking to Dawn at the reception desk and as I push open the door, they both look up.

'I'm sorry I'm a bit late,' I say, shrugging out of my coat. 'I got caught up.'

PC Lilley smiles. 'Mrs Abbott, isn't it?'

'Yes, that's right. Thank you for coming.'

She turns to her colleague. 'This is PC Knowles.'

Dawn is looking at me curiously, her expression changing to one of disappointment when she realises I'm not going to tell her what's going on. I point down the corridor. 'I thought we could talk in Studio Two as it's not being used at the moment.'

The policewoman smiles. 'Wherever you like.' She steps aside to let me pass. 'After you.'

I start walking and the officers follow, but when she reaches the board with our photographs on, PC Lilley stops. She stares at the pictures displayed there, although I'm sure she must have seen them when she was here before.

'Is this everyone who works here?' she asks.

'All the presenters, yes.'

She nods and touches a finger to the photograph of Charl. 'And this is the young lady who spoke to us the other day... about being followed?'

'Yes, that's right.'

'Is she back at work yet?'

I'm surprised to be asked. Does she think there might be a link? 'Yes, she says she's okay but Simon's not so sure.'

'Simon Winner?'

'Yes... from the Breakfast Show. I used to work with him.' Feeling my cheeks redden, I lead the way down the corridor. As we pass Studio One, one of our youngest presenters, Paul James, looks up, not bothering to cover his surprise when he sees us. I give him a nod and continue walking. When I reach the next door, I push it open.

'This is the studio where I broadcast the Late-Night Show. Luckily, it's empty at this time of the morning.'

I open the door and let them go through. 'Here we are.'

'Thank you. Before we ask you more about what happened last night, would you be able to show us the equipment you use and how it works when you get a call to the show?'

'Yes, you'll need to come round this side.'

I show the police officers the phone system, explaining the computer software we use and how the six phone lines flash on the screen to indicate when a call is coming in.

PC Lilley leans her elbows on the desk and scrutinises it. 'And you store a list of those numbers?'

'Yes, that way we can see if the same person is calling in regularly. The one last night came from a number that the system didn't recognise as having been used before.'

PC Lilley nods. 'Shall we sit down? There are a few questions we need to ask you.'

'Yes, of course.'

I pull out the swivel chair that I use when I'm broadcasting and sit, waiting as the police officers go round to the other side. PC

Lilley settles herself in Chris's chair and flips over the cover of her notebook. 'It might be best if you start at the beginning, Mrs Abbot.'

'Please, it's Melanie.'

She smiles. 'You mentioned last night, Melanie, that you had a phone call from a listener that you found threatening.'

I look at the desk. 'Well, maybe not threatening...'

She swipes back a few pages in her notebook and reads aloud. 'You said, and I quote, *the caller sounded desperate, as though he'd done something wrong. Maybe harmed someone and I'm worried he might do it again.*' She looks up at me. 'That sounds pretty threatening to me.'

I look down at my lap. What happened last night now seems like a dream. I fully expect PC Lilley to get up and close her notebook. Tell me I'm wasting their time and suggest that in future I end a call from a listener before they can divulge their fantasies. But she doesn't. Instead, she puts her notebook on the table and steeples her fingers.

'I want you to know that we take threats of this nature seriously.'

Unsure of what to say to that, I say nothing.

PC Lilley looks down at her pad. 'And you say it happened on the True Confessions part of the show. I've listened to that myself on the odd occasion.' She turns to the young officer beside her. 'What about you? Have you heard it?'

PC Knowles folds his arms and gives a boyish smile. 'Never have. I need my beauty sleep.'

'Well, you're missing something. A show like that gives a great insight into the human psyche.'

I think of all the varied things people have confessed to over the last few weeks, how candid they've been, and know she's right. The confessions part of the show tends to bring out people's deepest thoughts and beliefs. Last night's caller's in particular.

PC Lilley fixes her eyes on me again. 'I want you to tell me everything you can remember about the call. What he said and what you replied. If he had a regional accent. What his tone of voice was like. That sort of thing.'

I make myself think back. 'He sounded odd. Flat and matter-of-fact. Robotic almost. I'm sorry, that's probably not especially useful.'

'Are the calls recorded? If they are, we'd like to listen to it.'

I shake my head. 'They are on the daytime shows but not the late one. We like to take each call live – audience surveys have shown it's what makes the show special. Listeners are much more likely to open up to you if they know you won't be vetting what they say first. It's especially true on the True Confessions slot. The programme's recorded though – I can find it for you now, if you like.'

I put on my headphones and turn to the studio computer to access the log. It doesn't take long for me to locate yesterday's programme and download the audio. 'Here we are. I just need to find the exact bit.'

As I locate it, I feel my stomach tighten. The thought of hearing the man's words again is making me feel physically sick.

PC Lilley looks at me kindly. 'Are you okay, Melanie?'

'Yes, I just need a minute.'

I get up and move away from the mixer desk. Turning my back on the two of them, I take a few deep breaths. I'd been fine earlier but now my stomach is clenched so tightly it hurts. I force myself to relax and go back to my seat. Without looking at them, I turn to the computer and press play.

As his voice fills the studio, I feel the fine hairs on my arms rise. I rub at them, trying not to concentrate on the words that are causing my heart to thud in my chest.

The two officers listen in silence and when it's over, PC Lilley looks across at her colleague then back again. 'We'll need to take a copy of this.'

'Yes, of course.'

She looks at me, her eyes steady. 'It might be a silly question, but we have to ask. Did you recognise the voice? Have you any idea who it might be? It feels personal.'

'No. I didn't recognise it. I'm sorry.'

'Not to worry. Callers can be quite devious. There are apps they can use to change the sound of their voice... all sorts of tricks. But you say there was a number?'

'Yes, I made a note of it. Here.' I hand her a copy.

'Thanks, we'll take a look later, but chances are the call will have been made from a cheap pay-as-you-go and won't be registered to anyone. Whoever it was that called in may well have ditched the phone by now, but you never know, we might be lucky.' She leans on the desk and makes a note. 'And this Natalie you mentioned? What can you tell me about her?'

I look down at my hands; I can't explain why but I don't want to talk about her. 'She's just someone who's been calling in to the show.'

PC Lilley's eyes are a light brown flecked with gold. They're pretty eyes but they're looking at me as though I'm hiding something.

'And what does she say?'

I know it's stupid, as thousands of listeners would have heard Natalie over the airwaves, but I feel uncomfortable talking about her – as though I'm about to betray her secret.

That's what late-night radio does to you.

I pick up the headphones that are lying next to me and press the soft padding with my thumb. It's a distraction. Makes talking about her easier.

'When Natalie called in, she told me she had feelings for someone who wasn't good for her. The word she used was *damaged*.'

'I see.' She waits for me to say more and when I don't she leans forward. 'Are you thinking that the person she was talking about could be the same man who phoned in yesterday?'

I nod. 'He might be.'

Beside her, PC Knowles is frowning, the expression changing

his face from boyish to something harder, more calculating. It makes me realise how many different facets there are to a person. How we only see glimpses of some and others not at all.

He looks up at me and smiles, his face transforming again. 'How did she sound?'

'She was scared of him. I heard it in her voice.'

PC Lilley scribbles some notes. 'Did she say he hurt her?'

'Not in so many words, but the first time she phoned in, she mentioned that she thought he'd killed someone.'

Her hand stops its writing and she looks up. 'How long ago was this?'

'A few weeks. I can find out the exact date for you if you want.'

'And you didn't think to tell us?'

I feel my cheeks flush. 'Di said—'

'Di?'

'Our programme controller. She said it was probably just a crank call. Alan, the presenter before me, was always getting them apparently. He used to cut them off straight away before they could go too far.'

PC Lilley puts down her pen. 'Yet *you* didn't, Melanie. Why's that?'

My neck's prickling and I rub at it, hating where this is going. I could lie but the woman sitting in front of me with her neat blonde bun and gold-flecked eyes is no fool.

'Because I recognised some of what she was saying.' My voice wavers and I clear my throat. 'It was like we had a connection.'

'Go on.' She looks at me steadily. There's a glimpse of something in her expression but it's gone before I can work out what it is. 'It's important you tell us everything you know.'

My body feels light, as if it might float away, and I grip the desk to centre myself. 'What she said about the man she was seeing. The things he did...' I clear my throat again. 'The same things have happened to me.'

Although I'm not looking at him I see, out of the corner of my eye, PC Knowles's head lift. 'What things are we talking about here, Melanie?'

'The way he blew hot and cold.' I swallow. 'How he went out at night and locked her in his room.'

I see the glance the two of them share. They don't even try to hide it.

'You say this has happened to you too?' PC Lilley says gently.

I force myself to answer. 'Yes.'

She looks at me steadily. 'Can you tell me a little more about it? Where you were?'

'A friend's... my blind date.' I start again. 'I was in the home of a man I was dating. Malik.'

I stop, realising what I've done. Put a voice to my fears. I hadn't meant to give his name. Yet, even if I hadn't, it would have come to light one way or another.

PC Lilley smiles at me kindly. 'What can you tell us about this Malik, Melanie?'

'Malik...' I stop. The word conjures up his face. The caramel skin between his shoulder and his neck, where my lips pressed kisses. The dark curling hair on his chest, so soft beneath my palm.

PC Lilley leans forward encouragingly.

I blink away the tears that have come into my eyes.

'Even now, I barely know anything about him...'

THIRTY-SEVEN

PC Lilley shifts in her chair. 'Who set you up on this blind date?'

'A friend of mine... well, I thought he did anyway.'

She lifts her eyebrows fractionally. 'What do you mean?'

'Chris – I used to work with him on the Breakfast Show. He wanted to set me up with someone but I hadn't been keen. To be honest I hadn't even wanted to go out that night, but I changed my mind later and met him at the pub.' I think back to that time. It seems so long ago now. 'When I got there, Chris had had too much to drink and was hanging off this guy who I later found out was Malik. I just assumed it was the blind date he'd talked about. I'd forgotten that when Chris has had a drink, he'll talk to anyone.'

'Can you fill us in with a few more details about your relationship with this man? How long you've known him. How many times you've seen each other and when you last saw him. Things like that. Anything that you think might be helpful.'

I know what she's thinking but she's wrong.

'It can't be him who rang. He's not like that.'

'With all due respect, it was you who said the caller could be the man Natalie was seeing, the one she was scared of. You've also just told us Malik locked you in his bedroom the same way Natalie's lover did.' PC Lilley's voice is patient. If she wasn't a police officer, she'd have made a good teacher. 'We're just putting two and two together here.'

'I know but...' I stop, realising the futility of arguing. That is *exactly* what I've just said.

I think of Malik's smile. The way he would hold me like I was something precious. As though he never wanted to let go. Why would he do something like this?

A voice is in my head. A voice that could be anyone's: Simon's, Chris's... even Niall's. Anyone who's ever cared for me. *Because you left him. Because he's angry. Because a man who locks a woman in their room and wakes from violent nightmares he can't explain could be capable of so much worse.*

'There are many reasons why people do things,' PC Lilley continues. 'Not all of them obvious to the person on the receiving end. I'd like to ask you a few more questions about this friend of yours and then we'll leave you in peace. As soon as we know more about the number, we'll let you know.'

'Yes, please do.'

PC Lilley looks towards the door. Through the glass panel, the windowless corridor is dark. 'Before we do that, there's something I've been meaning to ask.'

'Yes?'

'Did the outside security camera get fixed?'

'I'm not sure. I presume so. Di was going to get onto it.' I stop, not wanting to ask the question but knowing I must. 'Why? You don't think I'm in danger, do you?'

'I didn't say that. I just think that with the radio station so isolated, it would be prudent to take all precautions. We can't ignore the fact that your tyre was slashed. Of course, that could just be teenagers with nothing better to do but we can't be sure.'

'I'll check with Di.'

'You do that. You can't be too careful.' She flips a page of her notebook and smiles. 'Shall we continue?'

. . .

Half an hour later, I'm putting on my coat ready to leave. I've told the police everything I know about the calls and about Malik and am overwhelmingly tired. I just want to go home and get some more sleep.

I'm just leaving the studio when Di catches me. 'Got a minute?'

'Yes, of course.'

'That's good. I wanted to have a quick word with you about last night.' She gives me a hard look. 'I really wish you'd spoken to me before bringing the police into it.'

Immediately, I feel defensive; I know exactly why I didn't. It's because she'd have brushed it off as unimportant. Told me that if I wasn't up to the job then maybe I should consider leaving. I'd already guessed, from our talk before, that she and Alan had shared a mutually beneficial working relationship. She'd let him get on with things his way and in return he hadn't bothered her with all the strange things working on the Late-Night Show would throw up. I'd thought that was what she wanted.

'It wasn't an ordinary call, Di. There was something disturbing about it. Darker. He knew about Natalie. He knew that—'

Di closes her eyes as if in pain and shakes her head. 'Natalie. Everyone knows about Natalie if they have their radios on at midnight. She's hardly a secret as she's called in practically every night since you took over.'

'But it's like he knew her.' I desperately think back. Was it? Or had I just put that idea into the caller's head? I'm now wondering if what I'd told the police had been accurate? 'She stopped calling in and now this... you can't blame me for being worried that something might have happened to her.'

'I've told you before, Mel. We can't go running to the police every time we get a call that's a bit difficult. If we do, no one will want to phone in and where will we be then? We might just as well be one of those stations that play music, give the news and weather and bore everyone to death.'

'I understand what you're saying, but what if you're wrong?

What if ignoring this puts Natalie, or some other woman, in danger?' I grow cold as a terrible thought occurs to me. 'What if last night's caller had something to do with the disappearance of the woman in the tunnel? Or Charl's attack?'

Di's face hardens. She looks down the corridor towards the reception then back again. 'Now you're getting melodramatic. Take my advice and leave well alone. You don't know what hornets' nest you might be stirring up.'

I fight to keep my frustration in check. Di's my boss and I need to tread carefully, but what she's saying doesn't make any sense. 'What hornets' nest? Is something going on that I don't know about?'

Di looks at me steadily. 'Of course not, but there are cranks and desperate people out there wanting an outlet to vent their paranoia and give voice to their fantasies.' She breathes in loudly through her nose. 'I thought with Alan gone and someone sane at the helm I'd be done with all this.'

At her words, my frustration turns to anger. 'You shouldn't speak about him like that. The man's dying. Don't you have any compassion?'

Di folds her arms and leans back against the wall of the corridor. 'Dying? What gave you that idea?'

I frown. Down the end of the corridor, in the brightly lit reception, Simon and Chris are deep in conversation. My paranoid brain wonders if Simon is telling him about the messages he sent to me, but of course he isn't. Chris doesn't know about our drunken tryst and that's the way we both want it to stay. As far as he knows, the message he saw was from Malik.

I turn my attention back to Di. 'It's what Phil told me.' I stop, remembering Alan's late-night visit to the studio. 'And what *Alan* told me himself.'

She nods slowly. 'So that's his story, is it? I shouldn't be surprised, as there was bound to be some gossip around his swift departure. I suppose he thought it was better to let people think that than the alternative. It meant he could leave and enjoy his retirement with his reputation still intact.'

'So he lied.' I'm trying to take it in. 'I can't believe I felt sorry for him. I was *nice* to him, even though he did everything he could to make me feel uncomfortable.'

Di's expression is sympathetic. 'There's no point in wasting your anger on him. He's gone now and Lock Radio is a better place without him.'

She starts walking down the corridor and I hurry to catch up with her. 'What did he do, Di?'

'You know I can't tell you that. It's confidential.' We go through into reception and as Simon looks up, she gives him a hard look. 'Why are you two still here? I thought you had a pregnant wife at home, Simon?'

Simon's jaw is set. 'We were just leaving.'

He glances at me then away again, and I will him to keep it together. To act normally. All I can think about is getting out of this building that's beginning to feel like the inside of a pressure cooker.

Luckily, he says nothing else and I make my escape, not wanting to speak to him. When I reach my car, I put my phone on the passenger seat and am just putting my seat belt on when I see Chris and Simon pushing through the door of the building. Simon heads across the car park to his car, his head bent to his phone, but Chris takes the path to the canal, turning right when he reaches the water. He'll be passing Malik's block of flats on his way home.

The thought of Malik brings with it an image of the depressing bedroom, the sheet barely covering the dirty window. Then the image changes, shifts away from the window to the bed where Malik lies asleep on his stomach, a stripe of moonlight caressing his skin.

There's a ping from the passenger seat and I glance down at my phone. Seeing it's a message from Simon, I pick the phone up and read it.

Sorry. I've been thinking about what you said and you're right.

I look at the screen, wondering what to reply. Whether I should. I feel torn two ways. It's impossible to forget what Simon did, but I know also, now that I've had time to calm down, that it wasn't malicious. He just hadn't been thinking. That's always been his problem: act now, think later.

Okay, I type. *But if we're to remain friends, I need you to stop acting like an idiot.*

The reply pings back. *I know. I will.*

When my phone rings, I presume it's Simon wanting to continue the conversation.

'Can we talk about this later?' I say, starting the engine.

But as soon as the caller says my name, I know it's not Si.

A blackthorn hedge edges the car park and a paper bag flaps in the breeze, one corner speared on one of the sharp spikes. I stare at it, through my windscreen, with blind eyes. My breath held tight within my chest.

'Melanie,' the voice says again.

I let my breath out. 'It's you.'

Taking my mobile from my ear, I lower my eyes to the screen, wishing I'd checked the caller's name before answering.

It's Malik.

THIRTY-EIGHT

'What do you want?'

I look out of the window at the car parked next to mine, sunlight reflecting off its windows.

'I need to see you.'

Thank goodness he can't hear my heartbeat. See the flush that has risen to my cheeks. He mustn't know how flustered I am.

'That's not a good idea, Malik. I meant what I said. We had fun but I'm not interested in taking it any further.'

I bite my lip, hating how I'm sounding. How pompous. As though I'm severing a business deal.

'I just want to talk to you. Nothing more.'

'I don't think it's a good idea,' I repeat.

'Five minutes. Ten. That's all I ask. I can meet you by the canal.'

I feel a pang of guilt that he has no idea about the things I've just told PC Lilley. How I gave his name with no hard evidence. Because I was scared. They won't have contacted him yet, but they will do soon. I press my phone to my ear, my disloyalty lying heavy on me.

'I don't know.'

Should I meet him? I'm still angry about Simon's messages and that anger has taken up some of the space I'd reserved for Malik.

What would be the harm in talking to him and finding out what he wants? The canal is a public place after all. There will be people around.

I make my decision.

'All right but I haven't long. I'll meet you on the towpath outside your flat.' I've no wish for anyone at the station to see what I'm doing.

'Thank you, Melanie.'

I switch off my phone and put it in my back pocket, then get out of my car and walk through the car park, stepping around potholes filled with brown water. As I hurry along the towpath, telling myself the thumping of my heart is due to the exertion, I focus on what I'll say to Malik when I see him. Or maybe I'll just let him do the talking.

He's waiting for me, standing with his hands behind his back, his dark hair falling into his face as he stares down at the water.

The sun that had been behind a cloud comes out briefly, throwing light over everything, turning the canal warm caramel. I stop a metre from him, not trusting myself to go closer, and when he sees me, he straightens. 'Hello.'

I look at him, remembering everything we did. 'You wanted to see me.'

'Yes, I did. I do. I wanted to explain that I understand there are things I have done that some people might think strange. Disturbing maybe.' He looks away from me towards a mallard half-hidden in the reeds and I wonder if he's thinking about the locked door. 'There are reasons for everything, Melanie, and that is what I need you to understand.'

I see how tired he looks, shadows darkening the skin under his eyes. His white trainers are worn. The bottoms of his jeans frayed and dirty. He looks flustered. Vulnerable. Tormented.

And I've never felt the need to hold someone so much.

Last night, I'd thought so many things, had made so many assumptions because I'd been scared. Under pressure. It was the middle of the night and outside the building the car park was empty. The dark canal beyond it moving imperceptibly towards a tunnel where a young woman had disappeared. Now though, with the sunlight playing on the surface of the water, those thoughts seem nothing more than the vestige of a bad dream. Last night, my imagination had gone into overdrive. What stands before me now is what is real.

I move closer. 'You look tired.'

'I am. This is a bad time for me.' He looks at me with haunted eyes. 'You are the one light in my darkness.' He turns his head away again but not before I've seen the glint of a tear. 'I wanted to tell you that I am sorry.'

'What for?'

He reaches out and takes my hand, and I let him, feeling his fingers curl around my own. 'For the things I have done. I understand why you don't wish to see me but couldn't live with myself if I didn't reach out to you one more time. Please forgive me.'

My brain is in turmoil. It was me who broke things off, yet Malik's plea is so heartfelt. I don't know whether it's my lack of sleep or the stress of the last few days, but without stopping to think what I'm doing, I let go of his hand. Reaching up, I place my palms on either side of his face and pull his head towards me, his stubble rough beneath my touch. The kiss is like refilling a dry well, taking away all thoughts except for the taste of him. The feel of his fingers in my hair.

Too soon, he takes my wrists and lowers my hands, gently breaking away.

'I should go,' he says, tucking a strand of hair behind my ear.

Without his arms around me, I feel empty. 'I'll come with you.'

'Are you sure?' He looks uncertain.

'I wouldn't say it if I wasn't.'

Later, as I'm lying with my head on his chest, the breeze through the open window ruffling the edges of the sheet that's tacked there, I know I must warn him. It's been eating away at me.

'Malik?'

'Yes?' He runs a hand down my shoulder, making me shiver.

'The police might be contacting you.'

His hand stops. 'Why?'

Even though the police will be questioning him about it, I can't bring myself to tell him about last night's call to the show. In the afterglow of our lovemaking, the idea that he might have had anything to do with it now seems preposterous. For now at least, I want him to remain ignorant of my suspicions. So I take another tack.

'A few days ago, a colleague of mine was followed and assaulted on the way to the radio station. It was very early in the morning. We were all questioned, and your name came up as I'd been seeing you. They'll be talking to a lot of people. You'll be one of many.'

He turns on his back. 'And you think that is what I do when I walk at night?'

'No, of course not. I just didn't want it to come as a surprise.'

Malik rests the heels of his hands on his forehead. 'And you think I'll be able to explain it? You think they'll see it as *normal*? It could easily have been me... it's not far from here and I would have no way to explain myself.'

I look at him in desperation, thinking of the people who listen to my show. Those who are awake when others are asleep: coming home from a night shift, walking a fretful baby, rolling home late from a club. 'Surely there must be someone who would see you when you're out?'

He thinks for a moment. 'There's the old guy who sleeps under the bridge by the canal. I see him most nights. I stop and talk. He listens.'

I smile, reassured. 'That's good then. They'll be able to speak to him.' I run the back of my hand down Malik's cheek. 'Look, I'd better go. I need to get some proper sleep before tonight's show.'

I get dressed and he doesn't try to stop me. As I'm letting

myself out of the door, he props himself on one elbow and looks at me.

'Goodbye, Melanie. Stay safe.'

I close the door behind me, thinking it's an odd thing for him to say.

PC Lilley calls just as I'm rubbing the sleep from my eyes. I push myself up to a sitting position.

'Hello?'

'Melanie, I'm ringing about that number you gave us earlier.'

I squash the pillow behind my back to get more comfortable. 'Did you manage to find out who it belonged to?'

'I'm afraid not. Like we thought, it's an unregistered pay-as-you-go so we don't know who used it to call, but we've managed to obtain some data. We know the network they were using and a general idea of where the person was when they made the call. To pinpoint where they were with more accuracy, we would need to catch them phoning in live and use GPS to track them.'

'So where were they when they called?' I ask her.

'As I said, we can't be exact, but it wasn't far from the studio.'

'And Malik? Have you spoken to him yet?' At the thought of him, my heart gives a small leap, which I try to ignore. Should I tell her I've seen him again?

'We've had a short chat. He said he had nothing to do with the call last night, but he did tell us about his little night walks. Not that his alibi holds up on the morning of your colleague's attack. That homeless man he talks to is a known alcoholic and doesn't remember one day from the next.'

I rub at my arms. 'So you still think it could be him?'

There's a pause on the other end of the phone. 'I can't say at present. There is something else though.'

'Yes?'

'We've found a link between Malik and the girl in the tunnel. They've been seen together.'

The room has turned suddenly cold. 'How did he know her?'

'That's all I can tell you, I'm afraid, and it might not mean anything. These things are complicated though, and we need to be careful how we play it. We don't want to frighten him off.'

'Do you think he'll call in to the show again?' I'm rigid with alarm.

'It's quite likely, yes. People who phone in to shows like yours are often narcissists. They want the attention. I doubt our friend would be satisfied calling in just the once... his ego wouldn't allow that. What we want is to catch him if and when he rings into the show again and get a trace on the call. We really need to do this sooner rather than later.'

I'm filled with disgust at myself for being so weak. For coming as soon as Malik called me and for going back to the flat with him. Those fingers that touched my body... what else had they done? I press down the panic that's rising inside me. 'Do you need to be in the studio to do it?'

'No, it can all be done from our end. We'd like it to be tonight if possible.'

'Tonight?'

'Yes, as I said, the sooner the better. There'll be someone listening in and we just need you to be natural. The last thing we want is for him to be scared off. I know it's hard but pretend it's a normal night. Are you okay with that?'

'Yes, yes, of course.'

'Oh, and another thing. You said that you're on your own in the building. As a precaution, do you want to check with your station controller to see if someone can be with you?'

The thought of Di considering paying for a second presenter to come in is laughable. I know it's never going to happen, and besides, having another person in the studio would add a different dynamic to the evening. It will be hard enough knowing the police will be listening in, but having someone there with me would break the atmosphere of the confessional.

PC Lilley takes my hesitation as a sign that I'm not happy. 'I can talk to her if you want?'

'No,' I say quickly. 'It's okay. I can do it.'

I give her some more details and end the call. My fingertips move to my lips where the skin is tender, then to my neck where Malik's stubble grazed my flesh. This is the man whose touch I'd longed for.

As I pull clean underwear from my drawer, I try to imagine him standing on the towpath, the moonlight glittering on the water, his mouth pressed to a pay-as-you-go he's picked up cheaply somewhere. I can't ignore what PC Lilley has just told me. If he knew the girl who is missing, was he involved in her disappearance? How did he know her? Why didn't he identify himself to the police during their investigation? What is he capable of?

Every part of me wants to believe he's innocent, but however much I want to, I can't ignore his clenched fist. The panicked words he'd shouted. His strange behaviour – the walking at night. My fear. No, I can't ignore that any more than I can the fact that he'd locked me in his room when he'd gone out. Or the passion in his eyes when he'd looked at me. His need for me had been as great as mine for him.

Maybe that was why I'd told him about me and Simon. Why I'd told the secret I'd kept to myself for over a year. It was the night he'd woken from his nightmare and I'd wanted to share something with him. Hoping that if I did, he'd do the same and open up. I'd had the stupid thought that it might help me to understand him better. Get closer to him. Now I know that all I'd managed to do was hand him something he could use against me.

There's the rest of the afternoon and evening to get through and I can't settle. Eventually, I make myself something to eat and curl up on the settee to watch some mindless comedy on the TV. As the opening credits roll, I message Simon.

I'm worried, Si. The police think the crazy guy will phone back tonight. They're going to try and trace the call.

It doesn't take long for him to answer.

That's good. You don't need to worry, Mel. We all have your back.

It's as though a weight has lifted from my shoulders. Knowing I'm not alone in this helps to settle my nerves. Despite what I said to Simon at the canal, he's been a good friend to me over the years. My only real one. And I need all the friends I can get.

As I pick up my fork to twist spaghetti around it, I see that my hand is shaking. If PC Lilley is right, tonight I'll find out who the caller is and, to be perfectly honest, the thought terrifies me.

THIRTY-NINE

It's nearing two thirty in the morning and the flat is silent when I let myself in after the show. I listen, wondering whether Nathan is in or not then, seeing no evidence of him, go into the living area and throw my bag onto the settee.

I'm tired. Disappointed. I'd hoped that by the time tonight's show was over I'd have found out what was going on, but the man hadn't called in to True Confessions again and I know no more than I did before.

I sink down next to my bag. I don't know what I expected from the police but I don't feel reassured. I feel scared. Helpless.

Frustration is making me irritable. I get up again and walk round to the other side of the breakfast bar. Reaching up, I open the cupboard next to the cooker and take out the bottle of gin I keep there for emergencies. I empty a large measure into a glass and add tonic from a can in the fridge, not caring that in just a few short hours the rest of the town will be waking.

I'm not usually much of a drinker, unless you count the night in The Junction, but my head is buzzing with unanswered questions. Ones I'm desperate to silence. When I feel this way, I know I'll find it hard to sleep so I've decided that the mind-numbing effect of alcohol is the only thing that might work.

I take the glass over to the settee and sit with it cradled between my hands. A part of me is relieved he didn't call in again, and yet another part is telling me that until he does, there can't be closure. I'll be forever wondering whether it was Malik, and if it wasn't, who else could be out there wanting to frighten me? Because I *am* frightened. The evidence is in the way the clear liquid shivers in my glass and in the pale face I'd seen reflected back at me in the hall mirror.

I lay my head back against the settee and view my surroundings. The place is nice enough but it's more like somewhere a student might rent. I think of Nathan in the small bedroom along the hall from mine. I'd been hoping that over time we'd have developed if not a friendship then some sort of amicable sharing of the space we live in... but it hasn't happened like that. We don't talk. In fact, we hardly ever see each other. And even though I should feel glad that I have my own space and don't have to make conversation at the breakfast bar, or share meals, it's oddly lonely. I feel as if my life's on hold. That I'm treading water.

I'm too old to be living like this.

When my glass is empty, I get up and pour myself another. The gin is starting to work its magic and my eyelids are getting heavy. I drink this one quickly and am just thinking about making a move to bed when I notice something I hadn't seen earlier – a bag tucked between two of the stools at the breakfast bar. I stare at it through half-closed eyes. It's a grey and black rucksack that can only belong to Nathan. Inside will be things that might give me a clearer idea of the man I'm sharing my home with. Surely it can't be wrong to want to find out.

If I hadn't had the second drink, I wouldn't consider doing it, but as it is, curiosity has got the better of me. Pushing myself up from the settee, I go over to the bag, and with a glance over my shoulder at the half-open door, start to unzip it.

I don't know what I'd been expecting to find but it's nothing noteworthy, just a pair of tracksuit bottoms and some muddy running shoes There's also a battered copy of Shakespeare's *As You*

Like It and a sheaf of paper, covered in yellow highlighter that's held together with a green paper clip.

Hearing a noise, I stop, my eyes trained on the door. The sound was the click and squeak of a door opening and now I can hear footsteps in the hall. Quickly, I stuff the pages back into the bag and zip it back up, my heart racing, then hurry back to the settee.

The footsteps have stopped and there's the sound of the bathroom door opening and closing. I close my eyes in relief. What if he'd come in and found me rummaging through his things? How would I have explained it? And even though there's no way he'll ever know, I feel sick with embarrassment at what I've just done – how I've invaded his privacy. What if he'd done the same to me?

I wait until I hear the toilet flush and the sound of footsteps returning to the bedroom then take my glass over to the sink and rinse it out. When all is silent again, I turn the light off and go into my own bedroom, aware as I take off my clothes and pull on my vest top and pyjama bottoms of the person on the other side of the wall. It makes me feel ill at ease knowing he's there, but that's not surprising as everything is making me nervous at the moment. I have to get a grip. He's just a young man who reads Shakespeare and enjoys going for a run – just as I do. What's happened over the last few weeks has made my imagination turn everyone into someone they're not.

I pull back the duvet and get into bed, spending a moment catching up on people's Facebook posts before lying back on the pillow and waiting for sleep to come. But it doesn't, even with the gin I've just drunk. Instead, things continue to go round in my head. The call to True Confessions, Natalie, the messages Simon left on my phone.

As if the act of thinking about it is enough to make it happen, my phone pings. I look at the clock on my bedside table. It's almost four and there's only one person I know who is awake at this time every morning. What does he want? Without looking at the screen, I reach over to my phone and click on the message, my eyes squinting as the phone lights up.

I read the first line and stop, my breath catching in my throat.

I won't let you go. You know that, don't you?

A cold lick of fear stops me from reading any further and I sit without moving until, eventually, the screen goes black and I'm in darkness. I lie back down, but even when I turn over and press my face into the pillow, I can't get the words out of my head. Realising sleep is never going to come if I don't read the rest of what he's said, I sit up again and turn on my bedside light. Quickly, before I can change my mind, I find the message again and open it.

I read, my chest so tight it hurts.

When you think you're alone, I'll be watching you. As you go to work. When you walk the canal. When you're just a silhouette at your window. You tempt and tease but you're nothing but a common slut. Women like you need to be punished.

I drop the phone on the duvet as though by continuing to hold it, the vile words might infect me. Why is he saying this? My heart is thudding and I'm just wondering what to do when the phone rings, making me jump. Simon's name comes up on the screen and I stare at it.

How can he think I'd want to talk to him after this?

Lack of sleep and the gin I've drunk are making my head ache. There's no way I want to deal with this now, but I know that if I don't it's never going to go away. What an idiot he is... and after everything I said.

I snatch the phone up again and answer. 'For God's sake, Simon. Leave me alone.'

His voice comes back laced with confusion. 'Sorry. I saw you were online and thought I'd check in to see how tonight went. What happened? Did the guy call again?'

I massage my temples, fed up with his games. 'Stop it. I'm too tired for this. You know what I'm talking about.'

'Actually, I don't. I have no idea.'

'The message you just sent.' My voice has risen and I lower it again, hoping that Nathan won't have heard any of this through the wall. 'I don't know what you're trying to achieve but it isn't funny. In fact, if I had to give it a name, I'd call it stalking.'

There's a pause. 'I didn't send you a message, Mel.'

'Oh, really? Well explain this then.' I read it out to him and wait.

'You have to be kidding.' He sounds shocked. 'How could you think I'd send something as fucked up as that?'

'Why do you think?'

'Look at the phone number,' he continues, 'and you'll see it wasn't from me.'

I stare at the unknown number. I'd been too tired and shocked to take it in. 'What's to stop you from having used a different phone?'

His voice is weary. 'You really believe I'd do that? I know I'm an idiot and a bit obsessive, but I'd never pull a stunt like this. I care for you too much.'

'Don't.'

'I'm sorry, but I need to know you believe me.'

'I don't know if I can.'

But even as I say it, I know that the message is different to the others and the knowledge sends a chill through me. 'If you didn't send it, who did?'

But the question is unnecessary; I already know. The only person it could be is Malik.

Simon lets out a breath and I wonder if he's thinking this too. 'Whoever it is, you need to tell the police. I've got a bad feeling about this.'

'I'll do it in the morning.'

'No, do it now. He could be anywhere. He could be outside your flat at this very moment. I mean it, Mel. Just do it.'

I look towards the window. There's no moon tonight and

there's nothing to see but a rectangle of grey. Maybe the person who messaged me is standing outside watching the house. Could it be Malik? When he woke from his nightmare, I'd seen a different man to the one I'd fallen asleep with. A man who relived his past while he slept. A past he didn't want to tell me about. One that made him capable of violence.

With my phone pressed to my ear, I get up and pad across the room. When I reach the window, I push aside the curtain and look out. I don't know what I'm expecting to see but there's nothing but the dark street. I shiver.

'Yes, I'll call them.'

Simon doesn't answer. On the other end of the phone there's whispering. I hear the words *message* and *bastard*. Hear my name. There's another voice – Anne's. We must have woken her.

'Sorry.' Simon's back. 'I've just been telling Anne what happened. She's worried about you and says you need to tell the police straight away. I've told her you will.'

'She mustn't worry about me,' I say. 'She has enough on her plate as it is. Tell her I'm fine.'

But I'm not fine. I'm shaking, my eyes still scouring the street for a shadow. A movement.

'Are you okay? Do you want me to come over?'

I picture Simon and Anne in their living room. Simon on the settee in just his sweatpants, Anne standing behind him with her chin resting on top of his head, her pregnancy showing under the soft material of her nightdress. So trusting of her husband.

But *I* don't trust him.

Not his words or his motive for suggesting he come over.

'No. There's no need.'

I end the call and, with a last look out at the street, go back to my cold bed. In the next room I hear movement and the sound of Nathan coughing. A few minutes later, there are footsteps in the hall followed by the click of the front door. I get up again and part the curtain in time to see him jog down the front path and unlatch the gate. He's wearing the tracksuit bottoms I saw in the rucksack and a sweatshirt with a hood, which he pulls over his head before running past the house and out of view.

It seems I'm not the only one who can't sleep tonight.

FORTY

It's not PC Lilley who comes to the flat the next morning, it's a young, stocky man in a black bomber jacket and baggy jeans. He introduces himself as Detective Constable Forrest and his colleague, a pretty woman with long dark hair and dimples, as Detective Constable Atwood.

I invite them in and lead the way to the living area.

'Would you like some coffee?'

'No, thank you. We're good.' DC Forrest leans his back against the breakfast bar. 'PC Lilley has filled us in with what's been happening at the radio station, so you don't need to go over any of that. You say that last night you received an unsavoury phone message.'

'Yes, and I don't recognise the number.'

DC Atwood smiles and indicates the settee. 'May I sit down?'

It's only then I notice the swell of her pregnancy beneath her denim jacket. 'Yes, sorry. I should have said.' I wait until she's settled on the settee. 'How long before...?'

'Oh, still another four months. Plenty of time to get used to the idea. Do you have any children?'

'No, I've never been very maternal,' I say awkwardly.

DC Forrest remains where he is, his arms folded. 'Nor me. Got three boys though so I clearly didn't get that across to my wife. This message. What time did you receive it?'

'It was around four. My show doesn't finish until two then when I got home I couldn't sleep.' I think of the gin bottle in the cupboard and decide there's no need to mention it.

'Late then... or early.' He shrugs and pulls a face. 'Depending on how you want to look at it.'

DC Atwood shifts on the settee to get more comfortable. 'The message will be time stamped so we'll be able to get an exact timing from that. We'll need to take your phone away with us if that's okay. We'll get it back to you just as soon as we've looked at it.'

I know my cheeks are reddening. 'Can't I just show you now?'

'I'm afraid we'll need it back at the station so we can download the data and have a record of the message. We'll give it a read now though to get a better idea of what we're dealing with.'

I think of what else is on my phone. The messages from Simon for a start. If they read them, it won't reflect well on either of us. I try to gauge the likelihood of them looking at anything else while the phone is in their possession and decide it's unlikely, but I don't want to take the chance.

'Yes, of course,' I say, sliding down from the stool. 'My mobile's in the bedroom. I'll just go and get it.'

I leave the living area and cross the hall to my room. When I'm inside, I pull the door closed behind me, go over to my bedside table and unplug my phone from the charger. With a quick look at the door, I open my messages. Ignoring the one at the top, the one I haven't had the stomach to look at again since I got it, I scroll down a few more until I come to Simon's name. Without opening the messages, I delete them.

DC Forrest and DC Atwood have been talking while I've been out of the room, but they stop as I come back in. DC Atwood smiles and holds out her hand. 'Better have a look then.'

'Yes.' I click on the message I received last night and hand her the phone.

I watch as she reads, my arms folded, my thumbnails digging

half-moons into the soft skin on the underside of my elbows. 'Do you think it could be Malik? The guy I told the other officers about? Do you think it could have been him who phoned in to the show too?'

DC Forrest takes the phone from his colleague and studies what's written there, his lips a thin line. When he finishes, he looks up. 'That's not something we can say for sure until we talk to him again but we'll find out. As PC Lilley told you, the only thing we know for sure about the call to the studio is that it wasn't made from that far away. We also know that Malik's flat is in the area covered by the data, but because there was no repeat call to your show, there's been no way of getting a more precise location.' He taps his finger against the screen. 'My guess is that the number this message has been sent from won't tell us much either. But if it *was* Malik, once we interview him, he should stop all of this before it escalates.'

I stare at him. 'Escalates?'

He leans back against the breakfast bar again and crosses one foot over the other. 'That was probably a poor choice of word.'

DC Atwood frowns at him. 'Yes it was, and he didn't mean to alarm you. What he meant was stalkers will sometimes want to find ways to lash out, but a warning from us will usually make them see sense. They tend to be put off once they know the police are aware of their behaviour.'

I look at her doubtfully. 'I hope you're right.'

'I was wondering. Do you still have the tyre? The one that was slashed?'

'Yes. When the AA mechanic changed it, he put the old one in my boot. I haven't got around to getting rid of it.'

'That's good. We'll take that too if we may?'

I frown. 'Why would you need it?'

'You never know.' He says no more.

'So that's it?'

'For the moment.' DC Atwood gets up. 'We'll be in touch.'

I press my lips together, thinking of something. 'But what about Natalie?'

I see the way DC Atwood glances at her colleague, but I can't tell what they're thinking. It's been a week since Natalie called in to the show.

'She's not our priority at the moment. We need to concentrate on the man who sent the message and why he's targeted you.'

'Do you think he'll call the show again... the man?' Even now, my brain wants so much not to believe it's him that I find it impossible to say Malik's name.

DC Forrest folds his arms. 'I think if he was going to, it would have been last night.' He's still holding my phone and he waggles it. 'Looks like he's changed his tactic. We'll have a look at this and get it straight back to you. As I said earlier, we'll pay your friend Malik a visit and see if that brings anything to light. Leave it with us and please don't worry.'

He walks to the door and DC Atwood follows. Before she gets there, she turns. 'I know PC Lilley suggested it before and you weren't keen, but I really think you should consider having someone with you tonight when you're doing your show. Just until we know what's what.'

I nod. I hadn't wanted anyone with me last night but the message on my phone has rattled me.

'Yes, I'll talk to the station controller after you've gone and arrange something.'

'Good.' She smiles at me, deep dimples forming in her cheeks. 'Shall we get that tyre?'

I pick my car keys up from the side and lead the way out. We've just reached the ground floor when DC Atwood turns and surveys the entrance hallway with its row of metal post boxes, each with a flat number on. 'I forgot to ask, Mrs Abbott. Do you live alone?'

I think of Nathan's closed door. I didn't hear him come in after his early morning run and, as far as I know, he hasn't come home. 'No, I don't. I have a flatmate, Nathan King, but he's out at the moment.'

'I see.' She gets out her notebook and jots down his name. 'Thank you for that. We'll need to talk to him too at some stage.'

We go out into the street. My car's parked outside and I open the boot for them. DC Forrest reaches in and lifts the tyre out. 'Thank you. We'll be in touch.'

'Okay. Thank you for coming.'

'It's what we're here for.'

I say goodbye and go back up to the flat. As I open the front door, I stop, my hand pressed to my heart – the shock of seeing someone there having sent it racing. Nathan is standing in the hall just outside my open bedroom door. If I didn't know any better, I'd say he'd been in there.

'What are you doing?'

There's a collection of small pimples on the side of his neck, which darken to red as the colour creeps up his flesh. 'I wasn't doing anything. I'm going to work if you must know. They've changed my shift from late to early.'

In his navy nurse's tunic, he looks older than he does in the logo-printed T-shirts I've seen him in before. He must have come home while I was asleep. I don't like the thought of him creeping around, not when I'm so on edge with the messages I've been getting, but he's harmless enough. He reads Shakespeare plays for goodness' sake.

'I don't know if you heard but the police were round. They've just gone.'

He nods. 'Yeah, I heard.'

I look at his pale face. The overlong ginger hair. Why hadn't he come out of his room if he knew?

'I expect you'd like to know why they were here?'

He rubs the palms of his hands down the sides of his blue trousers. 'Of course. What did they want?'

'I've been getting these messages.'

He shifts from one foot to the other. 'What sort of messages?'

'Disturbing ones. One was to my phone but the other was a call to the radio station. The police thought you ought to know in case you see anything... you know... suspicious.'

'Like what?'

'I don't know. Someone hanging around outside. Anything.'

'Sure, but I'm late for my shift.'

Without another word, he pushes past me and leaves the flat, the door slamming behind him.

As I stand alone in the hallway, listening to his footsteps on the stairs, I can't help feeling like I can't trust anyone anymore.

FORTY-ONE

The studio is brightly lit, the main light on. It's not what I'm used to, and it makes the room stark. Impersonal. Chris sits across from me, his hands linked behind his head, his feet up on the desk. His eyes are closed, and I know that he's bored. Late-night radio really isn't his thing, but I'm grateful that he's here.

I fade in a music track and take off my headphones. 'Are you okay?'

Chris opens his eyes, the whites more bloodshot than usual in the harsh overhead light. He rubs at them with the heels of his hands and frowns.

'Sure.'

'Do you want to get a coffee or something?'

'I'm all right.'

He sounds irritable, and I feel guilty that he had to come in. When I'd phoned Di earlier and told her what the police had said about me being on my own, she'd suggested Simon, but I'd quickly put her off. I'd told her that Anne needed him at home just in case she started to get more unexplained pains. That's not the only reason though. After everything that's happened, my friendship with Simon is fragile and being alone with him in an empty radio building is not going to help it mend.

'It's only for tonight. Just until the police can talk to Malik.'

Chris gives a tut of derision. 'Thought they hadn't been able to pin anything on the nutter?'

'Even so, they still think it's pretty likely it was him. They also think that after they've spoken to him, he won't try anything like this again.'

When they'd dropped my phone back this afternoon, the police had confirmed what they'd suspected. The message had come from the same unregistered phone as the one from which the call to the radio station had been made.

'So that's it then.' Chris rakes fingers yellowed with nicotine through his hair. 'The police aren't going to do anything other than have a little chat with him.'

'No, like I said to Di, there's no reason to believe he'll call the show again. They don't have the manpower to listen in night after night just in case he does.'

He shakes his head in disbelief but doesn't say anything.

'It's fine. I'm not bothered.'

But, despite my show of bravado, I clearly am. Although I've deleted the message, the memory of it is still with me. *Women like you need to be punished.* Just the thought of those words makes me shudder. When I'd told Chris, the word *bastard* had escaped his lips. Nothing more.

'Why am I here, Mel?' A muscle works in his jaw. 'Really... Why did you ask me?'

I frown at him, unsure why he's asked. He knows what's happened and how unnerved I've been. 'Because I didn't think you'd mind. Because you're my friend.'

'That's not what I meant, and you know it. Why *me*? Because Simon wasn't available? Because he was too busy playing happy families?'

'What's that supposed to mean?' I stare at him in shock until, eventually, he slides his eyes away from mine.

'It doesn't mean anything.' He pushes his chair away from the desk with his feet and jumps up. 'Fuck this place. This bloody fucked-up place.'

I can't hide my surprise. I've never seen him like this before. 'Calm down, Chris. What the hell's got into you?'

'Nothing.'

I want to say more but the track is coming to an end. Just a few more minutes and then it will be time for True Confessions. Chris is pacing now, clearly agitated. His skin is mottled, and I wonder, not for the first time this evening, if he's been drinking.

My mobile is doing a merry dance on the desk in front of me. Anyone who knows me will also know that I work at this time of night, so my guess is it must be important. When I answer it, I'm surprised to hear DC Forrest's voice.

'I'm sorry it's such an inconvenient time but we have an update. When we went round to talk to your friend Malik earlier, we found a flick knife on him and there were what looked like traces of rubber on the blade. When we suggested to him that if forensics looked at it, there was every likelihood that it would match the slash in your tyre, he broke down and admitted to it.'

I run a hand down my face. 'So it *was* him.'

'Yes. His explanation was that it was his way of getting you to go back to his flat. He said that the first night you were with him, he'd woken in the morning to find you gone. He didn't want it to be just a one-nighter and thought the knight-in-shining-armour routine would work better than just asking to see you again. He also seems to have a bit of an obsession about the dangers of the area. Odd if you ask me, and we think there could be more to it than that. We have him at the station and are going to question him again about the calls and messages. I just thought you ought to know.'

'Thank you. I'm glad you did.'

Part of me is relieved yet a larger part is sad. Malik couldn't have known that I would have gone back with him anyway. Despite his odd behaviour, and how scared I'd felt after he'd woken from one of his nightmares, there was a gentle side to him too. He'd listened to me, really listened. More than Niall had done during our marriage.

I shake my head at my thoughts. From what DC Forrest has said, the police clearly believe he could be behind the calls and messages, so how can I feel pity for a man who has terrorised me? Made me feel unsafe not only in my place of work but in my own home? The only emotion I should be feeling is revulsion at having given him so much of myself.

Chris is standing in front of me, looking at me inquisitively, but there's no time to fill him in. Ignoring him, I get up and dim the overhead lights until only the area where I'm sitting is lit. I lift my headphones and position them on my head then fade out the song, bringing in the True Confessions theme tune at the same time.

I lean in close to the microphone. 'Now, dear listeners, it's time for True Confessions. Why don't you tell me your secrets?'

As always, the lines go crazy, the flashing numbers begging to be answered. Chris has sat down again, his forehead resting against the heels of his hands. He's not himself and I'm worried about him, but I've no time to dwell on what's wrong as my first caller is speaking.

'Good evening, Melanie. I want to confess to killing my brother's goldfish while he was at scout camp. It was in 1973...'

The night drags on. Lines flash. Voices come and go. *I want to confess. I want to confess.*

Eventually, Chris pushes back his chair. 'Sod this. I need to pee.'

'I'm not stopping you,' I mouth.

I wave him away with a flap of my hand, glad to have the studio to myself again. I can't breathe with him there. Can't think. Can't do my job.

When the caller has finished telling me his anecdote, I stifle a yawn and click on another phone line. With any luck, the next confession will be more interesting than the one I've just had.

'Hello, caller,' I say. 'What do you want to confess?'

Settling myself back in my chair, I get ready for another mundane confession. I wait but there's nothing.

'Hello?'

And then the voice comes: through the phone line, through the mixer desk, through my headphones. It's flat. Devoid of emotion. Robotic.

'Melanie.'

That's all he says but it's enough. I sit up straight, my hand clamped to my mouth. Too scared to speak.

Eventually, I find my voice. 'Who are you?'

'Who do you want me to be? That's the question you need to ask yourself. Who can you trust?'

I turn to the door, willing Chris to come back. How long does it take to have a pee? The toilet is only down the corridor.

As I force my frozen brain to think of a reply, a different thought occurs to me. When he'd phoned in to the show before, everyone, including the police, had presumed the caller to be Malik. He'd been the link between me and Natalie. But Malik is being questioned at the police station.

The realisation it's not him speaking to me is chilling.

Knowing it won't help me if I panic, I try to push down the fight or flight instinct that's threatening to take over. If the crazy guy had called yesterday when the police were listening in, they'd have been able to trace it and catch them in the act. But it isn't yesterday; it's tonight, and the only blessing is that I'm not alone in the building.

A needle of doubt is prickling me. Why is Chris taking so long? Where is he?

For now, it's just me and the voice on the end of the phone. I have to keep it together.

'I've been watching you, Melanie. Biding my time and wondering if you'd confess. That time has come. Don't think you're safe because you're not on your own.'

It's as if his words are filling the whole studio. Every inch. Every corner. I rip off my headphones and cover my ears, but even though I can no longer hear him, I know he's still speaking.

My phone is vibrating and I snatch it up, not caring who it is. Any voice is better than the one through my headphones.

When I hear the voice on the other end, I think I might cry with relief.

'Cut the call, Melanie,' DC Forrest says. 'We've heard enough.'

It's as if a spell has been broken and I reach across to my computer and end it, not caring what my listeners might think as I push the button to play the next music track.

'You were listening?' I slump back in my chair, letting out a long breath. 'Thank God.'

'It's PC Lilley you must thank for it. She wasn't happy when she knew we weren't going to be listening in on the show tonight, so she tuned in herself. As soon as she heard the caller, she started the trace.' His voice turns serious. 'I want you to listen carefully to me, Melanie. We've a patrol car on its way, but I need you to make sure the building is secure and the doors locked.'

I look at the dark panel of the door. Where is Chris? What's taking him so long?

'Why?' My heart's pounding. 'Do you know something?'

DC Forrest's voice is calm but there's an edge to it. 'Malik's not at the station – we've already let him go home.'

My breathing becomes shorter. 'So it could be him who made the call?'

With the spotlight shining on me in the dark studio, I feel exposed.

'It's possible.' He pauses a fraction too long. 'Also, we have news on the phone trace. It's given us a precise location of the caller.'

'Then you'll be able to find him.'

'That's the idea.' He clears his throat. 'Do you have someone with you?'

'Yes, my old colleague from the Breakfast Show, Chris Riggs.'

'That's good.'

I get up and go to the door. Through the glass panel, I can see nothing but the unlit corridor. 'Why are you asking? You're worrying me now. What did the phone trace show?'

'I want you to stay calm, but what the trace has told us is that the call was made in the vicinity of the Lock Radio building.'

I stand immobile as the shock courses through me. He's trying not to frighten me, but I hear in my head the words he hasn't said.

The caller is outside and he might be trying to get in.

FORTY-TWO

I stand frozen to the spot, telling myself over and over that it's all right. That the police will be here soon and all I have to do is wait. It's not as if Malik can get in as the outside door is locked. Chris is here somewhere and soon it will all be over. But I can't just stay in the studio. I need to be doing something.

Opening the door, I step into the dark corridor and immediately the overhead lights flick on. I walk briskly, stopping outside Studio One with the thought that Chris might be in there, but he isn't. The room is in darkness.

The toilets are a little further on and when I get to the gents, I put my ear to the door and listen. Nothing.

I rap loudly against the shiny wood. 'Chris? Are you in there?'

When there's no reply, I push the door open. The light comes on as I step inside, illuminating the empty cubicles. No one is there.

A ripple of unease runs through me as I remember what the caller said. Just because I'm not alone doesn't mean I'm safe. What if he went outside and Malik was waiting for him?

Jesus, Chris. Where are you?

Leaving the toilets, I walk through to the reception area, stopping at the board on which our photographs have been mounted. They're the ones that are used in all our publicity leaflets and online. I look at the faces of the people I work with, some of whom I've known for years. They stare back at me with expressions carefully chosen to give their fans a face to match the image their voice has conjured across the airwaves. Chris with his overlong hair and cheeky-chap grin. Simon the charming matinee idol with his carefully gelled hair. Me...

I stare at my large eyes, the dark hair I'd cropped short so that each morning when I looked in the mirror, I wouldn't have to see the person I'd been before. But despite the disguise, she's still there. The adulteress. The woman who had given in to her base urges when she was drunk. Someone who should have known better.

I think of what the police told me... that they'd tracked the phone message to somewhere outside the building. Out there in the shadows of the car park, far enough away that the security light won't be activated, Malik is watching, waiting. His phone in his hand, realising his call has been cut off.

I'm scared of him.

His obsession with me is dangerous.

How could I have been so stupid as to trust a man I didn't know?

Hurrying to the door, I lock it from the inside, even though I know he won't be able to get in without the key code. Thank God I never had a reason to give it to him.

On the wall above the keypad is the security camera Di had promised to get fixed. I just need to bring the picture up on the reception computer, then I'll be able to see where he is. I'll know if he's in the car park. Or, worse still, if he's coming to the door.

With a glance at the front door, I go behind the reception desk and sit in Dawn's chair. I search the home screen for the security camera programme, click on it and wait, my forehead prickling with perspiration.

A black screen greets me with the words *camera inactive* and immediately, the relief I'd felt at having shut Malik out of the building disappears. I have no way of knowing where he is.

There's a noise to my left and I turn, the flat of my hand to my

chest, but there's nobody there, just the curved side of the reception desk, the architectural plant in the corner of the room, the
large screen on the wall that for once is blank. Normally, there
would be news items flashing across the display, but not tonight.

I'm just wondering why not when the monitor springs to life,
its vibrant blue background hurting my eyes. As I watch, a ticker
tape of white writing slides across the screen like a newsflash.

... SLUT... WHORE... WOMEN LIKE YOU NEED TO BE
PUNISHED...

I stare at it, horrified.

FORTY-THREE

I sit rigid, staring at the screen. However much I want to drag my eyes away from the words, I can't. It's the truth in them that stops me from doing what I should. Running out of the building to the safety of my car. Phoning the police and finding out why they're not here yet.

The words continue their never-ending journey. Round and round. Disappearing off the end of the screen to return again. A sushi conveyor belt of loathing. Those words are meant for me, I know that. Whoever has done it wants to punish me.

The truth hits me like a sledgehammer. I've been wrong all the time. The police too. This has nothing to do with Malik. Whoever's behind this knows the radio-station computer system. Another thought follows on, one that hasn't occurred to me before: the police only said the message had come from the *vicinity* of the building. How could I have been so stupid as to overlook the obvious? That could mean outside... or *in*.

Whoever typed out those words not only had access to the computer, they also know the code to the shiny keypad on the door. While Chris and I were in the studio, they'd let themselves in and logged on to the system. They could still be here.

Where are they? Blood hammers at my temples. Chris has

been gone too long and I know, with utter certainty, that something's happened to him.

I back towards the front door, stopping when my shoulder makes contact with the hard wood. I've locked myself inside with my nemesis. My chest is so tight I can barely breathe. Whoever they are, why don't they show themselves?

I think of everyone who works here. The ones I might have upset. Who might bear a grudge. My eyes flick to the noticeboard, the faces of the people I've worked with coming in and out of focus. Then my eyes stop at my own photo. My face smiling out from where my predecessor's had once been. The man who'd left under a cloud.

Alan.

His face with its hooded eyes and sunken cheeks comes into my head. I remember how uncomfortable he'd made me feel when I'd gone into the studio to talk to him about his show. He'd said he was testing me, but what if it wasn't an act? What if after I'd taken over the show, he'd listened in with both resentment and lust?

I was just a tease. A slut. A whore. The words are still travelling across the screen, pressing their message home. He'd found out about me and Simon and it proved it. Simon was the poster boy for Lock Radio and Alan would have known he wouldn't have a chance with me. He might hate me but he might also want to take what he knew he couldn't ask for.

He was, after all, a man with nothing to lose.

'I know it's you, Alan.' My shaky words fill the empty reception area. I've no idea if he's even here, let alone whether he's heard. 'We can talk about this. No one need ever know.'

All the time I'm speaking, the vile words are tracking across the blue screen.

...SLUT... LIAR... I WON'T LET YOU GO...

What had PC Lilley said about people who called in to shows like mine? She'd called them narcissists – people so wrapped up in their own self-importance that they can't see where reality ends and fantasy starts. Was it the same for the presenters? Alan has been on both sides of the airwaves and I know, instinctively, that even if he wanted to, talking will do no good.

With my eyes flicking from each closed door to the corridor and back again, I change tack. 'Chris is here too. If anything happens to me, he'll know.'

I hear the tremor in my voice, knowing he'll hear it too. Because we both know Chris *isn't* here. He's been gone too long, and dread is creeping through my body at the thought of what might have happened if he'd met Alan. If he'd been taken by surprise.

I clasp my head in my hands. I can't think like this. Mustn't.

I need to get out of here.

I'm just reaching for the door when I hear a sound that makes my blood freeze. A metallic crash as though something's been knocked over. I look towards the kitchen. When I'd come into the reception, I'd been so intent on locking the front door that I hadn't thought to check in there. My phone is in my pocket, but I don't take it out. I'm too paralysed by my fear.

The door opens. Someone is coming out. 'All for one and one for all.'

I step away from the door, confused. 'Simon?'

But it's not Simon who comes out of the darkened kitchen – it's Chris. His face pale. His pupils shrunk to dark pinpricks in the bright reception light. He's rubbing at his shoulder and the agitation I'd seen earlier is more pronounced, as if a layer of his skin has been stripped away to leave the nerve endings exposed. I'd suspected he'd been drinking when I'd been doing my show, but this is different. He's clearly taken something but I've no idea what. Despite this, I'm desperately glad to see him.

He stares at me through bloodshot eyes.

'I'm not Simon. Sorry to disappoint.'

My relief at seeing him quickly turns to concern. I don't like the way he's looking at me. It's like he's someone else. Someone I don't know. There's no sign of the ironic smile or the brotherly teasing. Nothing like that. He looks like a coiled spring about to release.

I put my hand out to placate him. 'Don't be stupid, Chris. It was what you said... You sounded just like him. Look, we need to get out of here.'

Ignoring what I've said, Chris takes a step forward.

'Fuck Simon! Why is everything always about *him*? Lording it over the Breakfast Show. Di's golden boy. Every woman's fucking dream.'

My throat tightens. My thoughts, my suspicions, my fears turned on their head once again. I'm struggling to anchor myself to reality, but a voice in my head is telling me I must stay calm. This isn't Chris speaking; it's the drink. The comedown from whatever drug he's taken.

'That's not true. And even if it was, why should it bother you? You've never had a problem taking someone home with you at the end of an evening.'

'His cast-offs... the ones he's turned down.' He spits the words. 'Don't pretend you don't know that. The ones who sleep with me are the little tramps who'll go with anyone well known so they can brag to their mates. And the tosser just laughs, knowing he can get whoever he wants.'

I know I have to mollify him. We need to get out of here. 'You might think that about Simon but it's not true. He's all show. He's weak.'

Chris's face, so pale a minute ago, darkens. 'That's good coming from someone who fucked their co-presenter when his wife was pregnant.'

My blood runs cold. I want to deny it, but how can I when it's true?

'How did you find out?'

He gives a sharp bark of laughter. 'How do you think? Because Simon couldn't keep his mouth shut. He thought he'd rub my face in it.'

'No, he wouldn't...'

It only takes a few steps for Chris to be in front of me. This close, he seems even bigger than usual, his large head with its glassy eyes staring down at me. 'Yet you didn't think twice about fucking him. Just one click of his fingers and you were there.' He clicks his fingers sharply in my face, making me flinch.

'Stop it. That's not fair. You don't know anything about it.'

'What do you know about fair?' He steps away and leans heavily on the reception desk. 'You think it's fair when you're picking up strangers in a bar?' His expression hardens and he sweeps his arm across the top of the desk, sending a glass vase of flowers and the Perspex stand containing our publicity leaflets crashing to the floor. 'You think it's fair when you're fucking Simon? Or when you're knocking me back?'

'But it was you who wanted me to meet someone. You tried to set me up. Why would you do that if you feel this way?'

'Why do you think? It was only a matter of time before you went back to him. Better someone else than that gloating bastard.'

I try to blank out what he's saying. Even though his words sting, I need to make him listen.

'Please, Chris. It's not like that. We'll talk about it another time, but I'm scared and I really think we should go.' I try to take his arm, but he shakes me off.

'Get your hands off me, slut.'

I stare at him, shocked. Across the blue screen behind Chris, the foul words keep moving.

... SLUT... LIAR.... WHORE...

He's looking at me coldly and it's only now that I really take in what he's just said. *Or when you're knocking me back.*

I'm back in Chris's flat, the night I'd found him drunk outside the radio station. I'm leaning over him, giving him the hug he's asked for, but he's turned his head, wanting to kiss me. I'd pushed him away, thinking he'd only done it because he was drunk, but maybe I'd been wrong.

The words keep moving across the bottom of the blue screen, each one reaching their target, and I stare at Chris in horror. Realising the truth at last. I'd thought the danger had come from someone I didn't know well, when all the time it had been one of my closest friends who'd been the threat. What a fool I've been.

I take a step back, but the locked door stops me from going any further. Malik and Alan might have their troubles and Simon might be weak, but the man who stands in front of me, his hands balled into fists, his brain addled with whatever drugs he's been taking, is more dangerous by far. His true nature is exposed, the chip on his shoulder growing and festering with every bottle of whisky drunk. With every chemical ingested.

'Let's talk about this,' I say, but even as I speak, my hand is reaching to turn the metal knob that will unlock the door.

'Bitch.' He lurches back to me, his feet crunching on the broken glass.

My fingers work at the lock, desperately trying to release it, but they're slippery with sweat, and it won't turn. Chris has reached me. He grabs my arm and pulls me towards him. Forcing the flat of my hand between us, I try to push him away, but he's too strong. He cups my chin between his fingers and thumb, forcing me to look at him.

'You gave yourself to them, but you thought I was nothing but a joke. Well, let's see if you think *this* is funny.'

He crushes his lips against mine, making my skull bang against the door. I wrench my head sideways, the cold glass pressing against my cheek. 'Chris, stop it. It's me. You don't know what you're doing.'

'Oh, I know what I'm doing all right. What I should have done every time you walked into the studio in your skintight jeans... the top with your tits hanging out. Loving how much it tortured that idiot Simon. Rubbing your sexuality in our faces.'

His fingers are digging into the flesh of my jaw, and he's

looking at me with someone else's eyes. There's no getting through to him.

I close my eyes and start to scream, knowing how this is going to end, but then everything changes. Chris's head jerks back and he falls away from me. He slumps to the floor, the whites of his eyes exposed, blood seeping from the back of his head onto the carpet tiles.

I'm shaking, staring at the person who's looking down at him, one of the stools from behind the reception desk in his hand, the metal back now stained with Chris's blood.

FORTY-FOUR

I stare at him, white-faced. 'Oh, Jesus. What have you done?'

Simon stands statue-still, his fingers still clenched around the legs of the stool. I watch in horror as a trickle of dark blood runs down the shiny metal surface and drips onto the carpet tiles. He says nothing, his own face twisted into an expression I can't read. Is it triumph? Anger? Hatred? I don't know.

My limbs are frozen, the urgent messages my brain is sending not reaching them, and I can't think straight. Despite everything, I know I should go to Chris. Check he's okay. But I'm scared. Scared of the person who's done this. The force he must have used to fell such a large man.

Chris is lying on his back, his skin ashen, the hair at the side of his head sticky and matted. I take a step forward and Simon looks up sharply as if woken from a dream.

'No!'

I stop, looking from one man to the other. I'm shaking now, the adrenaline sending tremors through my limbs. We were once the Three Musketeers, but now we are three strangers, separated by our thoughts and our actions. Where I'd once seen friendship, I now see something quite different.

I stare at Simon, my heart beating into the silence.

Drugs had exposed the dark underbelly of Chris's part in this horror but what role does Simon play? Why is he here and how did he get in? I no longer know who to trust.

Despite my shock and fear, there's still a part of my brain that's functioning. A part that wants to keep me safe from harm. *You must get away from here*, it whispers. *Get to somewhere safe.*

But Simon is no longer looking at me. Instead, he's staring down at Chris, devastation at what he's done now clearly written across his boyish face. He's white with shock, and the stool he's holding falls to the floor with a loud clatter.

He claps a hand to his mouth. 'Oh God. What if I've killed him?'

My stomach is knotted so tight I'm afraid I might pass out but I can't. I won't. Someone needs to take control. 'We need to check he's breathing.'

Simon runs a hand down his face. 'Yes.'

Without saying anything more, he drops to his knees and places a hand on Chris's chest, his ear to his mouth. Looking up at me, he nods.

A breath escapes me but my relief is short-lived. Chris has moved his head. He's facing me now and although his eyes are still closed, the deep groan he gives signals he's regaining consciousness.

I wrap my arms around myself, panic taking hold once more. It pulls me back to a few moments ago when Chris's fingertips had been clamped around my jaw. At the memory, my throat constricts, making my voice alien to my ears. 'What should we do?'

Beads of moisture have broken out on Simon's forehead and he wipes them away with his forearm. 'We leave him.'

'We can't do that.'

'We have to. What choice do we have? He's dangerous.'

I look desperately out at the black night. 'The police should be here.'

'But they're not. We have to go before he wakes up properly. Here, help me get him into the recovery position. We'll call an ambulance and I'll take you home. We can wait for the police there.'

'Are you sure?'

Simon doesn't answer. He's turned Chris's head to face him and is busy placing his right arm across his chest so it won't get trapped. As he pulls at his shoulder, I press my palms against Chris's broad back until, together, we manage to get him onto his side.

Chris groans again and Simon looks beseechingly at me. 'Come on. He'll be fully awake soon.'

I don't need to be told twice. Getting to my feet, I run to the door and unlock it, Simon behind me. As the door swings shut behind us, we run across the open area to where his car is parked. It's in the shadows, away from the stark security light. Only when we're safely inside and Simon's reversing out of his parking space do I feel brave enough to glance back at the brightly lit reception.

Chris is already sitting up, his hand pressed to his blood-soaked hair. As we drive away, he turns his head to the door.

FORTY-FIVE

For the first few minutes of our drive back to my flat, Simon and I have sat in silence. We've spoken to the police and now my head is tipped back against the headrest as I try to process everything that's happened.

Eventually, I turn to Simon. See how anxiety has tightened the muscles of his jaw.

'Don't blame yourself, Simon.'

He glances at me then turns his eyes back to the road. 'What if I'd hit him harder? What if I'd killed him?'

My skin is puckered with goosebumps and I rub at my arms. 'But you didn't, and if it hadn't been for you, who knows what Chris might have done. I'm so sorry for how I reacted when I saw you but I was terrified. You appeared out of nowhere and I didn't know what to think.'

'It doesn't matter. The main thing is you're okay.' His knuckles whiten on the steering wheel. 'I listened in to the show because I had a bad feeling about it... like a sixth sense.'

'And you were right.'

Simon grimaces. 'I wish I hadn't been. As soon as I heard that fucked-up call, I jumped straight in the car. I would have phoned you but I was in such a rush, I left my mobile behind.' He thumps his forehead with the heel of his hand. 'What an idiot!'

I take his wrist and gently lower his hand, placing it back on the wheel. 'You acted on instinct and I'm grateful. Please don't let's talk about it anymore. Not until the police come.'

But Simon's not listening. 'When I saw you and Chris through the glass, I wasn't sure what was going on, but it didn't look good.' His face twists as he remembers. 'I knew if I went in through the back entrance, you wouldn't see me.'

I can't get the picture of Chris out of my head – his expression as he'd gripped my face between his fingers. The disgust. The hatred. Maybe I'm wrong to not want to talk about it. Maybe sharing my fears will lessen them.

'He was off his head, Si. I've never seen him like that before.' I grow cold at the memory. 'I really thought he was going to—'

Simon nods. 'Me too. I hit him because I didn't know how else to stop him. You wouldn't have stood a chance against him.' He shudders and I know his thoughts have moved on to the moment the stool made contact. 'We believed we knew him. How could we have been so blind?'

I shake my head into the darkness. 'I don't know. Had you any idea he was feeling this way? So jealous. So resentful of us both?'

Simon indicates right, even though at this hour there are no other cars on the road to see. 'Of course not. But then clowns are often sad bastards, hiding their true feelings behind their big fake smiles. What I can't understand is how we didn't recognise his voice when he called in. He's a radio presenter, for God's sake. It's not as if we don't hear him every day.'

The curtains at the windows of the terraced houses we pass are all closed; it will be a while before the streets wake up.

'DC Forrest said there are apps he could have used to change his voice, but even if he hadn't, it's amazing what your brain can miss when you're not expecting it.'

Simon breathes in sharply. 'Ten years I've worked with him and he's been like a brother to me. We used to share everything.' His eyes flick across to me. 'I just wish I'd known how much he'd wanted to share you too. If I had, maybe I could have done something to stop things getting this far.'

The way he says it makes me uncomfortable. If we're to remain friends, he's got to stop this, but I'm too exhausted to tell him now.

'You shared too much, Simon. If you hadn't told Chris about us, things might have turned out differently. He used that knowledge against me.'

'I'm sorry.'

'I know you are, but I've been thinking about it. We're lucky really. I've moved on, and things are back on track with you and Anne. It could have been so much worse.'

'Worse? How do you make that out?'

I turn my head and look at him meaningfully, staggered that he hasn't thought about it himself. 'You know full well Chris can never keep his mouth shut when he's had a few. Did you not think who else he might have told given the chance?'

We stop at a red light and Simon's fingers tighten on the steering wheel. 'But he didn't.'

'No, but it would only have been a matter of time before he did.'

It's as I'm speaking that an even worse thought occurs to me. 'You didn't tell him anything else, did you?'

'Like what?' But the pause has been too long. He knows what I'm talking about.

My gut churns. 'You know what. Please, Simon. Say you didn't tell him *that*.'

The lights have changed to green. Simon says nothing. He crunches the gears and accelerates away too quickly.

And in that moment, I know that he did.

FORTY-SIX

I'd hoped that once we got to the flat, the familiarity of it would soothe me, but it hasn't. Instead, my hand shakes so much I'm finding it difficult to fit the key in the lock.

'Here, let me do it.'

Taking the key out of my hand, Simon unlocks the door and I follow him in. The hall light is on and I see, straight away, that Nathan's bedroom door is ajar. He must be working a late shift and I'm glad. I haven't the strength for explanations.

'I'll make us a drink.'

Simon stands in the hallway staring at the blood on his sleeve, now drying to a dark brown. 'Thanks. I need one. A black coffee. As strong as you can make it.'

The living room is in darkness. Reaching out a hand, I flick the switch on the wall. Light floods the room.

'Jesus!' My hand flies to my chest, shock rooting me to the spot.

Simon is behind me. 'What is it, Mel. What's the matter?'

I stare at the settee. At the person sitting there.

'Anne?' Confusion courses through me. What's she doing here and how did she get in?

Anne's face is strained. Waxen. It's not me she's looking at, it's her husband.

'I thought you'd come if I waited long enough. You're always telling me to trust my instincts, Simon, so this time I did. Lucky I've still got the spare key Tina gave me for emergencies.' She produces a key from her pocket. 'You can't keep away from her, can you?'

I glance back at Simon. In the dim light of the hallway, his face is pale.

'Don't say anything,' he whispers. 'I can handle this.'

Brushing past me, he goes into the room and perches on the edge of the settee next to his wife. He takes her hands in his and I'm surprised when she lets him. 'It's not what you think, Anne. Something bad happened at the radio station and I came back with Mel to make sure she was all right. Nothing more.'

She pulls her hands away. 'Don't lie to me. I want the truth. How long has it been going on?'

I hover in the doorway, like an extra in a bad play, not wanting to go any further. 'There's nothing going on, Anne,' I say. 'You have to believe me. Simon and I are just friends.'

Simon puts an arm around his wife's shoulders. 'It's the truth. I promise.'

Anne shrugs him away then holds her hand out to me, palm up. 'Your phone. Show it to me.'

I hand my mobile to her, relieved I've deleted all Simon's stupid messages. 'I've nothing to hide.'

Finding Simon's name, she scrolls through the messages before handing the phone back to me. 'This time maybe but what about before?'

My skin grows cold. 'Before?'

'Yes.' Her voice is tight. 'When you were screwing my husband.'

I try to regulate my breathing. I'd thought we'd got away with it but that was before I'd known that Simon had told Chris about our night together.

I need to make her understand.

'It should never have happened. We were drunk. Stupid. It

was a one-off and meant nothing to either of us. We never meant to hurt you.'

I hear the clichés fall from my lips, knowing they're true yet doubting Anne will believe them.

She links her fingers over her gently swollen belly. 'No?'

'Of course not.'

I watch her thumbs caress the growing child within her then look away. 'When did Chris tell you?'

'A while ago. He took great pleasure in it.' She gives a bitter laugh. 'That's not all he told me.'

My hands have gone clammy and I wipe them on the sides of my jeans.

'What do you mean?'

She looks down at her bump. 'Seems I'm not the only one who knows what this feels like.'

I feel the colour drain from my face. The knowledge she possesses sweeps away everything that has come before. All this time, she's known my secret and I never realised. I fix Simon with accusing eyes. He looks as sick as I feel.

'You should never have told him, Simon. It was private. It wasn't his secret to know.'

The decision not to go through with the pregnancy hadn't been a difficult one to make. After all, what choice did I have? I was married and so was Simon. The whole thing had been a terrible mistake and it wasn't as if I'd ever wanted children. Not even with Niall.

The sad irony of Simon and Anne losing their own child soon after my termination wasn't lost on me and I've carried the guilt with me ever since.

I can see from Simon's face that he has too.

He looks up at me now, his eyes dark with pain. 'I'm sorry, Mel, but I had no one else to tell. I was worried about Anne. She went into such a dark place after the miscarriage and I was desperate.' He pinches the bridge of his nose with his thumb and forefinger. 'I needed to offload. It was one night when we were drinking in The Junction.'

A wave of sadness passes through me at the mention of the place. The night I met Malik seems a lifetime ago; so much has happened since then. The poor guy had done nothing wrong. None of what had happened at the radio station had been his fault... unless you count criminal damage to my tyre. My heart clenches when I think of what might have been, but just as quickly my head overrules it. Locking me in his room at night hadn't been a normal way to behave... and then there were the violent, unsettling nightmares and the way he'd been with me after. He wasn't good for me. Not really.

Anne shifts in her chair. She's waiting for me to say something.

'Why didn't you confront me back then?' I ask her.

For the first time since we got back to the flat, she looks uncertain. Her eyes slide to Simon. 'I was scared that if I made a scene, he would leave me.'

'He would never do that,' I say, remembering the conversation I'd had with Simon on the canal bank. Hoping she can't see through the lie.

The sound of the front door opening then closing gives a welcome relief to the tension. Nathan must be back. There are footsteps in the hall then he pokes his head around the door, clearly surprised to find me up and with company.

He looks from me to the others. 'Anne?'

Anne's brow pinches but she doesn't say anything.

I raise my eyebrows. 'You know each other?'

Nathan nods. 'Yeah. We both used to belong to the theatre group that met above the pub in town, though I had to stop going when I went on to night shifts. We both had parts in *Take Me Back*.'

Simon leans forward. 'I remember... I picked up Anne from one of the rehearsals and caught the end of it. You played the university student.'

'That's right.' He looks at Anne. 'It was a shame when you had to pull out, but it can't have been fun having morning sickness in the evening. If you ever fancy coming back, they're doing *As You Like It* next. I'll be back on day shift by then and fancy trying out for Orlando. You should give it a go... that's if having a kid gives you any time for hobbies.'

My eyes alight on the holdall by his feet. The battered script I'd seen in his rucksack along with the highlighted sheaf of paper had been to help him prepare for the audition.

'Anyway, what did you have?' he asks. 'Boy or girl?'

Anne still hasn't spoken – her eyes are fixed on her swollen stomach.

It's only now that Nathan registers her small bump, his face creasing in confusion.

'Sadly, Anne miscarried,' I tell him quickly. 'But the great thing is, as you can see, she's expecting again.'

Nathan takes a breath. He looks up at the ceiling, clearly searching for the correct thing to say. 'I'm sorry.' Colour rises up his neck. 'But congratulations and I'm sure this time...'

'Yes. Things will be different this time.' It's the first time Anne's spoken since he arrived.

From the way he's shuffling his feet, it's obvious that Nathan is keen to be away from the awkward atmosphere. He raises a hand. 'Anyway, I'm off to bed. Good to see you again, Anne. Small world. As I say, if you fancied coming back to the group at any time, I'm sure they'd welcome you with open arms. The understudy for your part wasn't a patch on you and she had absolutely no idea how to do an Irish accent.'

He leaves us alone and I listen to the click of his bedroom door as he closes it. Simon and Anne say nothing. It's like they're both waiting for something. I walk over to the window and rest my forehead against the cold glass, my thoughts racing.

Eventually Simon speaks. 'We need to think carefully about all this. Tell the police everything we know about Chris and what he did then move on.'

I'm only half listening. It's impossible to concentrate on what he's saying when my head is filled with just one thing: Natalie's words when she'd phoned into the show.

He's not good for me, she'd said, the Irish lilt covering her true voice.

FORTY-SEVEN

The silence in the room expands and eventually I turn, different emotions fighting for space: anger, hurt and a sadness that I'm finding hard to disguise.

'You phoned in to my show. You were Natalie.'

'Yes,' she says, the reply short. To the point.

Although it's Anne I'm talking to, I'm aware of Simon taking one of her hands in his own. Covering it with his other.

'But why?'

Her eyes close a second as she takes a breath in.

'Is it so hard to understand? I know what Simon's like and suspected there might still be something between you. I hated that you worked together.'

'But I was moved onto the Late-Night Show. We hardly ever saw each other.'

Anne shrugs. 'I thought that would make things better, but then the thoughts came creeping back.' She thumps her forehead with the heel of her hand as though still seeing them. 'The images of you together. I needed to get under your skin and Natalie was my way of doing it. You'd just met Malik and I thought that if I could make you believe the two of you shared a psychotic lover, one who might be dangerous, it would screw you up. With any luck, you'd leave the radio station or, better still, move away completely.'

Simon sighs. 'And when Chris decided to give the man who was supposedly stalking you both a voice for his own ends, her work was done.' He pulls his wife to him and kisses her hair. 'Anne knows what she did was wrong and she's sorry.'

It's like the rug has been pulled from underneath me. 'You knew about this?'

'Yes.'

I stare at him in horror. 'And you never thought to tell me?'

'I've only known a week or so.' His eyes lower to their linked fingers. 'I know I should have told you but Anne begged me not to. We talked about it and thought it would all blow over.'

I look at them both in astonishment. 'Blow over! If you hadn't phoned in to the show, Anne, Chris would never have run with it and tonight would never have happened.' I think of Malik sitting in the interview room, two detectives on the opposite side of the table from him. 'Because of what you did, an innocent man was questioned, his reputation trashed. Have you any idea of the damage you've caused?'

Anne looks defensive. 'Things got out of control, but the pregnancy made me desperate. More determined than ever.'

'Determined about what?'

'To keep my husband.'

With his free hand, Simon runs his fingers through his fringe. What I'd thought were highlights are actually streaks of grey. If I had been in Anne's position, would I have gone to such lengths to keep the man who had betrayed me?

I don't think so.

Even though the room is warm, I'm shivering. 'Everything you knew about my relationship with Malik. Everything I told Simon. You used it all when you rang in to the show as Natalie. Without realising it, I gave you all you needed.'

'Yes. It was enough.'

I think of Anne in my flat – how well she'd played the part of a supportive, caring friend. I knew drama was her hobby, but it had never in a million years crossed my mind she'd use it to create a character of her own. One who would ensure that what had happened between me and her husband would never happen again.

Leaving the window, I pull a stool from the breakfast bar and sit. 'I was so pleased you wanted to see me again after all this time. After your breakdown, I should have made the first move, but how could I when I was consumed with guilt? Even though I had no idea you knew about us, supporting you after the loss of your baby would have felt so wrong after what Simon and I had done. Now I know why you rekindled our friendship.'

Anne levels her gaze at me. 'You know what they say. Keep your enemies close.'

'I'm not your enemy, Anne. I hate that you think that. Could you ever forgive me?'

Anne doesn't answer and I feel wretched. As wretched as I did when Natalie stopped phoning in. I'd missed the connection we'd had, but now I know who I'd been talking to, I feel stupid. 'Why did you stop phoning in to the show? What happened?'

Simon answers for her. 'She knew it would make you worry, think something had happened to her. She intended to call back eventually but after you and I had that argument on the towpath, when you more or less accused me of being a shit husband, she had no need to.' His eyes slip away from mine and I know what he's thinking. It was also when I'd confronted him with the phone messages. For the second time since Anne arrived at my door, I'm consumed with relief that I deleted them.

'After you'd gone,' he continues, 'I sat on one of the benches and thought about everything you'd said. At first I was angry, but after I'd calmed down, I realised that I only felt that way because I knew you were right. I'd been a selfish idiot and owed it to Anne to grow up, especially with the baby on the way. I stopped going out with Chris as much and made more of an effort. Anne had no need of Natalie anymore.'

A sadness settles on me. I can't tell them that I'd needed Natalie too. How, at the time, she'd seemed to be the only person who understood what I was going through with Malik... the person Natalie had accused of killing someone. I frown at the memory. The emotion in her voice as she'd said those terrible words had been so real. So raw. Was she really that good an actress?

'I understand why you did it, Anne. But to accuse someone of murder? Poor Malik. It's not as if you'd ever met him and even if...'

I stop, noticing how the colour has drained from Simon's face. 'What is it? What's the matter?'

He looks wretched. 'It wasn't Malik Anne was talking about, okay?'

Our eyes meet. 'Then who was it?'

Simon looks like he's about to throw up. 'She was talking about *me*.'

I stare from one to the other. 'That's not funny. You said he *killed* someone, Anne.'

Anne smooths her top over her small bump and the tension in the air shifts.

'That's because it's true,' she answers.

My breathing becomes shallow. This is Simon, I tell myself. The man I've shared a studio with every weekday for the last eight years. There must be some mistake. 'I don't understand.'

'She's right, Mel.' Simon's close to tears. 'I did kill someone.'

My concern turns to panic. 'Stop it, Simon. You're frightening me.' In my head, I'm picturing the screen in reception. A reporter stands at the mouth of the tunnel where the woman disappeared, his words transcribed across the bottom.

Did you see... please come forward... anniversary plea...

It's a mystery that has never been solved.

'It's not what you're thinking.' Simon's tone has hardened. He's seen where my imagination has taken me. 'Christ, Mel. Don't look at me like that.'

I'm staring at him in horror. 'What did you do?'

I see from the way his face closes the enormity of what I'm accusing him of, but it's too late to take it back.

'Simon?'

'It was the miscarriage Anne was talking about,' he says eventually, despair deadening his voice. 'She believes the stress of knowing what I'd done, how I'd betrayed her with you when she needed me most, had made it happen. Anne thinks I killed the baby.'

The palm of Anne's hand alights on her stomach. 'It's true. I held you responsible. Both of you. I still do.'

Simon takes his wife's hand. 'You can't blame her, Mel.'

I look from one to the other, eyes wide with incredulity, registering how calm they both are. What they're saying is crazy yet from the way they're telling me, you'd think they were discussing the weather. I have to put an end to the conversation.

'I'm sorry for everything that's happened but it's done and it's something we'll all have to live with. What else can we do?'

I'm addressing them both; it's something we will have to navigate together.

Simon lets his head fall into his hands. 'So, what happens next?'

'I don't know. Maybe it's time I moved away. I can get a job at another radio station... There's nothing to keep me here.'

He stays silent; he knows better than to say what he's thinking.

'It might be for the best,' Anne says, speaking for both of them. She links her arm with Simon's. Signalling their united front.

And I know she's right. It *is* for the best.

'I've already told Di I don't want to do the Late-Night Show anymore and she's found someone to stand in. As soon as I've worked out what I want to do, I'll start looking for a new place to live. Somewhere on my own this time. I'm too old to be flat sharing, and I'm sure Nathan would prefer to be living with someone his own age. Charl's been looking for a place, Simon. Maybe you could suggest it to her.'

'Yes, I'll do it tomorrow.' He looks uncomfortable. 'But we need to be thinking about what we say when the police arrive.'

Anne looks from him to me. 'There's no reason for me to be here when they talk to you both. What happened tonight had nothing to do with me.'

She gets up but Simon reaches out and circles her wrist. 'Why don't you wait? We can both go home in my car and I'll come back and collect yours tomorrow.'

She looks at him sharply. 'No. I want to go home. All this stress isn't good for the baby.'

He looks doubtful. 'Okay, if you're sure.'

Anne picks up her bag. 'I am. There's no need to see me out.'

Simon and I sit in silence until we hear the door of the flat shut. I wait a moment then get off my stool and go into my bedroom, parting the curtain to see Anne climb into her car, which she's parked on the opposite side of the street. We'd been too occupied with what had happened at the studio to notice it. I watch her drive away and when I turn back, Simon is standing in the doorway.

'This business with Anne and the calls,' he says. 'I need to know... Are you going to mention it to the police?'

I think about it. 'I should. What she did has had huge repercussions, and it's not as though what happened with us is a secret anymore.'

He joins me at the window and reaches for my hand. 'Please don't, Mel. I've promised Anne I won't leave her, but she's struggling big time. I don't think it will take much to tip her over the edge.'

I look at our joined hands then quickly pull mine away. 'She needs help, Si. Professional help. Have you thought about what will happen after the baby comes? She struggled so much after the miscarriage. What if having the baby makes her even more anxious?'

'I'll sort something, I promise. But I think when the baby arrives she'll be so consumed by it that what happened between you and me will become less important to her. Whatever happens, I beg you, please don't say anything to anyone.'

His plea is so impassioned it's impossible not to be swayed by it. 'Okay, if that's what you want.'

He gives an audible sigh. 'Thank you. It's hard, you know?'

'Yes, it's hard.'

I want to comfort him, but I can't. Instead, I turn back to the window in time to see a car pull up outside. I watch as DC Forrest gets out. He glances up at the window then walks to the front door.

I'm suddenly overwhelmed with a great tiredness. I'm done with all this. I need to leave – not just Lock Radio but my flat. This town.

FORTY-EIGHT

It doesn't take long to reach the towpath and follow it. As I walk, I don't look at the moored boats or the swans that glide silently under the bridge. I feel rather than see the canal water shift and breathe beside me.

I need to see Malik and apologise for doubting him. For stepping away so easily. If I'd stayed, in time he might have learnt to trust me and maybe talk about the things that were in his head. The past that only surfaced in his dreams.

As I hurry down the towpath, I'm not kidding myself that we can make a go of things. That's not what this is about. I just want him to understand what happened and I want to understand him too. This time when I see him, my eyes will be open. Not blind.

The path is getting narrower, more overgrown with weeds, and it isn't long before I see the muddy stretch of grass that leads to Malik's block of flats. I don't know if he'll see me or if he'll even be there, but I have to try.

I see the estate agent's sign, with For Sale written on it, as soon as I walk around the side of the building. A square of white plastic attached to one corner indicates the number of the flat and I know, even before I read it, that it's Malik's.

Retracing my steps to the back of the flats again, I see what I hadn't before – the sheet is no longer at the window and when I cup my hand to the glass and peer in, the room is empty.

'Can I help you?' A young man in a shiny grey suit and ginger hair cropped close to his head is looking at me questioningly. 'Are you here for a viewing? I wasn't expecting anyone until—'

'Yes.' It takes only a moment for me to decide. 'I'm a bit early I'm afraid.'

He looks at the clipboard he's holding. 'Ah yes, Mrs Alden. No problem. Come this way. You'll need to excuse the state of the property, but the tenant left without giving notice. To be honest,' he says conspiratorially, 'between you, me and the gatepost, I get the impression that the tenancy wasn't exactly legit.' He rubs fingers and thumb together to illustrate his meaning. 'The arrangement clearly suited them both, but now the owner wants to sell. He'll be getting industrial cleaners in, but until that happens, you'll just have to use your imagination.'

'Of course. I understand.'

I follow him around the side of the block and wait as he unlocks the main door.

He bends to pick up some circulars from the tatty linoleum floor then stands back to let me in.

'Was it for you or were you thinking of renting it out?'

The question catches me off guard. 'I... I haven't decided yet.'

'Well, whatever. As I said before, you need to look beyond what you see and imagine fresh paint. New carpet. It would make a nice little bolthole. Close to the centre of town and right on the canal too.'

I stand in the dark hallway and look around me. To my right is the tiny galley kitchen with its chipped worktop and damp-stained wall. The scratched refrigerator, against which Malik had made love to me with such passion, is no longer there and it makes me feel sad.

I don't know what I'd been expecting by coming into the flat. To see something of Malik's, maybe? Something he'd left behind in his hurry to leave? But as I go into the bed-sitting room and see how bare it is, no trace of the packing-case tables or the mattress where we'd lain, our legs entwined, I realise how stupid I've been. The place has been cleared of everything that was once us. There's nothing for me here.

I touch my fingers to my lips, remembering. My vision mists then swims.

'I'm sorry, Malik.'

The agent is looking at me, clearly unsure of what to make of this odd woman who's standing in the middle of the squalid room, tears running down her face. He shifts his feet awkwardly on the patched lino then holds out an A4 sheet of paper with the details on. 'Should have given this to you earlier.'

I brush at my cheeks with the heel of my hand and wave the page away. 'No, thank you. I've seen enough to know that it's not suitable. I'm sorry for wasting your time.'

The man shrugs. 'Can't say I blame you. Let's get out into the fresh air.'

'Yes,' I say, no longer wanting to be here.

Once outside, the agent glances back at the flat. 'He might have been here illegally, but you can't help feeling sorry for the guy.'

I frown my confusion. 'Who?'

He points to the blank window. 'Sorry, I meant the tenant. Seems it was his younger sister who disappeared in that tunnel. You know, the one that was on the news. He was pretty cut up about it, and the landlord said letting the poor sod stay until he could sort himself out was the least he could do.' He puts his hands in his pockets and jingles his keys. 'Apparently, when the two of them came over to this country, he'd promised his family back home he'd look after his sister. Don't think he could forgive himself.' He looks across to the canal. 'Wonder what happened to her.'

I don't want to hear any more; it's too sad.

'Thank you for showing me around.' A blue Fiesta has parked outside the block of flats and a middle-aged woman is getting out. Mrs Alden presumably. 'It looks like your next viewing is here.'

'Cheers.'

He hurries to greet her and, without looking back, I cross the grassy slope to the towpath. When I reach it, instead of turning right to go home, I turn left in the direction of the radio station and the tunnel. Head bowed. Thoughts crowding in. We believe we know people when, in reality, we see just the part that people want us to see.

I'd thought Malik was my blind date, but the truth was I'd been blind to them all. To everything they'd held back from me.

Simon.

Chris.

Anne.

Alan.

They'd all had their secrets and I had too.

In the end, it had been Malik who'd known me the best. It had been to him that I'd opened up, and in doing so had shown a part of me I'd kept hidden from everyone.

And I'd betrayed him.

Ahead of me is the tunnel, the brickwork of its wide mouth bearded with damp, dark moss, its sides grooved by decades of tow ropes. I try to imagine the boats that would have passed through the impenetrable blackness of its chamber, their bowels heavy with sand, timber and iron ore. But I struggle to make the picture clear. Instead, all I can see is Malik's sister, standing in the shadows watching as a man walks towards her. A man who will be the last to set eyes on her. A man they've never traced.

No wonder Malik's nightmares had tortured him. Sent him walking out in the black night, the guilt of not having been able to protect her, as a brother should, eating away at him.

I see now what I couldn't have seen before. He'd locked me in his room to keep me safe. Nothing more.

How I wish things could have turned out differently, but they didn't. And, despite today's revelations, I feel an odd sense of relief. The nightmare is over. Not for Malik, or for Simon and

Anne, whose relationship is held together by the finest of threads. But for me at least.

Weeks ago, when I'd woken up to my alarm trilling its early wake-up call for the final time, my life had been as slow-moving and stagnant as the brown water of the canal. I hadn't known that change was coming. There'd been no hint or inkling of the terrible chain of events that would unfold.

And I'm glad.

Sometimes it's best not to know.

FORTY-NINE

EIGHTEEN MONTHS LATER

The room is in semi-darkness, the only light coming from the glass panel above the door. I hate it, but changing the door is one of the things on our to-do list, along with stripping off the wallpaper in the downstairs loo and replacing all the windows.

Our project, Sean calls it.

Not that either of us had realised the huge amount of work we'd be taking on when we'd bought the run-down semi. No, putting in the offer had been as spontaneous as our engagement. Still, that's what I like most about the man who lies in bed next to me. His ability to constantly surprise me.

Sean's hand rests on my stomach, his thumb absently stroking the soft skin below my ribs, and I smile to myself. I haven't felt this happy in a long time and I don't want to do anything to jeopardise it. The bed is still rumpled from when we made love and I turn onto my side, studying Sean's face: the dark hair, the pale skin. Daydreaming about what our future children might look like. I'd never really wanted children and, after Anne's miscarriage and the abortion, hadn't allowed myself to consider that one day I might change my mind. Not comfortable with the idea of being a mother.

But now I'm with Sean I've changed. Forgiven myself. I know in my heart that he's the person I want to have a child with. Not that I would have known that the first time I'd spoken to him.

Unlike the instant attraction I'd had to Malik, our relationship had started slowly. Just a quick hello if we passed each other in the radio-station corridor or a locking of eyes at one of the weekly meetings.

Not that Sean and I see that much of each other as we work at different ends of the day. There had been a big shake-up at Lock Radio and when Phil had been swapped to the Breakfast Show, Sean had been his replacement. Meeting Sean had been the reason I'd stayed, despite my resolution to move on to pastures new.

To everyone's surprise, including my own, I'd been moved back to the Breakfast Show too. Charl had left to do something in PR, and I'd been the obvious person to take her place. I'd pushed against the idea at first, but then I'd reasoned that there was no rationale for not doing so. It wasn't as though I had to worry about what Anne thought, for after giving birth to a healthy baby boy, she'd settled happily into motherhood. The depression that had dogged her after her miscarriage hadn't reappeared, and with Simon continuing to play the role of dutiful husband, the two of them appeared settled. The perfect little family.

Having promised Simon I wouldn't, I've never told anyone about what happened, and, to this day, Natalie remains our little secret. Even to the police.

'We can't be lying here all day.' Sean sits up, the sheet wrapped around his waist, and looks at the bedside clock. 'I'd better get going.'

He twists round to get his phone and I trace my finger across the birthmark on his lower back. A brown heart-shaped island against the pale sea of his skin.

'Just a few more minutes?'

Turning his head, he smiles. 'And leave the listeners to fend for themselves? Now that would never do.' He slides his legs out of the bed and pulls on his boxers. 'Anyway, I'll be seeing you when you come in later. I'll make you a cup of coffee and bring it in to you after I've finished.'

I reach up and take his hand. 'As long as you don't put me off. It's a while since I've done the Late-Night Show.'

Sean buttons up his shirt. 'It will be a breeze. It's not as though you haven't done it before.'

'I know, it's just that...' I tail off. I've never really talked to Sean about what happened when I was working on the show. Just brushed it off as something and nothing. He's never asked me either.

As he continues to dress, I consider how I feel about doing the show tonight. When Di had called me to say the new presenter was ill, I'd agreed to her request to step into his shoes. Now I'm wondering why I'd been so generous as the graveyard shift holds nothing but bad memories. It will also be the first time I've been alone in the building since the night Chris attacked me. He'd been interviewed by the police about Charl's attack and Malik's sister's disappearance, but there'd been nothing to link him to these incidences. He's moved away from the area and has a court order stopping him from contacting me.

It will be fine, I tell myself. It's just for one night, after all. Besides, Di said Simon and Phil can do the Breakfast Show without me tomorrow, so I'll be able to have a welcome lie-in.

'Shall we do something tomorrow?' I ask Sean. 'Go out somewhere?'

He sits on the bed to put on his trainers. 'Not tomorrow – I've something on.'

'Really? You didn't say.'

He frowns. 'Did I need to?'

He bends and kisses the top of my head. It feels patronising but I try not to dwell on it. Despite our impromptu evening in bed, he's been a bit off with me recently. Distracted. I should ask him what it is, but the last thing I want is to appear clingy like his ex. Always wanting to know where he was. What he was doing. I never want to be like that.

'I'll see you later then,' he says, putting on his jacket.

'Yes, see you later.'

He goes out, closing the door behind him, and I lie there, my fingers seeking out the sharp crown of my engagement ring, wondering if he might be having regrets.

Sean has his head bowed to the microphone, his earphones covering his dark hair. I stand for a moment watching him through the glass, enjoying the warm feeling I get in my stomach whenever I see him. When he looks up, I blow him a kiss before carrying on to Studio Two.

I sit at the mixer desk and look at the computer screen, running through the topics I'm going to discuss, looking at the songs on the playlist and trying to get into the right headspace for the night's show.

When I've gone through everything, I get up again and dim the lights, leaving on just the one directly above my chair. I hear Sean sign out of his show and lean in to the microphone, telling my listeners that it's lovely to be back. That I've missed them.

Five minutes later, Sean appears at the door with a mug of coffee.

'Break a leg,' he says, handing it to me.

I'm not sure the sentiment is particularly appropriate in the setting of the radio station, but I thank him anyway.

'See you at home.'

'Yeah, I'll sleep in the spare room tonight. So you don't need to worry about waking me when you come in.'

I'm disappointed but cover it with a smile. 'Sure. I'll see you later.'

The door swings shut behind him and I'm left on my own. I look at my monitor then back at the dark corridor through the rectangle of glass, trying not to think of the night, eighteen months ago, when I'd done the same thing. Wondering where Chris was.

Thankfully, once the show is underway, I get into the swing of it, remembering how good it is to be so connected to the listeners. Feeling myself being drawn into their stories.

But, as it gets nearer to midnight, nearer to True Confessions, I find my heart is beginning to race – a hangover from the early days when I used to wait for Natalie to phone in.

I'm just being stupid.

I shake my head, the headphones heavy on my ears, and fade in the theme tune, the first bars of music bringing with it a rush of memories. Forcing myself to concentrate, I lean closer to the mic.

'You're through to Late-Night Radio and True Confessions. Why don't you tell me your secrets?'

The lines start to flash, and I work my way through them. Uttering words of encouragement. Questioning the motives for the callers' various indiscretions. I glance at the clock. It won't be long before I can leave the Late-Night Show behind me and climb into my bed. Press my body against Sean's. When I remember he'll be sleeping in the spare room tonight, a wave of disappointment washes over me.

Lines are still flashing. There's time for just one more call and then I'll be done. I click on one.

'Tell me your true confession, caller, so that I might absolve you.'

There's a silence but that's not unusual. Sometimes it takes the caller a while to pluck up courage. I wait, in the spotlight, until at last they speak.

When it comes, the voice is soft as a whisper. The Irish lilt, one I know so well.

'My name is Natalie,' she says. 'And I have a confession.'

I'm so shocked I can only repeat what she's just said. 'Natalie.'

I picture the regular listeners to the programme pricking up their ears, furrowing their brows trying to remember where they've heard the name before and why it's piqued their interest.

'How are you?' In my confusion, it's all I can think of to say.

'Life is good. I have a child now, a beautiful boy, and a loving husband.'

My mind's in a whirl and I'm unsure how to play this.

'I'm glad,' I say, at last, 'that things worked out for you, Natalie. But what's your confession?'

I'm still in shock that she's phoned in after all this time. I'd hoped that now she was happy it would be over. Somewhere in her house, Simon is sleeping. The baby too. Why is she doing this?

'I'm in love,' she says, her voice a smile.

'That's good,' I reply carefully. 'I'm sure your husband loves you too.'

She laughs. 'I'm not in love with my husband. I'm having an affair.'

My breath catches in my throat. 'An affair?'

'Yes, it's awkward. You see my husband works with him.'

I'm gripping the edges of my swivel chair, scared of where she'll go next. What if Simon's listening?

'Maybe it's best if we talk about this off air.'

'No. I have nothing to hide.'

I play for time. I could cut her off, but something is stopping me. 'Tell me about this man. What makes him special to you?'

'So many things. The way he looks at me. The feel of his skin against my fingertips. The taste of his kiss.'

I nod, recognising what she's saying. It's the way Sean makes me feel. Once more, Natalie and I have a connection.

But this isn't Natalie, it's Anne... I have to remember that. She's no longer in love with Simon – someone else has broken that spell, and in doing so they've released me.

'I don't think you should say any more,' I say quickly, scared now.

'No? But I want to tell everyone how beautiful he is, so they can understand why I did it. His dark hair. The cute birthmark... heart-shaped as though put there just for me.'

I grow cold.

'Maybe you know him,' she continues. 'Maybe you could ask him if he loves me too.'

I'm trying to hold myself together. 'Why are you doing this?'

But, of course, I know. It's her ultimate revenge.

'I'm sorry.' Natalie's soft voice comes to me through my headphones. 'I thought you would be happy for me... or is there something you wanted to get off your chest?'

It was just one drunken night. One mistake. But it was enough to set in motion a series of events I could never have foreseen. Women like Anne never forgive. Never forget. For all I know, it might have been she, not Chris, who'd been the one to follow and attack Charl. She was, after all, a threat. Young, pretty... just Simon's type. It's something we'll probably never know, but I can't help thinking it was just as well the girl left the radio station.

But this isn't about Charl; it's about me. I'd been wrong in thinking I'd be able to put what happened behind me. I know now that until I own up to my fateful indiscretion, Anne will be watching me. Playing me. There's only one way to end all this.

Closing my eyes, I draw in a breath then press my lips to the microphone.

It will be the hardest thing I've ever done but it's time to make my confession.

A LETTER FROM WENDY

Firstly, I would like to say a huge thank you for reading my fifth psychological thriller, *Blind Date*. It's been a joy to write and I hope you loved reading it as much as I loved writing it.

If you did enjoy it and want to keep up to date with all my latest releases, just sign up at the following link. Your email address will never be shared, and you can unsubscribe at any time.

www.bookouture.com/wendy-clarke

I remember, clearly, the moment the idea for *Blind Date* came to me. It was the summer of 2020 and I'd just finished writing my fourth thriller, *His Hidden Wife*. In the lull before edits, my lovely editor asked if I'd had any thoughts on ideas for more novels. Well, as luck would have it, I had! I'd recently read an article about a late-night radio presenter and had been mulling it over. It had left me with a strong impression of what it must be like to be that person sitting in a darkened studio, picked out by a single light. I could only imagine how lonely it must be but also how intimate, the late hour and the diverse strangers who call in to the show adding to the atmosphere. Each faceless person as unknown as a blind date.

It sparked questions in my mind: What if the radio station was isolated? What if the presenter was a woman at a turning point in her life? What if she formed an obsession with one of her callers? What if the caller knew her secret?

As you can see, *what ifs* always play an important role in my early thought process!

I sent the idea to my editor who, to my delight, said she loved it and suggested I start writing. I couldn't wait.

But what of the setting? In previous novels, the place where the action happens has always come to me before the plot. Not so in the case of *Blind Date*. In this psychological thriller, I already had my story idea so the need for an atmospheric setting where it could play out came later.

I like to use settings with which I'm familiar, and an image came to me of the canal-boat holidays I'd had with my husband – the slow-moving water sometimes mirror-flat and sunlit, at other times brown and frigid. I knew this contrasting scenery would be perfect. So, in some chapters, the willow-fringed canal side seen in picture postcards, where brightly coloured canal boats glide beneath cast-iron bridges, became my backdrop. In others, the action took place in an area where the towpath was overgrown, the earlier bucolic rural scene replaced by a canal flanked by dilapidated buildings. The brackish water moving towards the gaping mouth of the tunnel where a young woman had disappeared.

The theme of *Blind Date* is recognising the danger of thinking you know someone when in fact they are a stranger to you. Is that something you recognise? It might not be an actual blind date, just a first meeting with someone where you think or feel you know more about them than you actually do.

Would you trust your instincts in a situation like this? It was a question I felt I could take further.

I hope you enjoyed *Blind Date* and if you did, I would be extremely grateful if you could write a review. It would be great to hear what you think, and it makes such a difference to an author.

I love hearing from my readers – you can get in touch on my Facebook page, through Twitter, Goodreads, Instagram or my website.

Thanks,

Wendy x

wendyswritingnow.blogspot.com

facebook.com/WendyClarkeAuthor

twitter.com/WendyClarke99

instagram.com/wendyclarke99

ACKNOWLEDGEMENTS

I want to start by thanking my wonderful editor at Bookouture, Jennifer Hunt. Jennifer has been with me since day one when she read and loved my debut, *What She Saw*, and I shall always be grateful to her for that. She is a dream to work with and, five novels on, I'm still impressed with how her skill and dedication help make my novels the best they can be. How lucky I am to have someone like that behind me every step of the way! Thanks also to the rest of the Bookouture team who work tirelessly to get my novels in front of readers.

Thank you to my family for their continued support of my writing and to my friends – especially my writing buddy, Tracy, who has accompanied me on this roller-coaster ride since the day we met; Liz who knows exactly what I go through to get the book out there and the lovely Friday Girls: Carol, Linda, Helen, Barbara and Jill, who keep me on an even keel and have to put up with my erratic timetable in the lead-up to publication.

Blind Date contains a few police procedurals and once again it's to the fabulous Graham Bartlett I turned with my silly questions. Thanks, Graham, for your patience and any mistakes are entirely my own.

It would have been impossible to write a novel set in a radio station without help so I was incredibly lucky when Tom Evans from More Radio agreed to chat to me. I am indebted to him for his time and for his incredibly detailed descriptions and explanations of the working life of a presenter. Having been a listener of his various breakfast shows over the years, I am a huge fan and it was a great pleasure to talk to him. As before, any mistakes are my own.

But my final mention must, as always, go to my long-suffering husband, who is there by my side supporting me, putting up with a house filled with my writing detritus and taking care of the technical side of things that I hate. Thank you, Ian. I couldn't do it without you!